THE MAGIC EGG

AND OTHER STORIES

FRANK R. STOCKTON

1st WORLD
LIBRARY
Literary Society

The Magic Egg and Other Stories

Frank R. Stockton

© 1st World Library, 2007
PO Box 2211
Fairfield, IA 52556
www.1stworldlibrary.com
First Edition

LCCN: 2007927782

Softcover ISBN: 978-1-4218-4540-1
Hardcover ISBN: 978-1-4218-4456-5
eBook ISBN: 978-1-4218-4624-8

Purchase *"The Magic Egg and Other Stories"*
as a traditional bound book at:
www.1stWorldLibrary.com/purchase.asp?ISBN=978-1-4218-4540-1

1st World Library is a literary, educational organization
dedicated to:

- Creating a free internet library of downloadable ebooks

- Hosting writing competitions and offering book
publishing scholarships.

1ˢᵗ World Library Literary Society

Giving Back to the World

"If you want to work on the core problem, it's early school literacy."

- James Barksdale, former CEO of Netscape

"No skill is more crucial to the future of a child, or to a democratic and prosperous society, than literacy."

- Los Angeles Times

"Literacy... means far more than learning how to read and write... The aim is to transmit... knowledge and promote social participation."

- UNESCO

"Literacy is not a luxury, it is a right and a responsibility. If our world is to meet the challenges of the twenty-first century we must harness the energy and creativity of all our citizens."

- President Bill Clinton

"Parents should be encouraged to read to their children, and teachers should be equipped with all available techniques for teaching literacy, so the varying needs and capacities of individual kids can be taken into account."

- Hugh Mackay

CONTENTS

THE MAGIC EGG

The pretty little theatre attached to the building of the Unicorn Club had been hired for a certain January afternoon by Mr. Herbert Loring, who wished to give therein a somewhat novel performance, to which he had invited a small audience consisting entirely of friends and acquaintances.

Loring was a handsome fellow about thirty years old, who had travelled far and studied much. He had recently made a long sojourn in the far East, and his friends had been invited to the theatre to see some of the wonderful things he had brought from that country of wonders. As Loring was a club-man, and belonged to a family of good social standing, his circle of acquaintances was large, and in this circle a good many unpleasant remarks had been made regarding the proposed entertainment—made, of course, by the people who had not been invited to be present. Some of the gossip on the subject had reached Loring, who did not hesitate to say that he could not talk to a crowd, and that he did not care to show the curious things he had collected to people who would not thoroughly appreciate them. He had been very particular in regard to his invitations.

At three o'clock on the appointed afternoon nearly all the people who had been invited to the Unicorn Theatre were in their seats. No one had stayed away except for some very good reason, for it was well known that if Herbert Loring offered to show anything it was worth seeing.

About forty people were present, who sat talking to one another, or admiring the decoration of the theatre. As Loring stood upon the stage—where he was entirely alone, his exhibition requiring no assistants—he gazed through a loophole in the curtain upon a very interesting array of faces. There were the faces of many men and women of society, of students, of workers in various fields of thought, and even of idlers in all fields of thought; but there was not one which indicated a frivolous or listless disposition. The owners of those faces had come to see something, and they wished to see it.

For a quarter of an hour after the time announced for the opening of the exhibition Loring peered through the hole in the curtain, and then, although all the people he had expected had not arrived, he felt it would not do for him to wait any longer. The audience was composed of well-bred and courteous men and women, but despite their polite self-restraint Loring could see that some of them were getting tired of waiting. So, very reluctantly, and feeling that further delay was impossible, he raised the curtain and came forward on the stage.

Briefly he announced that the exhibition would open with some fireworks he had brought from Corea. It was plain to see that the statement that fireworks were about to be set off on a theatre stage, by an amateur, had rather startled some of the audience, and Loring hastened to explain that these were not real fireworks, but that they were contrivances made of colored glass, which were illuminated by the powerful lens of a lantern which was placed out of sight, and while the apparent pyrotechnic display would resemble fireworks of strange and grotesque designs, it would be absolutely without danger. He brought out some little

Frank R. Stockton

bunches of bits of colored glass, hung them at some distance apart on a wire which was stretched across the stage just high enough for him to reach it, and then lighted his lantern, which he placed in one of the wings, lowered all the lights in the theatre, and began his exhibition. As Loring turned his lantern on one of the clusters of glass lenses, strips, and points, and, unseen himself, caused them to move by means of long cords attached, the effects were beautiful and marvellous. Little wheels of colored fire rapidly revolved, miniature rockets appeared to rise a few feet and to explode in the air, and while all the ordinary forms of fireworks were produced on a diminutive scale, there were some effects that were entirely novel to the audience. As the light was turned successively upon one and another of the clusters of glass, sometimes it would flash along the whole line so rapidly that all the various combinations of color and motion seemed to be combined in one, and then for a time each particular set of fireworks would blaze, sparkle, and coruscate by itself, scattering particles of colored light as if they had been real sparks of fire.

This curious and beautiful exhibition of miniature pyrotechnics was extremely interesting to the audience, who gazed upward with rapt and eager attention at the line of wheels, stars, and revolving spheres. So far as interest gave evidence of satisfaction, there was never a better satisfied audience. At first there had been some hushed murmurs of pleasure, but very soon the attention of every one seemed so completely engrossed by the dazzling display that they simply gazed in silence.

For twenty minutes or longer the glittering show went on, and not a sign of weariness or inattention was made by any one of the assembled company. Then gradually the colors of the little fireworks faded, the stars and wheels revolved more slowly, the lights in the body of the theatre were gradually raised, and the stage curtain went softly down.

Anxiously, and a little pale, Herbert Loring peered through the loophole in the curtain. It was not easy to judge of the effects of his exhibition, and he did not know whether or not it had been a success. There was no applause, but, on the other hand, there was no signs that any one resented the exhibition as a childish display of colored lights. It was impossible to look upon that audience without believing that they had been thoroughly interested in what they had seen, and that they expected to see more.

For two or three minutes Loring gazed through his loophole, and then, still with some doubt in his heart, but with a little more color in his checks, he prepared for the second part of his performance.

At this moment there entered the theatre, at the very back of the house, a young lady. She was handsome and well dressed, and as she opened the door—Loring had employed no ushers or other assistants in this little social performance—she paused for a moment and looked into the theatre, and then noiselessly stepped to a chair in the back row and sat down.

This was Edith Starr, who, a month before, had been betrothed to Herbert Loring. Edith and her mother had been invited to this performance, and front seats had been reserved for them, for each guest had received a numbered card. But Mrs. Starr had a headache, and could not go out that afternoon, and for a time her daughter had thought that she, too, must give up the pleasure Loring had promised her, and stay with her mother. But when the elder lady dropped into a quiet sleep, Edith thought that, late as it was, she would go by herself, and see what she could of the performance.

Frank R. Stockton

She was quite certain that if her presence were known to Loring he would stop whatever he was doing until she had been provided with a seat which he thought suitable for her, for he had made a point of her being properly seated when he gave the invitations. Therefore, being equally desirous of not disturbing the performance and of not being herself conspicuous, she sat behind two rather large men, where she could see the stage perfectly well, but where she herself would not be likely to be seen.

In a few moments the curtain rose, and Loring came forward, carrying a small, light table, which he placed near the front of the stage, and for a moment stood quietly by it. Edith noticed upon his face the expression of uncertainty and anxiety which had not yet left it. Standing by the side of the table, and speaking very slowly, but so clearly that his words could be heard distinctly in all parts of the room, he began some introductory remarks regarding the second part of his performance.

"The extraordinary, and I may say marvellous, thing which I am about to show you," he said, "is known among East Indian magicians as the magic egg. The exhibition is a very uncommon one, and has seldom been seen by Americans or Europeans, and it was by a piece of rare good fortune that I became possessed of the appliances necessary for this exhibition. They are indeed very few and simple, but never before, to the best of my knowledge and belief, have they been seen outside of India.

"I will now get the little box which contains the articles necessary for this magical performance, and I will say that if I had time to tell you of the strange and amazing adventure which resulted in my possession of this box, I am sure you would be as much interested in that as I expect you to be in the contents of the box. But in order that none of you may think this is an ordinary trick, executed by means of concealed traps or doors, I wish you to take particular notice of this table, which is, as you see, a plain, unpainted pine table, with nothing but a flat top, and four straight legs at the corners. You can see under and around it, and it gives no opportunity to conceal anything." Then, standing for a few moments as if he had something else to say, he turned and stepped toward one of the wings.

Edith was troubled as she looked at her lover during these remarks. Her interest was great, greater, indeed, than that of the people about her, but it was not a pleasant interest. As Loring stopped speaking, and looked about him, there was a momentary flush on his face. She knew this was caused by excitement, and she was pale from the same cause.

Very soon Loring came forward, and stood by the table.

"Here is the box," he said, "of which I spoke, and as I hold it up I think you all can see it. It is not large, being certainly not more than twelve inches in length and two deep, but it contains some very wonderful things. The outside of this box is covered with delicate engraving and carving which you cannot see, and these marks and lines have, I think, some magical meaning, but I do not know what it is. I will now open the box and show you what is inside. The first thing I take out is this little stick, not thicker than a lead-pencil, but somewhat longer, as you see. This is a magical wand, and is covered with inscriptions of the same character as those on the outside of the box. The next thing is this little red bag, well filled, as you see, which I shall put on the table, for I shall not yet need it.

"Now I take out a piece of cloth which is folded into a very small compass, but as I unfold it you will perceive that it is more than a foot square, and is covered with embroidery. All those strange lines and figures in gold and red, which you can plainly see on the cloth as I hold it up, are also characters in the same magic language as those on the box and wand. I will now spread the cloth on the table, and then take out the only remaining thing in the box, and this is nothing in the world but an egg—a simple, ordinary hen's egg, as you all see as I hold it up. It may be a trifle larger than an ordinary egg, but then, after all, it is nothing but a common egg—that is, in appearance. In reality it is a good deal more.

"Now I will begin the performance." And as he stood by the back of the table, over which he had been slightly bending, and threw his eyes over the audience, his voice was stronger, and his face had lost all its pallor. He was evidently warming up with his subject.

"I now take up this wand," he said, "which, while I hold it, gives me power to produce the phenomena which you are about to behold. You may not all believe that there is any magic whatever about this little performance, and that it is all a bit of machinery; but whatever you may think about it, you shall see what you shall see.

"Now with this wand I gently touch this egg which is lying on the square of cloth. I do not believe you can see what has happened to this egg, but I will tell you. There is a little line, like a hair, entirely around it. Now that line has become a crack. Now you can see it, I know. It grows wider and wider! Look! The shell of the egg is separating in the middle. The whole egg slightly moves. Do you notice that? Now you can see something yellow showing itself between the two parts of the shell. See! It is moving a good deal, and the two halves of the shell are separating more and more. And now out tumbles this queer little object. Do you see what it is? It is a poor, weak, little chick, not able to stand, but alive—alive! You can all perceive that it is alive. Now you can see that it is standing on its feet, feebly enough, but still standing.

"Behold, it takes a few steps! You cannot doubt that it is alive, and came out of that egg. It is beginning to walk about over the cloth. Do you notice that it is picking the embroidery?

Now, little chick, I will give you something to eat. This little red bag contains grain, a magical grain, with which I shall feed the chicken. You must excuse my awkwardness in opening the bag, as I still hold the wand; but this little stick I must not drop. See, little chick, there are some grains! They look like rice, but, in fact, I have no idea what they are. But he knows, he knows! Look at him! See how he picks it up! There! He has swallowed one, two, three. That will do, little chick, for a first meal.

"The grain seems to have strengthened him already, for see how lively he is, and how his yellow down stands out on him, so puffy and warm! You are looking for some more grain, are you? Well, you cannot have it just yet, and keep away from those pieces of eggshell, which, by the way, I will put back into the box. Now, sir, try to avoid the edge of the table, and, to quiet you, I will give you a little tap on the back with my wand. Now, then, please observe closely. The down which just now covered him has almost gone. He is really a good deal bigger, and ever so much uglier. See the little pin-feathers sticking out over him! Some spots here and there are almost bare, but he is ever so much more active. Ha! Listen to that! He is so strong that you can hear his beak as he pecks at the table. He is actually growing bigger and bigger before our very eyes! See that funny little tail, how it begins to stick up, and quills are showing at the end of his wings.

"Another tap, and a few more grains. Careful, sir! Don't tear the cloth! See how rapidly he grows! He is fairly covered with feathers, red and black, with a tip of yellow in front. You could hardly get that fellow into an ostrich egg! Now, then, what do you think of him? He is big enough for a broiler, though I don't think any one would want to take him for that purpose. Some more grain, and another tap from my wand. See! He does not mind the little stick, for he has been used to it from his very birth. Now, then, he is what you would call a good half-grown chick. Rather more than half grown, I should say. Do you notice his tail? There is no mistaking him for a pullet. The long feathers are beginning to curl over already. He must have a little more grain. Look out, sir, or you will be off the table! Come back here! This table is too small for him, but if he were on the floor you could not see him so well.

"Another tap. Now see that comb on the top of his head; you scarcely noticed it before, and now it is bright red. And see his spurs beginning to show—on good thick legs, too. There is a fine young fellow for you! Look how he jerks his head from side to side, like the young prince of a poultry-yard, as he well deserves to be!"

The attentive interest which had at first characterized the audience now changed to excited admiration and amazement. Some leaned forward with mouths wide open. Others stood up so that they could see better. Ejaculations of astonishment and wonder were heard on every side, and a more thoroughly fascinated and absorbed audience was never seen.

"Now, my friends," Loring continued, "I will give this handsome fowl another tap. Behold the result—a noble, full-grown cock! Behold his spurs! They are nearly an inch long! See, there is a comb for you! And what a magnificent tail of green and black, contrasting so finely with the deep red of the rest of his body! Well, sir, you are truly too big for this table. As I cannot give you more room, I will set you up higher. Move over a little, and I will set this chair on the table. There! Upon the seat! That's right, but don't stop.

There is the back, which is higher yet! Up with you! Ha! There, he nearly upset the chair, but I will hold it. See! He has turned around. Now, then, look at him. See his wings as he flaps them! He could fly with such wings. Look at him! See that swelling breast! Ha, ha! Listen! Did you ever hear a crow like that? It fairly rings through the house. Yes, I knew it! There is another!"

At this point the people in the house were in a state of wild excitement. Nearly all of them were on their feet, and they were in such a condition of frantic enthusiasm that Loring was afraid some of them might make a run for the stage.

"Come, sir," cried Loring, now almost shouting, "that will do. You have shown us the strength of your lungs. Jump down on the seat of the chair; now on the table. There, I will take away the chair, and you can stand for a moment on the table and let our friends look at you; but only for a moment. Take that tap on your back. Now do you see any difference? Perhaps you may not, but I do. Yes, I believe you all do. He is not the big fellow he was a minute ago. He is really smaller—only a fine cockerel. A nice tail that, but with none of the noble sweep that it had a minute ago. No, don't try to get off the table. You can't escape my wand. Another tap. Behold a half-grown chicken, good to eat, but with not a crow in him. Hungry, are you? But you need not pick at the table that way. You get no more grain, but only this little tap. Ha, ha! What are you coming to? There is a chicken barely feathered enough for us to tell what color he is going to be.

"Another tap will take still more of the conceit out of him. Look at him! There are his pin-feathers, and his bare spots. Don't try to get away; I can easily tap you again. Now then. Here is a lovely little chick, fluffy with yellow down. He is active enough, but I shall quiet him. One tap, and now what do you see? A poor, feeble chicken, scarcely able to stand, with his down all packed close to him as if he had been out in the rain. Ah, little chick, I will take the two halves of the egg-shell from which you came, and put them on each side of you. Come, now get in! I close them up. You are lost to view. There is nothing to be seen but a crack around the shell! Now it has gone! There, my friends; as I hold it on high, behold the magic egg, exactly as it was when I first took it out of the box, into which I will place it again, with the cloth and the wand and the little red bag, and shut it up with a snap. I will let you take one more look at this box before I put it away behind the scenes. Are you satisfied with what I have shown you? Do you think it is really as wonderful as you supposed it would be?"

At these words the whole audience burst into riotous applause, during which Loring disappeared, but he was back in a moment.

"Thank you!" he cried, bowing low, and waving his arms before him in the manner of an Eastern magician making a salaam. From side to side he turned, bowing and thanking, and then, with a hearty "Good-by to you; good-by to you all!" he stepped back and let down the curtain.

For some moments the audience remained in their seats as if they were expecting something more, and then they rose quietly and began to disperse. Most of them were acquainted with one another, and there was a good deal of greeting and talking as they went out of the theatre.

When Loring was sure the last person had departed, he turned down the lights, locked the door, and gave the key to the steward of the club.

He walked to his home a happy man. His exhibition had been a perfect success, with not a break or a flaw in it from beginning to end.

"I feel," thought the young man, as he strode along, "as if I could fly to the top of that steeple, and flap and crow until all the world heard me."

That evening, as was his daily custom, Herbert Loring called upon Miss Starr. He found the young lady in the library.

"I came in here," she said, "because I have a good deal to talk to you about, and I do not want interruptions."

With this arrangement the young man expressed his entire satisfaction, and immediately began to inquire the cause of her absence from his exhibition in the afternoon.

"But I was there," said Edith. "You did not see me, but I was there. Mother had a headache, and I went by myself."

"You were there!" exclaimed Loring, almost starting from his chair. "I don't understand. You were not in your seat."

"No," answered Edith. "I was on the very back row of seats. You could not see me, and I did not wish you to see me."

"Edith!" exclaimed Loring, rising to his feet and leaning over the library table, which was between them. "When did you come? How much of the performance did you see?"

"I was late," she said. "I did not arrive until after the fireworks, or whatever they were."

For a moment Loring was silent, as if he did not understand the situation.

"Fireworks!" he said. "How did you know there had been fireworks?"

"I heard the people talking of them as they left the theatre," she answered.

"And what did they say?" he inquired quickly.

"They seemed to like them very well," she replied, "but I do not think they were quite satisfied. From what I heard some persons say, I inferred that they thought it was not very much of a show to which you had invited them."

Again Loring stood in thought, looking down at the table. But before he could speak again, Edith sprang to her feet.

"Herbert Loring," she cried, "what does all this mean? I was there during the whole of the exhibition of what you called the magic egg. I saw all those people wild with excitement at the wonderful sight of the chicken that came out of the egg, and grew to full size, and then dwindled down again, and went back into the egg, and, Herbert, there was no egg, and there was no little box, and there was no wand, and no embroidered cloth, and there was no red bag, nor any little chick, and there was no full-grown fowl, and there was no chair that you put on the table! There was nothing, absolutely nothing, but you and that table! Even the table was not what you said it was. It was not an unpainted pine table with four straight legs. It was a table of dark polished wood, and it stood on a single post with feet. There was nothing there that you said was there. Everything was a sham and a delusion; every word you spoke was untrue. And yet everybody in that theatre, excepting you and me, saw all the things that you said were on the stage. I know they saw them all, for I was with the people, and heard them, and saw them, and at times I fairly felt the thrill of enthusiasm which possessed them as they glared at the miracles and wonders you said were happening."

Loring smiled. "Sit down, my dear Edith," he said. "You are excited, and there is not the slightest cause for it. I will explain the whole affair to you. It is simple enough. You know that study is the great object of my life. I study all sorts of things; and just now I am greatly interested in hypnotism. The subject has become fascinating to me. I have made a great many successful trials of my power, and the affair of this afternoon was nothing but a trial of my powers on a more extensive scale than anything I have yet attempted. I wanted to see if it were possible for me to hypnotize a considerable number of people without any one suspecting what I intended to do. The result was a success. I hypnotized all those people by means of the first part of my performance, which consisted of some combinations of colored glass with lights thrown upon them. They revolved, and looked like fireworks, and were strung on a wire high up on the stage.

"I kept up the glittering and dazzling show—which was well worth seeing, I can assure you—until the people had been straining their eyes upward for almost half an hour. And this sort of thing—I will tell you if you do not know it—is one of the methods of producing hypnotic sleep.

"There was no one present who was not an impressionable subject, for I was very careful in sending out my invitations, and when I became almost certain that my audience was thoroughly hypnotized, I stopped the show and began the real exhibition, which was not really for their benefit, but for mine.

"Of course, I was dreadfully anxious for fear I had not succeeded entirely, and that there might be at least some one person who had not succumbed to the hypnotic influences, and so I tested the matter by bringing out that table and telling them it was something it was not. If I had had any reason for supposing that some of the audience saw the table as it really was, I had an explanation ready, and I could have retired from my position without any one supposing that I had intended making hypnotic experiments. The rest of the exhibition would have been some things that any one could see, and as soon as possible I would have released from their spell those who were hypnotized. But when I became positively assured that every one saw a light pine table with four straight legs, I confidently went on with the performances of the magic egg."

Edith Starr was still standing by the library table. She had not heeded Loring's advice to sit down, and she was trembling with emotion.

"Herbert Loring," she said, "you invited my mother and me to that exhibition. You gave us tickets for front seats, where we would be certain to be hypnotized if your experiment succeeded, and you would have made us see that false show, which faded from those people's minds as soon as they recovered from the spell, for as they went away they were talking only of the fireworks, and not one of them mentioned a magic egg, or a chicken, or anything of the kind. Answer me this: did you not intend that I should come and be put under that spell?"

Loring smiled. "Yes," he said, "of course I did. But then your case would have been different from that of the other spectators: I should have explained the whole thing to you, and I am sure we would have had a great deal of pleasure, and profit too, in discussing your experiences. The subject is extremely—"

"Explain to me!" she cried. "You would not have dared to do it! I do not know how brave you may be, but I know you would not have had the courage to come here and tell me that you had taken away my reason and my judgment, as you took them away from all those people, and that you had made me a mere tool of your will—glaring and panting with excitement at the wonderful things you told me to see where nothing existed. I have nothing to say about the others. They can speak for themselves if they ever come to know what you did to them. I speak for myself. I stood up with the rest of the people. I gazed with all my power, and over and over again I asked myself if it could be possible that anything was the matter with my eyes or my brain, and if I could be the only person there who could not see the marvellous spectacle that you were describing. But now I know that nothing was real, not even the little pine table—not even the man!"

"Not even me!" exclaimed Loring. "Surely I was real enough!"

"On that stage, yes," she said. "But you there proved you were not the Herbert Loring to whom I promised myself. He was an unreal being. If he had existed he would not have been a man who would have brought me to that public place, all ignorant of his intentions, to cloud my perceptions, to subject my intellect to his own, and make me believe a lie. If a man should treat me in that way once he would treat me so at other times, and in other ways, if he had the chance. You have treated me in the past as to-day you treated those people who glared at the magic egg. In the days gone by you made me see an unreal man, but you will never do it again! Good-by."

"Edith," cried Loring, "you don't—"

But she had disappeared through a side door, and he never spoke to her again.

Walking home through the dimly lighted streets, Loring involuntarily spoke aloud.

"And this," he said, "is what came out of the magic egg!"

"HIS WIFE'S DECEASED SISTER"

It is now five years since an event occurred which so colored my life, or rather so changed some of its original colors, that I have thought it well to write an account of it, deeming that its lessons may be of advantage to persons whose situations in life are similar to my own.

When I was quite a young man I adopted literature as a profession, and having passed through the necessary preparatory grades, I found myself, after a good many years of hard and often unremunerative work, in possession of what might be called a fair literary practice. My articles, grave, gay, practical, or fanciful, had come to be considered with a favor by the editors of the various periodicals for which I wrote, on which I found in time I could rely with a very comfortable certainty. My productions created no enthusiasm in the reading public; they gave me no great reputation or very valuable pecuniary return; but they were always accepted, and my receipts from them, at the time to which I have referred, were as regular and reliable as a salary, and quite sufficient to give me more than a comfortable support.

It was at this time I married. I had been engaged for more than a year, but had not been willing to assume the support of a wife until I felt that my pecuniary position was so assured that I could do so with full satisfaction to my own conscience. There was now no doubt in regard to this position, either in my mind or in that of my wife. I worked with great steadiness and regularity, I knew exactly where to place the productions of my pen, and could calculate, with a fair degree of accuracy, the sums I should receive for them. We were by no means rich, but we had enough, and were thoroughly satisfied and content.

Those of my readers who are married will have no difficulty in remembering the peculiar ecstasy of the first weeks of their wedded life. It is then that the flowers of this world bloom brightest; that its sun is the most genial; that its clouds are the scarcest; that its fruit is the most delicious; that the air is the most balmy; that its cigars are of the highest flavor; that the warmth and radiance of early matrimonial felicity so rarefy the intellectual atmosphere that the soul mounts higher, and enjoys a wider prospect, than ever before.

These experiences were mine. The plain claret of my mind was changed to sparkling champagne, and at the very height of its effervescence I wrote a story. The happy thought that then struck me for a tale was of a very peculiar character, and it interested me so much that I went to work at it with great delight and enthusiasm, and finished it in a comparatively short time. The title of the story was "His Wife's Deceased Sister," and when I read it to Hypatia she was delighted with it, and at times was so affected by its pathos that her uncontrollable emotion caused a sympathetic dimness in my eyes which prevented my seeing the words I had written. When the reading was ended and my wife had dried her eyes, she turned to me and said, "This story will make your fortune. There has been nothing so pathetic since Lamartine's 'History of a Servant Girl.'"

As soon as possible the next day I sent my story to the editor of the periodical for which I wrote most frequently, and in

Frank R. Stockton

which my best productions generally appeared. In a few days I had a letter from the editor, in which he praised my story as he had never before praised anything from my pen. It had interested and charmed, he said, not only himself, but all his associates in the office. Even old Gibson, who never cared to read anything until it was in proof, and who never praised anything which had not a joke in it, was induced by the example of the others to read this manuscript, and shed, as he asserted, the first tears that had come from his eyes since his final paternal castigation some forty years before. The story would appear, the editor assured me, as soon as he could possibly find room for it.

If anything could make our skies more genial, our flowers brighter, and the flavor of our fruit and cigars more delicious, it was a letter like this. And when, in a very short time, the story was published, we found that the reading public was inclined to receive it with as much sympathetic interest and favor as had been shown to it by the editors. My personal friends soon began to express enthusiastic opinions upon it. It was highly praised in many of the leading newspapers, and, altogether, it was a great literary success. I am not inclined to be vain of my writings, and, in general, my wife tells me, I think too little of them. But I did feel a good deal of pride and satisfaction in the success of "His Wife's Deceased Sister." If it did not make my fortune, as my wife asserted it would, it certainly would help me very much in my literary career.

In less than a month from the writing of this story, something very unusual and unexpected happened to me. A manuscript was returned by the editor of the periodical in which "His Wife's Deceased Sister" had appeared.

"It is a good story," he wrote, "but not equal to what you have just done. You have made a great hit, and it would not do to interfere with the reputation you have gained by publishing anything inferior to 'His Wife's Deceased Sister,' which has had such a deserved success."

I was so unaccustomed to having my work thrown back on my hands that I think I must have turned a little pale when I read the letter. I said nothing of the matter to my wife, for it would be foolish to drop such grains of sand as this into the smoothly oiled machinery of our domestic felicity, but I immediately sent the story to another editor. I am not able to express the astonishment I felt when, in the course of a week, it was sent back to me. The tone of the note accompanying it indicated a somewhat injured feeling on the part of the editor.

"I am reluctant," he said, "to decline a manuscript from you; but you know very well that if you sent me anything like 'His Wife's Deceased Sister' it would be most promptly accepted."

I now felt obliged to speak of the affair to my wife, who was quite as much surprised, though, perhaps, not quite as much shocked, as I had been.

"Let us read the story again," she said, "and see what is the matter with it." When we had finished its perusal, Hypatia remarked: "It is quite as good as many of the stories you have had printed, and I think it very interesting, although, of course, it is not equal to 'His Wife's Deceased Sister.'"

"Of course not," said I; "that was an inspiration that I cannot expect every day. But there must be something wrong about this last story which we do not perceive. Perhaps my recent success may have made me a little careless in writing it."

"I don't believe that," said Hypatia.

"At any rate," I continued, "I will lay it aside, and will go to work on a new one."

In due course of time I had another manuscript finished, and I sent it to my favorite periodical. It was retained some weeks, and then came back to me.

"It will never do," the editor wrote, quite warmly, "for you to go backward. The demand for the number containing 'His Wife's Deceased Sister' still continues, and we do not intend to let you disappoint that great body of readers who would be so eager to see another number containing one of your stories."

I sent this manuscript to four other periodicals, and from each of them it was returned with remarks to the effect that, although it was not a bad story in itself, it was not what they would expect from the author of "His Wife's Deceased Sister."

The editor of a Western magazine wrote to me for a story to be published in a special number which he would issue for the holidays. I wrote him one of the character and length he desired, and sent it to him. By return mail it came back to me.

"I had hoped," the editor wrote, "when I asked for a story from your pen, to receive something like 'His Wife's Deceased Sister,' and I must own that I am very much disappointed."

I was so filled with anger when I read this note that I openly objurgated "His Wife's Deceased Sister." "You must excuse me," I said to my astonished wife, "for expressing myself thus in your presence, but that confounded story will be the ruin of me yet. Until it is forgotten nobody will ever take anything I write."

"And you cannot expect it ever to be forgotten," said Hypatia, with tears in her eyes.

It is needless for me to detail my literary efforts in the course of the next few months. The ideas of the editors with whom my principal business had been done, in regard to my literary ability, had been so raised by my unfortunate story of "His Wife's Deceased Sister" that I found it was of no use to send them anything of lesser merit. And as to the other journals which I tried, they evidently considered it an insult for me to send them matter inferior to that by which my reputation had lately risen. The fact was that my successful story had ruined me. My income was at an end, and want actually stared me in the face; and I must admit that I did not like the expression of its countenance. It was of no use for me to try to write another story like "His Wife's Deceased Sister." I could not get married every time I began a new manuscript, and it was the exaltation of mind caused by my wedded felicity which produced that story.

"It's perfectly dreadful!" said my wife. "If I had had a sister, and she had died, I would have thought it was my fault."

"It could not be your fault," I answered, "and I do not think it was mine. I had no intention of deceiving anybody into the belief that I could do that sort of thing every time, and it ought not to be expected of me. Suppose Raphael's patrons had tried to keep him screwed up to the pitch of the Sistine Madonna, and had refused to buy anything which was not as good as that. In that case I think he would have occupied a much earlier and narrower grave than the one on which Mr. Morris Moore hangs his funeral decorations."

"But, my dear," said Hypatia, who was posted on such subjects, "the Sistine Madonna was one of his latest paintings."

Frank R. Stockton

"Very true," said I. "But if he had married as I did, he would have painted it earlier."

I was walking homeward one afternoon about this time, when I met Barbel, a man I had known well in my early literary career. He was now about fifty years of age, but looked older. His hair and beard were quite gray, and his clothes, which were of the same general hue, gave me the idea that they, like his hair, had originally been black. Age is very hard on a man's external appointments. Barbel had an air of having been to let for a long time, and quite out of repair. But there was a kindly gleam in his eye, and he welcomed me cordially.

"Why, what is the matter, old fellow?" said he. "I never saw you look so woe-begone."

I had no reason to conceal anything from Barbel. In my younger days he had been of great use to me, and he had a right to know the state of my affairs. I laid the whole case plainly before him.

"Look here," he said, when I had finished; "come with me to my room; I have something I would like to say to you there."

I followed Barbel to his room. It was at the top of a very dirty and well-worn house, which stood in a narrow and lumpy street, into which few vehicles ever penetrated, except the ash and garbage-carts, and the rickety wagons of the venders of stale vegetables.

"This is not exactly a fashionable promenade," said Barbel, as we approached the house, "but in some respects it reminds me of the streets in Italian towns, where the palaces lean over toward each other in such a friendly way."

Barbel's room was, to my mind, rather more doleful than the street. It was dark, it was dusty, and cobwebs hung from every corner. The few chairs upon the floor and the books upon a greasy table seemed to be afflicted with some dorsal epidemic, for their backs were either gone or broken. A little bedstead in the corner was covered with a spread made of New York "Heralds" with their edges pasted together.

"There is nothing better," said Barbel, noticing my glance toward this novel counterpane, "for a bed-covering than newspapers; they keep you as warm as a blanket, and are much lighter. I used to use 'Tribunes,' but they rattled too much."

The only part of the room which was well lighted was one end near the solitary window. Here, upon a table with a spliced leg, stood a little grindstone.

"At the other end of the room," said Barbel, "is my cook-stove, which you can't see unless I light the candle in the bottle which stands by it. But if you don't care particularly to examine it, I won't go to the expense of lighting up. You might pick up a good many odd pieces of bric-a-brac, around here, if you chose to strike a match and investigate. But I would not advise you to do so. It would pay better to throw the things out of the window than to carry them down-stairs. The particular piece of indoor decoration to which I wish to call your attention is this." And he led me to a little wooden frame which hung against the wall near the window. Behind a dusty piece of glass it held what appeared to be a leaf from a small magazine or journal. "There," said he, "you see a page from the 'Grasshopper,' a humorous paper which flourished in this city some half-dozen years ago. I used to write regularly for that paper, as you may remember."

"Oh, yes, indeed!" I exclaimed. "And I shall never forget

your 'Conundrum of the Anvil' which appeared in it. How often have I laughed at that most wonderful conceit, and how often have I put it to my friends!"

Barbel gazed at me silently for a moment, and then he pointed to the frame. "That printed page," he said solemnly, "contains the 'Conundrum of the Anvil.' I hang it there so that I can see it while I work. That conundrum ruined me. It was the last thing I wrote for the 'Grasshopper.' How I ever came to imagine it, I cannot tell. It is one of those things which occur to a man but once in a lifetime. After the wild shout of delight with which the public greeted that conundrum, my subsequent efforts met with hoots of derision. The 'Grasshopper' turned its hind legs upon me. I sank from bad to worse,—much worse,—until at last I found myself reduced to my present occupation, which is that of grinding points on pins. By this I procure my bread, coffee, and tobacco, and sometimes potatoes and meat. One day while I was hard at work, an organ-grinder came into the street below. He played the serenade from 'Trovatore' and the familiar notes brought back visions of old days and old delights, when the successful writer wore good clothes and sat at operas, when he looked into sweet eyes and talked of Italian airs, when his future appeared all a succession of bright scenery and joyous acts, without any provision for a drop-curtain. And as my ear listened, and my mind wandered in this happy retrospect, my every faculty seemed exalted, and, without any thought upon the matter, I ground points upon my pins so fine, so regular, and so smooth that they would have pierced with ease the leather of a boot, or slipped, without abrasion, among the finest threads of rare old lace. When the organ stopped, and I fell back into my real world of cobwebs and mustiness, I gazed upon the pins I had just ground, and, without a moment's hesitation, I threw them into the street, and reported the lot as spoiled. This cost me a little money, but it saved me my livelihood."

After a few moments of silence, Barbel resumed:

"I have no more to say to you, my young friend. All I want you to do is to look upon that framed conundrum, then upon this grindstone, and then to go home and reflect. As for me, I have a gross of pins to grind before the sun goes down."

I cannot say that my depression of mind was at all relieved by what I had seen and heard. I had lost sight of Barbel for some years, and I had supposed him still floating on the sun-sparkling stream of prosperity where I had last seen him. It was a great shock to me to find him in such a condition of poverty and squalor, and to see a man who had originated the "Conundrum of the Anvil" reduced to the soul-depressing occupation of grinding pin-points. As I walked and thought, the dreadful picture of a totally eclipsed future arose before my mind. The moral of Barbel sank deep into my heart.

When I reached home I told my wife the story of my friend Barbel. She listened with a sad and eager interest.

"I am afraid," she said, "if our fortunes do not quickly mend, that we shall have to buy two little grindstones. You know I could help you at that sort of thing."

For a long time we sat together and talked, and devised many plans for the future. I did not think it necessary yet for me to look out for a pin contract; but I must find some way of making money, or we should starve to death. Of course, the first thing that suggested itself was the possibility of finding some other business. But, apart from the difficulty of immediately obtaining remunerative work in occupations to which I had not been trained, I felt a great and natural reluctance to give up a profession for which I had carefully prepared myself, and which I had adopted as my life-work. It would be very hard for me to lay down my pen forever, and to close the top of my inkstand upon all the bright and happy fancies which I had seen mirrored in its tranquil pool. We talked and pondered the rest of that day and a good deal of the night, but we came to no conclusion as to what it would be best for us to do.

The next day I determined to go and call upon the editor of the journal for which, in happier days, before the blight of "His Wife's Deceased Sister" rested upon me, I used most frequently to write, and, having frankly explained my condition to him, to ask his advice. The editor was a good man, and had always been my friend. He listened with great attention to what I told him, and evidently sympathized with me in my trouble.

"As we have written to you," he said, "the only reason why we did not accept the manuscripts you sent us was that they would have disappointed the high hopes that the public had formed in regard to you. We have had letter after letter asking when we were going to publish another story like 'His Wife's Deceased Sister.' We felt, and we still feel, that it would be wrong to allow you to destroy the fair fabric which you yourself have raised. But," he added, with a kind smile, "I see very plainly that your well-deserved reputation will be of little advantage to you if you should starve at the moment that its genial beams are, so to speak, lighting you up."

"Its beams are not genial," I answered. "They have scorched and withered me."

"How would you like," said the editor, after a short reflection, "to allow us to publish the stories you have recently written under some other name than your own? That would satisfy us and the public, would put money in your pocket, and would not interfere with your reputation."

Joyfully I seized the noble fellow by the hand, and instantly accepted his proposition. "Of course," said I, "a reputation is a very good thing; but no reputation can take the place of food, clothes, and a house to live in, and I gladly agree to sink my over-illumined name into oblivion, and to appear before the public as a new and unknown writer."

"I hope that need not be for long," he said, "for I feel sure that you will yet write stories as good as 'His Wife's Deceased Sister.'"

All the manuscripts I had on hand I now sent to my good friend the editor, and in due and proper order they appeared in his journal under the name of John Darmstadt, which I had selected as a substitute for my own, permanently disabled. I made a similar arrangement with other editors, and John Darmstadt received the credit of everything that proceeded from my pen. Our circumstances now became very comfortable, and occasionally we even allowed ourselves to indulge in little dreams of prosperity.

Time passed on very pleasantly. One year, another, and then a little son was born to us. It is often difficult, I believe, for thoughtful persons to decide whether the beginning of their conjugal career, or the earliest weeks in the life of their first-born, be the happiest and proudest period of their existence. For myself I can only say that the same exaltation of mind, the same rarefication of idea and invention, which succeeded upon my wedding day came upon me now. As then, my ecstatic emotions crystallized themselves into a motive for a story, and without delay I set myself to work upon it. My boy was about six weeks old when the manuscript was finished, and one evening, as we sat before a comfortable fire in our sitting-room, with the curtains drawn, and the soft lamp lighted, and the baby sleeping soundly in the adjoining chamber, I read the story to my wife.

Frank R. Stockton

When I had finished, my wife arose and threw herself into my arms. "I was never so proud of you," she said, her glad eyes sparkling, "as I am at this moment. That is a wonderful story! It is, indeed I am sure it is, just as good as 'His Wife's Deceased Sister.'"

As she spoke these words, a sudden and chilling sensation crept over us both. All her warmth and fervor, and the proud and happy glow engendered within me by this praise and appreciation from one I loved, vanished in an instant. We stepped apart, and gazed upon each other with pallid faces. In the same moment the terrible truth had flashed upon us both. This story WAS as good as "His Wife's Deceased Sister"!

We stood silent. The exceptional lot of Barbel's super-pointed pins seemed to pierce our very souls. A dreadful vision rose before me of an impending fall and crash, in which our domestic happiness should vanish, and our prospects for our boy be wrecked, just as we had began to build them up.

My wife approached me, and took my hand in hers, which was as cold as ice. "Be strong and firm," she said. "A great danger threatens us, but you must brace yourself against it. Be strong and firm."

I pressed her hand, and we said no more that night.

The next day I took the manuscript I had just written, and carefully infolded it in stout wrapping-paper. Then I went to a neighboring grocery store and bought a small, strong, tin box, originally intended for biscuit, with a cover that fitted tightly. In this I placed my manuscript, and then I took the box to a tinsmith and had the top fastened on with hard solder. When I went home I ascended into the garret and brought down to my study a ship's cash-box, which had once belonged to one of my family who was a sea-captain. This box was very heavy, and firmly bound with iron, and was secured by two massive locks. Calling my wife, I told her of the contents of the tin case, which I then placed in the box, and having shut down the heavy lid, I doubly locked it.

"This key," said I, putting it in my pocket, "I shall throw into the river when I go out this afternoon."

My wife watched me eagerly, with a pallid and firm-set countenance, but upon which I could see the faint glimmer of returning happiness.

"Wouldn't it be well," she said, "to secure it still further by sealing-wax and pieces of tape?"

"No," said I. "I do not believe that any one will attempt to tamper with our prosperity. And now, my dear," I continued in an impressive voice, "no one but you, and, in the course of time, our son, shall know that this manuscript exists. When I am dead, those who survive me may, if they see fit, cause this box to be split open and the story published. The reputation it may give my name cannot harm me then."

THE WIDOW'S CRUISE

The Widow Ducket lived in a small village about ten miles from the New Jersey sea-coast. In this village she was born, here she had married and buried her husband, and here she expected somebody to bury her; but she was in no hurry for this, for she had scarcely reached middle age. She was a tall woman with no apparent fat in her composition, and full of activity, both muscular and mental.

She rose at six o'clock in the morning, cooked breakfast, set the table, washed the dishes when the meal was over, milked, churned, swept, washed, ironed, worked in her little garden, attended to the flowers in the front yard, and in the afternoon knitted and quilted and sewed, and after tea she either went to see her neighbors or had them come to see her. When it was really dark she lighted the lamp in her parlor and read for an hour, and if it happened to be one of Miss Mary Wilkins's books that she read she expressed doubts as to the realism of the characters therein described.

These doubts she expressed to Dorcas Networthy, who was a small, plump woman, with a solemn face, who had lived with the widow for many years and who had become her devoted disciple. Whatever the widow did, that also did Dorcas—not so well, for her heart told her she could never expect to do that, but with a yearning anxiety to do everything as well as she could. She rose at five minutes past six, and in a subsidiary way she helped to get the breakfast, to eat it, to wash up the dishes, to work in the garden, to quilt, to sew, to visit and receive, and no one could have tried harder than she did to keep awake when the widow read aloud in the evening.

All these things happened every day in the summertime, but in the winter the widow and Dorcas cleared the snow from their little front path instead of attending to the flowers, and in the evening they lighted a fire as well as a lamp in the parlor.

Sometimes, however, something different happened, but this was not often, only a few times in the year. One of the different things occurred when Mrs. Ducket and Dorcas were sitting on their little front porch one summer afternoon, one on the little bench on one side of the door, and the other on the little bench on the other side of the door, each waiting until she should hear the clock strike five, to prepare tea. But it was not yet a quarter to five when a one-horse wagon containing four men came slowly down the street. Dorcas first saw the wagon, and she instantly stopped knitting.

"Mercy on me!" she exclaimed. "Whoever those people are, they are strangers here, and they don't know where to stop, for they first go to one side of the street and then to the other."

The widow looked around sharply. "Humph!" said she. "Those men are sailormen. You might see that in a twinklin' of an eye. Sailormen always drive that way, because that is the way they sail ships. They first tack in one direction and then in another."

"Mr. Ducket didn't like the sea?" remarked Dorcas, for about the three hundredth time.

"No, he didn't," answered the widow, for about the two hundred and fiftieth time, for there had been occasions when she thought Dorcas put this question inopportunely. "He hated it, and he was drowned in it through trustin' a sailorman, which I never did nor shall. Do you really believe those men are comin' here?"

"Upon my word I do!" said Dorcas, and her opinion was correct.

The wagon drew up in front of Mrs. Ducket's little white house, and the two women sat rigidly, their hands in their laps, staring at the man who drove.

This was an elderly personage with whitish hair, and under his chin a thin whitish beard, which waved in the gentle breeze and gave Dorcas the idea that his head was filled with hair which was leaking out from below.

"Is this the Widow Ducket's?" inquired this elderly man, in a strong, penetrating voice.

"That's my name," said the widow, and laying her knitting on the bench beside her, she went to the gate. Dorcas also laid her knitting on the bench beside her and went to the gate.

"I was told," said the elderly man, "at a house we touched at about a quarter of a mile back, that the Widow Ducket's was the only house in this village where there was any chance of me and my mates getting a meal. We are four sailors, and we are making from the bay over to Cuppertown, and that's eight miles ahead yet, and we are all pretty sharp set for something to eat."

"This is the place," said the widow, "and I do give meals if there is enough in the house and everything comes handy."

"Does everything come handy to-day?" said he.

"It does," said she, "and you can hitch your horse and come in; but I haven't got anything for him."

"Oh, that's all right," said the man, "we brought along stores for him, so we'll just make fast and then come in."

The two women hurried into the house in a state of bustling preparation, for the furnishing of this meal meant one dollar in cash.

The four mariners, all elderly men, descended from the wagon, each one scrambling with alacrity over a different wheel.

A box of broken ship-biscuit was brought out and put on the ground in front of the horse, who immediately set himself to eating with great satisfaction.

Tea was a little late that day, because there were six persons to provide for instead of two, but it was a good meal, and after the four seamen had washed their hands and faces at the pump in the back yard and had wiped them on two towels furnished by Dorcas, they all came in and sat down. Mrs. Ducket seated herself at the head of the table with the dignity proper to the mistress of the house, and Dorcas seated herself at the other end with the dignity proper to the disciple of the mistress. No service was necessary, for everything that was to be eaten or drunk was on the table.

When each of the elderly mariners had had as much bread and butter, quickly baked soda-biscuit, dried beef, cold ham, cold tongue, and preserved fruit of every variety known, as his storage capacity would permit, the mariner in command, Captain Bird, pushed back his chair, whereupon the other mariners pushed back their chairs.

Frank R. Stockton

"Madam," said Captain Bird, "we have all made a good meal, which didn't need to be no better nor more of it, and we're satisfied; but that horse out there has not had time to rest himself enough to go the eight miles that lies ahead of us, so, if it's all the same to you and this good lady, we'd like to sit on that front porch awhile and smoke our pipes. I was a-looking at that porch when I came in, and I bethought to myself what a rare good place it was to smoke a pipe in."

"There's pipes been smoked there," said the widow, rising, "and it can be done again. Inside the house I don't allow tobacco, but on the porch neither of us minds."

So the four captains betook themselves to the porch, two of them seating themselves on the little bench on one side of the door, and two of them on the little bench on the other side of the door, and lighted their pipes.

"Shall we clear off the table and wash up the dishes," said Dorcas, "or wait until they are gone?"

"We will wait until they are gone," said the widow, "for now that they are here we might as well have a bit of a chat with them. When a sailorman lights his pipe he is generally willin' to talk, but when he is eatin' you can't get a word out of him."

Without thinking it necessary to ask permission, for the house belonged to her, the Widow Ducket brought a chair and put it in the hall close to the open front door, and Dorcas brought another chair and seated herself by the side of the widow.

"Do all you sailormen belong down there at the bay?" asked Mrs. Ducket; thus the conversation began, and in a few minutes it had reached a point at which Captain Bird thought it proper to say that a great many strange things happen to seamen sailing on the sea which lands-people never dream of.

"Such as anything in particular?" asked the widow, at which remark Dorcas clasped her hands in expectancy.

At this question each of the mariners took his pipe from his mouth and gazed upon the floor in thought.

"There's a good many strange things happened to me and my mates at sea. Would you and that other lady like to hear any of them?" asked Captain Bird.

"We would like to hear them if they are true," said the widow.

"There's nothing happened to me and my mates that isn't true," said Captain Bird, "and here is something that once happened to me: I was on a whaling v'yage when a big sperm-whale, just as mad as a fiery bull, came at us, head on, and struck the ship at the stern with such tremendous force that his head crashed right through her timbers and he went nearly half his length into her hull. The hold was mostly filled with empty barrels, for we was just beginning our v'yage, and when he had made kindling-wood of these there was room enough for him. We all expected that it wouldn't take five minutes for the vessel to fill and go to the bottom, and we made ready to take to the boats; but it turned out we didn't need to take to no boats, for as fast as the water rushed into the hold of the ship, that whale drank it and squirted it up through the two blow-holes in the top of his head, and as there was an open hatchway just over his head, the water all went into the sea again, and that whale kept working day and night pumping the water out until we beached the vessel on the island of Trinidad—the whale helping us wonderful on our way over by the powerful working of his tail, which, being outside in the water, acted like a propeller. I don't believe any thing stranger than that ever happened to a whaling ship."

"No," said the widow, "I don't believe anything ever did."

Captain Bird now looked at Captain Sanderson, and the latter took his pipe out of his mouth and said that in all his sailing around the world he had never known anything queerer than what happened to a big steamship he chanced to be on, which ran into an island in a fog. Everybody on board thought the ship was wrecked, but it had twin screws, and was going at such a tremendous speed that it turned the island entirely upside down and sailed over it, and he had heard tell that even now people sailing over the spot could look down into the water and see the roots of the trees and the cellars of the houses.

Captain Sanderson now put his pipe back into his mouth, and Captain Burress took out his pipe.

"I was once in an obelisk-ship," said he, "that used to trade regular between Egypt and New York, carrying obelisks. We had a big obelisk on board. The way they ship obelisks is to make a hole in the stern of the ship, and run the obelisk in, p'inted end foremost; and this obelisk filled up nearly the whole of that ship from stern to bow. We was about ten days out, and sailing afore a northeast gale with the engines at full speed, when suddenly we spied breakers ahead, and our Captain saw we was about to run on a bank. Now if we hadn't had an obelisk on board we might have sailed over that bank, but the captain knew that with an obelisk on board we drew too much water for this, and that we'd be wrecked in about fifty-five seconds if something wasn't done quick. So he had to do something quick, and this is what he did: He ordered all steam on, and drove slam-bang on that bank. Just as he expected, we stopped so suddint that that big obelisk bounced for'ard, its p'inted end foremost, and went clean through the bow and shot out into the sea. The minute it did that the vessel was so lightened that it rose in the water and we easily steamed over the bank. There was one man knocked overboard by the shock when we struck, but as soon as we missed him we went back after him and we got him all right. You see, when that obelisk went overboard, its butt-end, which was heaviest, went down first, and when it touched the bottom it just stood there, and as it was such a big obelisk there was about five and a half feet of it stuck out of the water. The man who was knocked overboard he just swum for that obelisk and he climbed up the hiryglyphics. It was a mighty fine obelisk, and the Egyptians had cut their hiryglyphics good and deep, so that the man could get hand and foot-hold; and when we got to him and took him off, he was sitting high and dry on the p'inted end of that obelisk. It was a great pity about the obelisk, for it was a good obelisk, but as I never heard the company tried to raise it, I expect it is standing there yet."

Captain Burress now put his pipe back into his mouth and looked at Captain Jenkinson, who removed his pipe and said:

"The queerest thing that ever happened to me was about a shark. We was off the Banks, and the time of year was July, and the ice was coming down, and we got in among a lot of it. Not far away, off our weather bow, there was a little iceberg which had such a queerness about it that the captain and three men went in a boat to look at it. The ice was mighty clear ice, and you could see almost through it, and right inside of it, not more than three feet above the waterline, and about two feet, or maybe twenty inches, inside the ice, was a whopping big shark, about fourteen feet long,—a regular man-eater,—frozen in there hard and fast. 'Bless my soul,' said the captain, 'this is a wonderful curiosity, and I'm going to git him out.' Just then one of the men said he saw that shark wink, but the captain wouldn't believe him, for he said that shark was frozen stiff and hard and couldn't wink. You see, the captain had his own idees about things, and he knew that whales was warm-blooded and would freeze if they was shut up in ice, but he forgot that sharks was not whales and that they're cold-blooded just like toads. And there is toads that has been shut up in rocks for thousands of years, and they stayed alive, no matter how cold the place was, because they was cold-blooded, and when the rocks was split, out hopped the frog. But, as I said before, the captain forgot sharks was cold-blooded, and he determined to git that one out.

"Now you both know, being housekeepers, that if you take a needle and drive it into a hunk of ice you can split it. The captain had a sail-needle with him, and so he drove it into the iceberg right alongside of the shark and split it. Now the minute he did it he knew that the man was right when he said he saw the shark wink, for it flopped out of that iceberg quicker nor a flash of lightning."

"What a happy fish he must have been!" ejaculated Dorcas, forgetful of precedent, so great was her emotion.

"Yes," said Captain Jenkinson, "it was a happy fish enough, but it wasn't a happy captain. You see, that shark hadn't had anything to eat, perhaps for a thousand years, until the captain came along with his sail-needle."

"Surely you sailormen do see strange things," now said the widow, "and the strangest thing about them is that they are true."

"Yes, indeed," said Dorcas, "that is the most wonderful thing."

"You wouldn't suppose," said the Widow Ducket, glancing from one bench of mariners to the other, "that I have a sea-story to tell, but I have, and if you like I will tell it to you."

Captain Bird looked up a little surprised.

"We would like to hear it—indeed, we would, madam," said he.

"Ay, ay!" said Captain Burress, and the two other mariners nodded.

"It was a good while ago," she said, "when I was living on the shore near the head of the bay, that my husband was away and I was left alone in the house. One mornin' my sister-in-law, who lived on the other side of the bay, sent me word by a boy on a horse that she hadn't any oil in the house to fill the lamp that she always put in the window to light her husband home, who was a fisherman, and if I would send her some by the boy she would pay me back as soon as they bought oil. The boy said he would stop on his way home and take the oil to her, but he never did stop, or perhaps he never went back, and about five o'clock I began to get dreadfully worried, for I knew if that lamp wasn't in my sister-in-law's window by dark she might be a widow before midnight. So I said to myself, 'I've got to get that oil to her, no matter what happens or how it's done.' Of course I couldn't tell what might happen, but there was only one way it could be done, and that was for me to get into the boat that was tied to the post down by the water, and take it to her, for it was too far for me to walk around by the head of the bay. Now, the trouble was, I didn't know no more about a boat and the managin' of it than any one of you sailormen knows about clear starchin'. But there wasn't no use of thinkin' what I knew and what I didn't know, for I had to take it to her, and there was no way of doin' it except in that boat. So I filled a gallon can, for I thought I might as well take enough while I was about it, and I went down to

Frank R. Stockton

the water and I unhitched that boat and I put the oil-can into her, and then I got in, and off I started, and when I was about a quarter of a mile from the shore—"

"Madam," interrupted Captain Bird, "did you row or—or was there a sail to the boat?"

The widow looked at the questioner for a moment. "No," said she, "I didn't row. I forgot to bring the oars from the house; but it didn't matter, for I didn't know how to use them, and if there had been a sail I couldn't have put it up, for I didn't know how to use it, either. I used the rudder to make the boat go. The rudder was the only thing I knew anything about. I'd held a rudder when I was a little girl, and I knew how to work it. So I just took hold of the handle of the rudder and turned it round and round, and that made the boat go ahead, you know, and—"

"Madam!" exclaimed Captain Bird, and the other elderly mariners took their pipes from their mouths.

"Yes, that is the way I did it," continued the widow, briskly. "Big steamships are made to go by a propeller turning round and round at their back ends, and I made the rudder work in the same way, and I got along very well, too, until suddenly, when I was about a quarter of a mile from the shore, a most terrible and awful storm arose. There must have been a typhoon or a cyclone out at sea, for the waves came up the bay bigger than houses, and when they got to the head of the bay they turned around and tried to get out to sea again. So in this way they continually met, and made the most awful and roarin' pilin' up of waves that ever was known.

"My little boat was pitched about as if it had been a feather in a breeze, and when the front part of it was cleavin' itself down into the water the hind part was stickin' up until the rudder whizzed around like a patent churn with no milk in it. The thunder began to roar and the lightnin' flashed, and three seagulls, so nearly frightened to death that they began to turn up the whites of their eyes, flew down and sat on one of the seats of the boat, forgettin' in that awful moment that man was their nat'ral enemy. I had a couple of biscuits in my pocket, because I had thought I might want a bite in crossing, and I crumbled up one of these and fed the poor creatures. Then I began to wonder what I was goin' to do, for things were gettin' awfuller and awfuller every instant, and the little boat was a-heavin' and a-pitchin' and a-rollin' and h'istin' itself up, first on one end and then on the other, to such an extent that if I hadn't kept tight hold of the rudder-handle I'd slipped off the seat I was sittin' on.

"All of a sudden I remembered that oil in the can; but just as I was puttin' my fingers on the cork my conscience smote me. 'Am I goin' to use this oil,' I said to myself, 'and let my sister-in-law's husband be wrecked for want of it?' And then I thought that he wouldn't want it all that night, and perhaps they would buy oil the next day, and so I poured out about a tumblerful of it on the water, and I can just tell you sailormen that you never saw anything act as prompt as that did. In three seconds, or perhaps five, the water all around me, for the distance of a small front yard, was just as flat as a table and as smooth as glass, and so invitin' in appearance that the three gulls jumped out of the boat and began to swim about on it, primin' their feathers and lookin' at themselves in the transparent depths, though I must say that one of them made an awful face as he dipped his bill into the water and tasted kerosene.

"Now I had time to sit quiet in the midst of the placid space I had made for myself, and rest from workin' of the rudder. Truly it was a wonderful and marvellous thing to look at. The waves was roarin' and leapin' up all around me higher than the roof of this house, and sometimes their tops would reach over so that they nearly met and shut out all view of the stormy sky, which seemed as if it was bein' torn to pieces by blazin' lightnin', while the thunder pealed so tremendous that it almost drowned the roar of the waves. Not only above and all around me was every thing terrific and fearful, but even under me it was the same, for there was a big crack in the bottom of the boat as wide as my hand, and through this I could see down into the water beneath, and there was—"

"Madam!" ejaculated Captain Bird, the hand which had been holding his pipe a few inches from his mouth now dropping to his knee; and at this motion the hands which held the pipes of the three other mariners dropped to their knees.

"Of course it sounds strange," continued the widow, "but I know that people can see down into clear water, and the water under me was clear, and the crack was wide enough for me to see through, and down under me was sharks and swordfishes and other horrible water creatures, which I had never seen before, all driven into the bay, I haven't a doubt, by the violence of the storm out at sea. The thought of my bein' upset and fallin' in among those monsters made my very blood run cold, and involuntary-like I began to turn the handle of the rudder, and in a moment I shot into a wall of ragin' sea-water that was towerin' around me. For a second I was fairly blinded and stunned, but I had the cork out of that oil-can in no time, and very soon—you'd scarcely believe it if I told you how soon—I had another placid mill-pond surroundin' of me. I sat there a-pantin' and fannin' with my straw hat, for you'd better believe I was flustered, and then I began to think how long it would take me to make a line of mill-ponds clean across the head of the bay, and how much oil it would need, and whether I had enough. So I sat and calculated that if a tumblerful of oil would make a smooth place about seven yards across, which

I should say was the width of the one I was in,—which I calculated by a measure of my eye as to how many breadths of carpet it would take to cover it,—and if the bay was two miles across betwixt our house and my sister-in-law's, and, although I couldn't get the thing down to exact figures, I saw pretty soon that I wouldn't have oil enough to make a level cuttin' through all those mountainous billows, and besides, even if I had enough to take me across, what would be the good of goin' if there wasn't any oil left to fill my sister-in-law's lamp?

"While I was thinkin' and calculatin' a perfectly dreadful thing happened, which made me think if I didn't get out of this pretty soon I'd find myself in a mighty risky predicament. The oil-can, which I had forgotten to put the cork in, toppled over, and before I could grab it every drop of the oil ran into the hind part of the boat, where it was soaked up by a lot of dry dust that was there. No wonder my heart sank when I saw this. Glancin' wildly around me, as people will do when they are scared, I saw the smooth place I was in gettin' smaller and smaller, for the kerosene was evaporatin', as it will do even off woollen clothes if you give it time enough. The first pond I had come out of seemed to be covered up, and the great, towerin', throbbin' precipice of sea-water was a-closin' around me.

"Castin' down my eyes in despair, I happened to look through the crack in the bottom of the boat, and oh, what a blessed relief it was! for down there everything was smooth and still, and I could see the sand on the bottom, as level and hard, no doubt, as it was on the beach. Suddenly the thought struck me that that bottom would give me the only chance I had of gettin' out of the frightful fix I was in. If I could fill that oil-can with air, and then puttin' it under my arm and takin' a long breath if I could drop down on that smooth bottom, I might run along toward shore, as far as I could, and then, when I felt my breath was givin' out, I could take a pull at the oil-can and take another run, and then take another pull and another run, and perhaps the can would hold air enough for me until I got near enough to shore to wade to dry land. To be sure, the sharks and other monsters were down there, but then they must have been awfully frightened, and perhaps they might not remember that man was their nat'ral enemy. Anyway, I thought it would be better to try the smooth water passage down there than stay and be swallowed up by the ragin' waves on top.

"So I blew the can full of air and corked it, and then I tore up some of the boards from the bottom of the boat so as to make a hole big enough for me to get through,—and you sailormen needn't wriggle so when I say that, for you all know a divin'-bell hasn't any bottom at all and the water never comes in,—and so when I got the hole big enough I took the oil-can under my arm, and was just about to slip down through it when I saw an awful turtle a-walkin' through the sand at the bottom. Now, I might trust sharks and swordfishes and sea-serpents to be frightened and forget about their nat'ral enemies, but I never could trust a gray turtle as big as a cart, with a black neck a yard long, with yellow bags to its jaws, to forget anything or to remember anything. I'd as lieve get into a bath-tub with a live crab as to go down there. It wasn't of no use even so much as thinkin' of it, so I gave up that plan and didn't once look through that hole again."

"And what did you do, madam?" asked Captain Bird, who was regarding her with a face of stone.

"I used electricity," she said. "Now don't start as if you had a shock of it. That's what I used. When I was younger than I was then, and sometimes visited friends in the city, we often amused ourselves by rubbing our feet on the carpet until we got ourselves so full of electricity that we could put up our fingers and light the gas. So I said to myself that if I could get full of electricity for the purpose of lightin' the gas I could get full of it for other purposes, and so, without losin' a moment, I set to work. I stood up on one of the seats, which was dry, and I rubbed the bottoms of my shoes backward and forward on it with such violence and swiftness that they pretty soon got warm and I began fillin' with electricity, and when I was fully charged with it from my toes to the top of my head, I just sprang into the water and swam ashore. Of course I couldn't sink, bein' full of electricity."

Captain Bird heaved a long sigh and rose to his feet, whereupon the other mariners rose to their feet "Madam," said Captain Bird, "what's to pay for the supper and—the rest of the entertainment?"

"The supper is twenty-five cents apiece," said the Widow Ducket, "and everything else is free, gratis."

Whereupon each mariner put his hand into his trousers pocket, pulled out a silver quarter, and handed it to the widow. Then, with four solemn "Good evenin's," they went out to the front gate.

"Cast off, Captain Jenkinson," said Captain Bird, "and you, Captain Burress, clew him up for'ard. You can stay in the bow, Captain Sanderson, and take the sheet-lines. I'll go aft."

All being ready, each of the elderly mariners clambered over a wheel, and having seated themselves, they prepared to lay their course for Cuppertown.

But just as they were about to start, Captain Jenkinson asked that they lay to a bit, and clambering down over his wheel, he reentered the front gate and went up to the door of the house, where the widow and Dorcas were still standing.

"Madam," said he, "I just came back to ask what became of your brother-in-law through his wife's not bein' able to put no light in the window?"

"The storm drove him ashore on our side of the bay," said she, "and the next mornin' he came up to our house, and I told him all that had happened to me. And when he took our boat and went home and told that story to his wife, she just packed up and went out West, and got divorced from him. And it served him right, too."

"Thank you, ma'am," said Captain Jenkinson, and going out of the gate, he clambered up over the wheel, and the wagon cleared for Cuppertown.

When the elderly mariners were gone, the Widow Ducket, still standing in the door, turned to Dorcas.

"Think of it!" she said. "To tell all that to me, in my own house! And after I had opened my one jar of brandied peaches, that I'd been keepin' for special company!"

"In your own house!" ejaculated Dorcas. "And not one of them brandied peaches left!"

The widow jingled the four quarters in her hand before she slipped them into her pocket.

"Anyway, Dorcas," she remarked, "I think we can now say we are square with all the world, and so let's go in and wash the dishes."

"Yes," said Dorcas, "we're square."

CAPTAIN ELI'S BEST EAR

The little seaside village of Sponkannis lies so quietly upon a protected spot on our Atlantic coast that it makes no more stir in the world than would a pebble which, held between one's finger and thumb, should be dipped below the surface of a millpond and then dropped. About the post-office and the store—both under the same roof—the greater number of the houses cluster, as if they had come for their week's groceries, or were waiting for the mail, while toward the west the dwellings become fewer and fewer, until at last the village blends into a long stretch of sandy coast and scrubby pine-woods. Eastward the village ends abruptly at the foot of a windswept bluff, on which no one cares to build.

Among the last houses in the western end of the village stood two neat, substantial dwellings, one belonging to Captain Eli Bunker, and the other to Captain Cephas Dyer. These householders were two very respectable retired mariners, the first a widower about fifty, and the other a bachelor of perhaps the same age, a few years more or less making but little difference in this region of weather-beaten youth and seasoned age.

Each of these good captains lived alone, and each took entire charge of his own domestic affairs, not because he was poor, but because it pleased him to do so. When Captain Eli retired from the sea he was the owner of a good vessel, which he sold at a fair profit; and Captain Cephas had made money in many a voyage before he built his house in Sponkannis and settled there.

When Captain Eli's wife was living she was his household manager. But Captain Cephas had never had a woman in his house, except during the first few months of his occupancy, when certain female neighbors came in occasionally to attend to little matters of cleaning which, according to popular notions, properly belong to the sphere of woman.

But Captain Cephas soon put an end to this sort of thing. He did not like a woman's ways, especially her ways of attending to domestic affairs. He liked to live in sailor fashion, and to keep house in sailor fashion. In his establishment everything was shipshape, and everything which could be stowed away was stowed away, and, if possible, in a bunker. The floors were holystoned nearly every day, and the whole house was repainted about twice a year, a little at a time, when the weather was suitable for this marine recreation. Things not in frequent use were lashed securely to the walls, or perhaps put out of the way by being hauled up to the ceiling by means of blocks and tackle. His cooking was done sailor fashion, like everything else, and he never failed to have plum-duff on Sunday. His well was near his house, and every morning he dropped into it a lead and line, and noted down the depth of water. Three times a day he entered in a little note-book the state of the weather, the height of the mercury in barometer and thermometer, the direction of the wind, and special weather points when necessary.

Captain Eli managed his domestic affairs in an entirely different way. He kept house woman fashion—not, however, in the manner of an ordinary woman, but after the manner of his late wife, Miranda Bunker, now dead some seven years. Like his friend, Captain Cephas, he had had the assistance of his female neighbors during the earlier days of his widowerhood. But he soon found that these women did not do things as Miranda used to do them, and, although he frequently suggested that they should endeavor to imitate the methods of his late consort, they did not even try to do things as she used to do them, preferring their own ways. Therefore it was that Captain Eli determined to keep house by himself, and to do it, as nearly as his nature would allow, as Miranda used to do it. He swept his doors and he shook his door-mats; he washed his paint with soap and hot water; he dusted his furniture with a soft cloth, which he afterwards stuck behind a chest of drawers. He made his bed very neatly, turning down the sheet at the top, and setting the pillow upon edge, smoothing it carefully after he had done so. His cooking was based on the methods of the late Miranda. He had never been able to make bread rise properly, but he had always liked ship-biscuit, and he now greatly preferred them to the risen bread made by his neighbors. And as to coffee and the plainer articles of food with which he furnished his table, even Miranda herself would not have objected to them had she been alive and very hungry.

The houses of the two captains were not very far apart, and they were good neighbors, often smoking their pipes together and talking of the sea. But this was always on the little porch in front of Captain Cephas's house, or by his kitchen fire in the winter. Captain Eli did not like the smell of tobacco smoke in his house, or even in front of it in summer-time, when the doors were open. He had no objection himself to the odor of tobacco, but it was contrary to the principles of woman housekeeping that rooms should smell of it, and he was always true to those principles.

It was late in a certain December, and through the village there was a pleasant little flutter of Christmas preparations. Captain Eli had been up to the store, and he had stayed there a good while, warming himself by the stove, and watching the women coming in to buy things for Christmas. It was strange how many things they bought for presents or for holiday use—fancy soap and candy, handkerchiefs and little woollen shawls for old people, and a lot of pretty little things which he knew the use of, but which Captain Cephas would never have understood at all had he been there.

As Captain Eli came out of the store he saw a cart in which were two good-sized Christmas trees, which had been cut in the woods, and were going, one to Captain Holmes's house, and the other to Mother Nelson's. Captain Holmes had grandchildren, and Mother Nelson, with never a child of her own, good old soul, had three little orphan nieces who never wanted for anything needful at Christmas-time or any other time.

Captain Eli walked home very slowly, taking observations in his mind. It was more than seven years since he had had anything to do with Christmas, except that on that day he had always made himself a mince-pie, the construction and the consumption of which were equally difficult. It is true that neighbors had invited him, and they had invited Captain Cephas, to their Christmas dinners, but neither of these worthy seamen had ever accepted any of these invitations. Even holiday food, when not cooked in sailor fashion, did not agree with Captain Cephas, and it would have pained the good heart of Captain Eli if he had been forced to make believe to enjoy a Christmas dinner so very inferior to those which Miranda used to set before him.

But now the heart of Captain Eli was gently moved by a Christmas flutter. It had been foolish, perhaps, for him to go up to the store at such a time as this, but the mischief had been done. Old feelings had come back to him, and he would be glad to celebrate Christmas this year if he could think of any good way to do it. And the result of his mental observations was that he went over to Captain Cephas's house to talk to him about it.

Captain Cephas was in his kitchen, smoking his third morning pipe. Captain Eli filled his pipe, lighted it, and sat down by the fire.

"Cap'n," said he, "what do you say to our keepin Christmas this year? A Christmas dinner is no good if it's got to be eat alone, and you and me might eat ourn together. It might be in my house, or it might be in your house—it won't make no great difference to me which. Of course, I like woman housekeepin', as is laid down in the rules of service fer my house. But next best to that I like sailor housekeepin', so I don't mind which house the dinner is in, Cap'n Cephas, so it suits you."

Captain Cephas took his pipe from his mouth. "You're pretty late thinkin' about it," said he, "fer day after to-morrow's Christmas."

"That don't make no difference," said Captain Eli. "What things we want that are not in my house or your house we can easily get either up at the store or else in the woods."

"In the woods!" exclaimed Captain Cephas. "What in the name of thunder do you expect to get in the woods for Christmas?"

"A Christmas tree," said Captain Eli. "I thought it might be a nice thing to have a Christmas tree fer Christmas. Cap'n Holmes has got one, and Mother Nelson's got another. I guess nearly everybody's got one. It won't cost anything—I can go and cut it."

Captain Cephas grinned a grin, as if a great leak had been

Frank R. Stockton

sprung in the side of a vessel, stretching nearly from stem to stern.

"A Christmas tree!" he exclaimed. "Well, I am blessed! But look here, Cap'n Eli. You don't know what a Christmas tree's fer. It's fer children, and not fer grown-ups. Nobody ever does have a Christmas tree in any house where there ain't no children."

Captain Eli rose and stood with his back to the fire. "I didn't think of that," he said, "but I guess it's so. And when I come to think of it, a Christmas isn't much of a Christmas, anyway, without children."

"You never had none," said Captain Cephas, "and you've kept Christmas."

"Yes," replied Captain Eli, reflectively, "we did do it, but there was always a lackment—Miranda has said so, and I have said so."

"You didn't have no Christmas tree," said Captain Cephas.

"No, we didn't. But I don't think that folks was as much set on Christmas trees then as they 'pear to be now. I wonder," he continued, thoughtfully gazing at the ceiling, "if we was to fix up a Christmas tree—and you and me's got a lot of pretty things that we've picked up all over the world, that would go miles ahead of anything that could be bought at the store fer Christmas trees—if we was to fix up a tree real nice, if we couldn't get some child or other that wasn't likely to have a tree to come in and look at it, and stay awhile, and make Christmas more like Christmas. And then, when it went away, it could take along the things that was hangin' on the tree, and keep 'em fer its own."

"That wouldn't work," said Captain Cephas. "If you get a

child into this business, you must let it hang up its stockin' before it goes to bed, and find it full in the mornin', and then tell it an all-fired lie about Santa Claus if it asks any questions. Most children think more of stockin's than they do of trees—so I've heard, at least."

"I've got no objections to stockin's," said Captain Eli. "If it wanted to hang one up, it could hang one up either here or in my house, wherever we kept Christmas."

"You couldn't keep a child all night," sardonically remarked Captain Cephas, "and no more could I. Fer if it was to get up a croup in the night, it would be as if we was on a lee shore with anchors draggin' and a gale a-blowin'."

"That's so," said Captain Eli. "You've put it fair. I suppose if we did keep a child all night, we'd have to have some sort of a woman within hail in case of a sudden blow."

Captain Cephas sniffed. "What's the good of talkin'?" said he. "There ain't no child, and there ain't no woman that you could hire to sit all night on my front step or on your front step, a-waitin' to be piped on deck in case of croup."

"No," said Captain Eli. "I don't suppose there's any child in this village that ain't goin' to be provided with a Christmas tree or a Christmas stockin', or perhaps both—except, now I come to think of it, that little gal that was brought down here with her mother last summer, and has been kept by Mrs. Crumley sence her mother died."

"And won't be kept much longer," said Captain Cephas, "fer I've hearn Mrs. Crumley say she couldn't afford it."

"That's so," said Captain Eli. "If she can't afford to keep the little gal, she can't afford to give no Christmas trees nor stockin's, and so it seems to me, cap'n, that that little gal would be a pretty good child to help us keep Christmas."

"You're all the time forgettin'," said the other, "that nuther of us can keep a child all night."

Captain Eli seated himself, and looked ponderingly into the fire. "You're right, cap'n," said he. "We'd have to ship some woman to take care of her. Of course, it wouldn't be no use to ask Mrs. Crumley?"

Captain Cephas laughed. "I should say not."

"And there doesn't seem to be anybody else," said his companion. "Can you think of anybody, cap'n?"

"There ain't anybody to think of," replied Captain Cephas, "unless it might be Eliza Trimmer. She's generally ready enough to do anything that turns up. But she wouldn't be no good—her house is too far away for either you or me to hail her in case a croup came up suddint."

"That's so," said Captain Eli. "She does live a long way off."

"So that settles the whole business," said Captain Cephas. "She's too far away to come if wanted, and nuther of us couldn't keep no child without somebody to come if they was wanted, and it's no use to have a Christmas tree without a child. A Christmas without a Christmas tree don't seem agreeable to you, cap'n, so I guess we'd better get along just the same as we've been in the habit of doin', and eat our Christmas dinner, as we do our other meals in our own houses."

Captain Eli looked into the fire. "I don't like to give up things if I can help it. That was always my way. If wind and tide's ag'in' me, I can wait till one or the other, or both of them, serve."

"Yes," said Captain Cephas, "you was always that kind of a man."

"That's so. But it does 'pear to me as if I'd have to give up this time, though it's a pity to do it, on account of the little gal, fer she ain't likely to have any Christmas this year.

She's a nice little gal, and takes as natural to navigation as if she'd been born at sea. I've given her two or three things because she's so pretty, but there's nothing she likes so much as a little ship I gave her."

"Perhaps she was born at sea," remarked Captain Cephas.

"Perhaps she was," said the other; "and that makes it the bigger pity."

For a few moments nothing was said. Then Captain Eli suddenly exclaimed, "I'll tell you what we might do, cap'n! We might ask Mrs. Trimmer to lend a hand in givin' the little gal a Christmas. She ain't got nobody in her house but herself, and I guess she'd be glad enough to help give that little gal a regular Christmas. She could go and get the child, and bring her to your house or to my house, or wherever we're goin' to keep Christmas, and—"

"Well," said Captain Cephas, with an air of scrutinizing inquiry, "what?"

"Well," replied the other, a little hesitatingly, "so far as I'm concerned,—that is, I don't mind one way or the other,— she might take her Christmas dinner along with us and the little gal, and then she could fix her stockin' to be hung up, and help with the Christmas tree, and—"

"Well," demanded Captain Cephas, "what?"

Frank R. Stockton

"Well," said Captain Eli, "she could—that is, it doesn't make any difference to me one way or the other—she might stay all night at whatever house we kept Christmas in, and then you and me might spend the night in the other house, and then she could be ready there to help the child in the mornin', when she came to look at her stockin'."

Captain Cephas fixed upon his friend an earnest glare. "That's pretty considerable of an idea to come upon you so suddint," said he. "But I can tell you one thing: there ain't a-goin' to be any such doin's in my house. If you choose to come over here to sleep, and give up your house to any woman you can find to take care of the little gal, all right. But the thing can't be done here."

There was a certain severity in these remarks, but they appeared to affect Captain Eli very pleasantly.

"Well," said he, "if you're satisfied, I am. I'll agree to any plan you choose to make. It doesn't matter to me which house it's in, and if you say my house, I say my house. All I want is to make the business agreeable to all concerned. Now it's time fer me to go to my dinner, and this afternoon we'd better go and try to get things straightened out, because the little gal, and whatever woman comes with her, ought to be at my house to-morrow before dark. S'posin' we divide up this business: I'll go and see Mrs. Crumley about the little gal, and you can go and see Mrs. Trimmer."

"No, sir," promptly replied Captain Cephas, "I don't go to see no Mrs. Trimmer. You can see both of them just the same as you can see one—they're all along the same way. I'll go cut the Christmas tree."

"All right," said Captain Eli. "It don't make no difference to me which does which. But if I was you, cap'n, I'd cut a good big tree, because we might as well have a good one while we're about it."

When he had eaten his dinner, and washed up his dishes, and had put everything away in neat, housewifely order, Captain Eli went to Mrs. Crumley's house, and very soon finished his business there. Mrs. Crumley kept the only house which might be considered a boarding-house in the village of Sponkannis; and when she had consented to take charge of the little girl who had been left on her hands she had hoped it would not be very long before she would hear from some of her relatives in regard to her maintenance. But she had heard nothing, and had now ceased to expect to hear anything, and in consequence had frequently remarked that she must dispose of the child some way or other, for she couldn't afford to keep her any longer. Even an absence of a day or two at the house of the good captain would be some relief, and Mrs. Crumley readily consented to the Christmas scheme. As to the little girl, she was delighted. She already looked upon Captain Eli as her best friend in the world.

It was not so easy to go to Mrs. Trimmer's house and put the business before her. "It ought to be plain sailin' enough," Captain Eli said to himself, over and over again, "but, fer all that, it don't seem to be plain sailin'."

But he was not a man to be deterred by difficult navigation, and he walked straight to Eliza Trimmer's house.

Mrs. Trimmer was a comely woman about thirty-five, who had come to the village a year before, and had maintained herself, or at least had tried to, by dressmaking and plain sewing. She had lived at Stetford, a seaport about twenty miles away, and from there, three years before, her husband, Captain Trimmer, had sailed away in a good-sized schooner, and had never returned. She had come to Sponkannis because she thought that there she could live cheaper and get more work than in her former home. She had found the

Frank R. Stockton

first quite possible, but her success in regard to the work had not been very great.

When Captain Eli entered Mrs. Trimmer's little room, he found her busy mending a sail. Here fortune favored him. "You turn your hand to 'most anything, Mrs. Trimmer," said he, after he had greeted her.

"Oh, yes," she answered, with a smile, "I am obliged to do that. Mending sails is pretty heavy work, but it's better than nothing."

"I had a notion," said he, "that you was ready to turn your hand to any good kind of business, so I thought I would step in and ask you if you'd turn your hand to a little bit of business I've got on the stocks."

She stopped sewing on the sail, and listened while Captain Eli laid his plan before her. "It's very kind in you and Captain Cephas to think of all that," said she. "I have often noticed that poor little girl, and pitied her. Certainly I'll come, and you needn't say anything about paying me for it. I wouldn't think of asking to be paid for doing a thing like that. And besides,"—she smiled again as she spoke,—"if you are going to give me a Christmas dinner, as you say, that will make things more than square."

Captain Eli did not exactly agree with her, but he was in very good humor, and she was in good humor, and the matter was soon settled, and Mrs. Trimmer promised to come to the captain's house in the morning and help about the Christmas tree, and in the afternoon to go to get the little girl from Mrs. Crumley's and bring her to the house.

Captain Eli was delighted with the arrangements. "Things now seem to be goin' along before a spankin' breeze,"said he. "But I don't know about the dinner. I guess you will have to leave that to me. I don't believe Captain Cephas could eat a woman-cooked dinner. He's accustomed to livin sailor fashion, you know, and he has declared over and over again to me that woman-cookin' doesn't agree with him."

"But I can cook sailor fashion," said Mrs. Trimmer,—"just as much sailor fashion as you or Captain Cephas, and if he don't believe it, I'll prove it to him; so you needn't worry about that."

When the captain had gone, Mrs. Trimmer gayly put away the sail. There was no need to finish it in a hurry, and no knowing when she would get her money for it when it was done. No one had asked her to a Christmas dinner that year, and she had expected to have a lonely time of it. But it would be very pleasant to spend Christmas with the little girl and the two good captains. Instead of sewing any more on the sail, she got out some of her own clothes to see if they needed anything done to them.

The next morning Mrs. Trimmer went to Captain Eli's house, and finding Captain Cephas there, they all set to work at the Christmas tree, which was a very fine one, and had been planted in a box. Captain Cephas had brought over a bundle of things from his house, and Captain Eli kept running here and there, bringing, each time that he returned, some new object, wonderful or pretty, which he had brought from China or Japan or Corea, or some spicy island of the Eastern seas; and nearly every time he came with these treasures Mrs. Trimmer declared that such things were too good to put upon a Christmas tree, even for such a nice little girl as the one for which that tree was intended. The presents which Captain Cephas brought were much more suitable for the purpose; they were odd and funny, and some of them pretty, but not expensive, as were the fans and bits of shellwork and carved ivories which Captain Eli wished to tie upon the twigs of the tree.

There was a good deal of talk about all this, but Captain Eli had his own way.

"I don't suppose, after all," said he, "that the little gal ought to have all the things. This is such a big tree that it's more like a family tree. Cap'n Cephas can take some of my things, and I can take some of his things, and, Mrs. Trimmer, if there's anything you like, you can call it your present and take it for your own, so that will be fair and comfortable all round. What I want is to make everybody satisfied."

"I'm sure I think they ought to be," said Mrs. Trimmer, looking very kindly at Captain Eli.

Mrs. Trimmer went home to her own house to dinner, and in the afternoon she brought the little girl. She had said there ought to be an early supper, so that the child would have time to enjoy the Christmas tree before she became sleepy.

This meal was prepared entirely by Captain Eli, and in sailor fashion, not woman fashion, so that Captain Cephas could make no excuse for eating his supper at home. Of course they all ought to be together the whole of that Christmas eve. As for the big dinner on the morrow, that was another affair, for Mrs. Trimmer undertook to make Captain Cephas understand that she had always cooked for Captain Trimmer in sailor fashion, and if he objected to her plum-duff, or if anybody else objected to her mince-pie, she was going to be very much surprised.

Captain Cephas ate his supper with a good relish, and was still eating when the rest had finished. As to the Christmas tree, it was the most valuable, if not the most beautiful, that had ever been set up in that region. It had no candles upon it, but was lighted by three lamps and a ship's lantern placed in the four corners of the room, and the little girl was as happy as if the tree were decorated with little dolls and glass balls. Mrs. Trimmer was intensely pleased and interested to see the child so happy, and Captain Eli was much pleased and interested to see the child and Mrs. Trimmer so happy, and Captain Cephas was interested, and perhaps a little amused in a superior fashion, to see Captain Eli and Mrs. Trimmer and the little child so happy.

Then the distribution of the presents began. Captain Eli asked Captain Cephas if he might have the wooden pipe that the latter had brought for his present. Captain Cephas said he might take it, for all he cared, and be welcome to it. Then Captain Eli gave Captain Cephas a red bandanna handkerchief of a very curious pattern, and Captain Cephas thanked him kindly. After which Captain Eli bestowed upon Mrs. Trimmer a most beautiful tortoise-shell comb, carved and cut and polished in a wonderful way, and with it he gave a tortoise-shell fan, carved in the same fashion, because he said the two things seemed to belong to each other and ought to go together; and he would not listen to one word of what Mrs. Trimmer said about the gifts being too good for her, and that she was not likely ever to use them.

"It seems to me," said Captain Cephas, "that you might be giving something to the little gal."

Then Captain Eli remembered that the child ought not to be forgotten, and her soul was lifted into ecstasy by many gifts, some of which Mrs. Trimmer declared were too good for any child in this wide, wide world. But Captain Eli answered that they could be taken care of by somebody until the little girl was old enough to know their value.

Then it was discovered that, unbeknown to anybody else,

Mrs. Trimmer had put some presents on the tree, which were things which had been brought by Captain Trimmer from somewhere in the far East or the distant West. These she bestowed upon Captain Cephas and Captain Eli. And the end of all this was that in the whole of Sponkannis, from the foot of the bluff to the east, to the very last house on the shore to the west, there was not one Christmas eve party so happy as this one.

Captain Cephas was not quite so happy as the three others were, but he was very much interested. About nine o'clock the party broke up, and the two captains put on their caps and buttoned up their pea-jackets, and started for Captain Cephas's house, but not before Captain Eli had carefully fastened every window and every door except the front door, and had told Mrs. Trimmer how to fasten that when they had gone, and had given her a boatswain's whistle, which she might blow out of the window if there should be a sudden croup and it should be necessary for any one to go anywhere. He was sure he could hear it, for the wind was exactly right for him to hear a whistle from his house. When they had gone Mrs. Trimmer put the little girl to bed, and was delighted to find in what a wonderfully neat and womanlike fashion that house was kept.

It was nearly twelve o'clock that night when Captain Eli, sleeping in his bunk opposite that of Captain Cephas, was aroused by hearing a sound. He had been lying with his best ear uppermost, so that he should hear anything if there happened to be anything to hear. He did hear something, but it was not a boatswain's whistle; it was a prolonged cry, and it seemed to come from the sea.

In a moment Captain Eli was sitting on the side of his bunk, listening intently. Again came the cry. The window toward the sea was slightly open, and he heard it plainly.

"Cap'n! " said he, and at the word Captain Cephas was sitting on the side of his bunk, listening. He knew from his companion's attitude, plainly visible in the light of a lantern which hung on a hook at the other end of the room, that he had been awakened to listen. Again came the cry.

"That's distress at sea," said Captain Cephas. "Harken!"

They listened again for nearly a minute, when the cry was repeated.

"Bounce on deck, boys!" said Captain Cephas, getting out on the floor. "There's some one in distress off shore."

Captain Eli jumped to the floor, and began to dress quickly.

"It couldn't be a call from land?" he asked hurriedly. "It don't sound a bit to you like a boatswain's whistle, does it?"

"No," said Captain Cephas, disdainfully. "It's a call from sea." Then, seizing a lantern, he rushed down the companionway.

As soon as he was convinced that it was a call from sea, Captain Eli was one in feeling and action with Captain Cephas. The latter hastily opened the draughts of the kitchen stove, and put on some wood, and by the time this was done Captain Eli had the kettle filled and on the stove. Then they clapped on their caps and their pea-jackets, each took an oar from a corner in the back hall, and together they ran down to the beach.

The night was dark, but not very cold, and Captain Cephas had been to the store that morning in his boat.

Whenever he went to the store, and the weather permitted, he rowed there in his boat rather than walk. At the bow of the boat, which was now drawn up on the sand, the two men stood and listened. Again came the cry from the sea.

"It's something ashore on the Turtle-back Shoal," said Captain Cephas.

"Yes," said Captain Eli, "and it's some small craft, fer that cry is down pretty nigh to the water."

"Yes," said Captain Cephas. "And there's only one man aboard, or else they'd take turns a-hollerin'."

"He's a stranger," said Captain Eli, "or he wouldn't have tried, even with a cat-boat, to get in over that shoal on ebb-tide."

As they spoke they ran the boat out into the water and jumped in, each with an oar. Then they pulled for the Turtle-back Shoal.

Although these two captains were men of fifty or thereabout, they were as strong and tough as any young fellows in the village, and they pulled with steady strokes, and sent the heavy boat skimming over the water, not in a straight line toward the Turtle-back Shoal, but now a few points in the darkness this way, and now a few points in the darkness that way, then with a great curve to the south through the dark night, keeping always near the middle of the only good channel out of the bay when the tide was ebbing.

Now the cries from seaward had ceased, but the two captains were not discouraged.

"He's heard the thumpin' of our oars," said Captain Cephas.

"He's listenin', and he'll sing out again if he thinks we're goin' wrong," said Captain Eli. "Of course he doesn't know anything about that."

And so when they made the sweep to the south the cry came again, and Captain Eli grinned. "We needn't to spend no breath hollerin'," said he. "He'll hear us makin' fer him in a minute."

When they came to head for the shoal they lay on their oars for a moment, while Captain Cephas turned the lantern in the bow, so that its light shone out ahead. He had not wanted the shipwrecked person to see the light when it would seem as if the boat were rowing away from him. He had heard of castaway people who became so wild when they imagined that a ship or boat was going away from them that they jumped overboard.

When the two captains reached the shoal, they found there a cat-boat aground, with one man aboard. His tale was quickly told. He had expected to run into the little bay that afternoon, but the wind had fallen, and in trying to get in after dark, and being a stranger, he had run aground. If he had not been so cold, he said, he would have been willing to stay there till the tide rose; but he was getting chilled, and seeing a light not far away, he concluded to call for help as long as his voice held out.

The two captains did not ask many questions. They helped anchor the cat-boat, and then they took the man on their boat and rowed him to shore. He was getting chilled sitting out there doing nothing, and so when they reached the house they made him some hot grog, and promised in the morning, when the tide rose, they would go out and help him bring his boat in. Then Captain Cephas showed the stranger to a bunk, and they all went to bed. Such experiences had not enough of novelty to the good captains to keep them awake five minutes.

In the morning they were all up very early, and the stranger, who proved to be a seafaring man with bright blue eyes, said that, as his cat-boat seemed to be riding all right at its anchorage, he did not care to go out after her just yet. Any time during flood-tide would do for him, and he had some business that he wanted to attend to as soon as possible.

This suited the two captains very well, for they wished to be on hand when the little girl discovered her stocking.

"Can you tell me," said the stranger, as he put on his cap, "where I can find a Mrs. Trimmer, who lives in this village?"

At these words all the sturdy stiffness which, from his youth up, had characterized the legs of Captain Eli entirely went out of them, and he sat suddenly upon a bench. For a few moments there was silence.

Then Captain Cephas, who thought some answer should be made to the question, nodded his head.

"I want to see her as soon as I can," said the stranger. "I have come to see her on particular business that will be a surprise to her. I wanted to be here before Christmas began, and that's the reason I took that cat-boat from Stetford, because I thought I'd come quicker that way than by land. But the wind fell, as I told you. If either one of you would be good enough to pilot me to where Mrs. Trimmer lives, or to any point where I can get a sight of the place, I'd be obliged."

Captain Eli rose and with hurried but unsteady steps went into the house (for they had been upon the little piazza), and beckoned to his friend to follow. The two men stood in the kitchen and looked at each other. The face of Captain Eli was of the hue of a clam-shell.

"Go with him, cap'n," he said in a hoarse whisper. "I can't do it."

"To your house?" inquired the other.

"Of course. Take him to my house. There ain't no other place where she is. Take him along."

Captain Cephas's countenance wore an air of the deepest concern, but he thought that the best thing to do was to get the stranger away.

As they walked rapidly toward Captain Eli's house there was very little said by either Captain Cephas or the stranger. The latter seemed anxious to give Mrs. Trimmer a surprise, and not to say anything which might enable another person to interfere with his project.

The two men had scarcely stepped upon the piazza when Mrs. Trimmer, who had been expecting early visitors, opened the door. She was about to call out "Merry Christmas!" but, her eyes falling upon a stranger, the words stopped at her lips. First she turned red, then she turned pale, and Captain Cephas thought she was about to fall. But before she could do this the stranger had her in his arms. She opened her eyes, which for a moment she had closed, and, gazing into his face, she put her arms around his neck. Then Captain Cephas came away, without thinking of the little girl and the pleasure she would have in discovering her Christmas stocking.

When he had been left alone, Captain Eli sat down near the kitchen stove, close to the very kettle which he had filled with water to heat for the benefit of the man he had helped bring in from the sea, and, with his elbows on his knees and his fingers in his hair, he darkly pondered.

"If I'd only slept with my hard-o'-hearin' ear up," he said to himself, "I'd never have heard it."

In a few moments his better nature condemned this thought.

"That's next to murder," he muttered, "fer he couldn't have kept himself from fallin' asleep out there in the cold, and when the tide riz held have been blowed out to sea with this wind. If I hadn't heard him, Captain Cephas never would, fer he wasn't primed up to wake, as I was."

But, notwithstanding his better nature, Captain Eli was again saying to himself, when his friend returned, "If I'd only slept with my other ear up!"

Like the honest, straightforward mariner he was, Captain Cephas made an exact report of the facts. "They was huggin' when I left them," he said, "and I expect they went indoors pretty soon, fer it was too cold outside. It's an all-fired shame she happened to be in your house, cap'n, that's all I've got to say about it. It's a thunderin' shame."

Captain Eli made no answer. He still sat with his elbows on his knees and his hands in his hair.

"A better course than you laid down fer these Christmas times was never dotted on a chart," continued Captain Cephas. "From port of sailin' to port of entry you laid it down clear and fine. But it seems there was rocks that wasn't marked on the chart."

"Yes," groaned Captain Eli, "there was rocks."

Captain Cephas made no attempt to comfort his friend, but went to work to get breakfast.

When that meal—a rather silent one—was over, Captain Eli felt better. "There was rocks," he said, "and not a breaker to show where they lay, and I struck 'em bow on. So that's the end of that voyage. But I've tuk to my boats, cap'n, I've tuk to my boats."

"I'm glad to hear you've tuk to your boats," said Captain Cephas, with an approving glance upon his friend.

About ten minutes afterwards Captain Eli said, "I'm goin' up to my house."

"By yourself?" said the other.

"Yes, by myself. I'd rather go alone. I don't intend to mind anything, and I'm goin' to tell her that she can stay there and spend Christmas,—the place she lives in ain't no place to spend Christmas,—and she can make the little gal have a good time, and go 'long just as we intended to go 'long— plum-duff and mince-pie all the same. I can stay here, and you and me can have our Christmas dinner together, if we choose to give it that name.

And if she ain't ready to go to-morrow, she can stay a day or two longer. It's all the same to me, if it's the same to you, cap'n."

Captain Cephas having said that it was the same to him, Captain Eli put on his cap and buttoned up his pea-jacket, declaring that the sooner he got to his house the better, as she might be thinking that she would have to move out of it now that things were different.

Before Captain Eli reached his house he saw something which pleased him. He saw the sea-going stranger, with his back toward him, walking rapidly in the direction of the village store.

Frank R. Stockton

Captain Eli quickly entered his house, and in the doorway of the room where the tree was he met Mrs. Trimmer, beaming brighter than any morning sun that ever rose.

"Merry Christmas!" she exclaimed, holding out both her hands. "I've been wondering and wondering when you'd come to bid me 'Merry Christmas'—the merriest Christmas I've ever had."

Captain Eli took her hands and bid her "Merry Christmas" very gravely.

She looked a little surprised. "What's the matter, Captain Eli?" she exclaimed. "You don't seem to say that as if you meant it."

"Oh, yes, I do," he answered. "This must be an all-fired—I mean a thunderin' happy Christmas fer you, Mrs. Trimmer."

"Yes," said she, her face beaming again. "And to think that it should happen on Christmas day—that this blessed morning, before anything else happened, my Bob, my only brother, should—"

"Your what!" roared Captain Eli, as if he had been shouting orders in a raging storm.

Mrs. Trimmer stepped back almost frightened. "My brother," said she. "Didn't he tell you he was my brother— my brother Bob, who sailed away a year before I was married, and who has been in Africa and China and I don't know where? It's so long since I heard that he'd gone into trading at Singapore that I'd given him up as married and settled in foreign parts. And here he has come to me as if he'd tumbled from the sky on this blessed Christmas morning."

Captain Eli made a step forward, his face very much flushed.

"Your brother, Mrs. Trimmer—did you really say it was your brother?"

"Of course it is," said she. "Who else could it be?" Then she paused for a moment and looked steadfastly at the captain.

"You don't mean to say, Captain Eli," she asked, "that you thought it was—"

"Yes, I did," said Captain Eli, promptly.

Mrs. Trimmer looked straight in the captain's eyes, then she looked on the ground. Then she changed color and changed back again.

"I don't understand," she said hesitatingly, "why—I mean what difference it made."

"Difference!" exclaimed Captain Eli. "It was all the difference between a man on deck and a man overboard—that's the difference it was to me. I didn't expect to be talkin' to you so early this Christmas mornin', but things has been sprung on me, and I can't help it I just want to ask you one thing: Did you think I was gettin' up this Christmas tree and the Christmas dinner and the whole business fer the good of the little gal, and fer the good of you, and fer the good of Captain Cephas?"

Mrs. Trimmer had now recovered a very fair possession of herself. "Of course I did," she answered, looking up at him as she spoke. "Who else could it have been for!"

"Well," said he, "you were mistaken. It wasn't fer any one of you. It was all fer me—fer my own self."

"You yourself?" said she. "I don't see how."

"But I see how," he answered. "It's been a long time since I wanted to speak my mind to you, Mrs. Trimmer, but I didn't ever have no chance. And all these Christmas doin's was got up to give me the chance not only of speakin' to you, but of showin' my colors better than I could show them in any other way. Everything went on a-skimmin' till this mornin', when that stranger that we brought in from the shoal piped up and asked fer you. Then I went overboard—at least, I thought I did—and sunk down, down, clean out of soundin's."

"That was too bad, captain," said she, speaking very gently, "after all your trouble and kindness."

"But I don't know now," he continued, "whether I went overboard or whether I am on deck. Can you tell me, Mrs. Trimmer?"

She looked up at him. Her eyes were very soft, and her lips trembled just a little. "It seems to me, captain," she said, "that you are on deck—if you want to be."

The captain stepped closer to her. "Mrs. Trimmer," said he, "is that brother of yours comin' back?"

"Yes," she answered, surprised at the sudden question. "He's just gone up to the store to buy a shirt and some things. He got himself splashed trying to push his boat off last night."

"Well, then," said Captain Eli, "would you mind tellin' him when he comes back that you and me's engaged to be married? I don't know whether I've made a mistake in the lights or not, but would you mind tellin' him that?"

Mrs. Trimmer looked at him. Her eyes were not so soft as

they had been, but they were brighter. "I'd rather you'd tell him that yourself," said she.

The little girl sat on the floor near the Christmas tree, just finishing a large piece of red-and-white candy which she had taken out of her stocking. "People do hug a lot at Christmas-time," said she to herself. Then she drew out a piece of blue-and-white candy and began on that.

Captain Cephas waited a long time for his friend to return, and at last he thought it would be well to go and look for him. When he entered the house he found Mrs. Trimmer sitting on the sofa in the parlor, with Captain Eli on one side of her and her brother on the other, and each of them holding one of her hands.

"It looks as if I was in port, don't it?" said Captain Eli to his astonished friend. "Well, here I am, and here's my fust mate," inclining his head toward Mrs. Trimmer. "And she's in port too, safe and sound. And that strange captain on the other side of her, he's her brother Bob, who's been away for years and years, and is just home from Madagascar."

"Singapore," amended Brother Bob.

Captain Cephas looked from one to the other of the three occupants of the sofa, but made no immediate remark. Presently a smile of genial maliciousness stole over his face, and he asked, "How about the poor little gal? Have you sent her back to Mrs. Crumley's?"

The little girl came out from behind the Christmas tree, her stocking, now but half filled, in her hand. "Here I am," she said. "Don't you want to give me a Christmas hug, Captain Cephas? You and me's the only ones that hasn't had any."

The Christmas dinner was as truly and perfectly a sailor-cooked meal as ever was served on board a ship or off it. Captain Cephas had said that, and when he had so spoken there was no need of further words.

It was nearly dark that afternoon, and they were all sitting around the kitchen fire, the three seafaring men smoking, and Mrs. Trimmer greatly enjoying it. There could be no objection to the smell of tobacco in this house so long as its future mistress enjoyed it. The little girl sat on the floor nursing a Chinese idol which had been one of her presents.

"After all," said Captain Eli, meditatively, "this whole business come out of my sleepin' with my best ear up. Fer if I'd slept with my hard-o'-hearin' ear up—" Mrs. Trimmer put one finger on his lips. "All right," said Captain Eli, "I won't say no more. But it would have been different."

Even now, several years after that Christmas, when there is no Mrs. Trimmer, and the little girl, who has been regularly adopted by Captain Eli and his wife, is studying geography, and knows more about latitude and longitude than her teacher at school, Captain Eli has still a slight superstitious dread of sleeping with his best ear uppermost.

"Of course it's the most all-fired nonsense," he says to himself over and over again. Nevertheless, he feels safer when it is his "hard-o'-hearin' ear" that is not upon the pillow.

LOVE BEFORE BREAKFAST

I was still a young man when I came into the possession of an excellent estate. This consisted of a large country house, surrounded by lawns, groves, and gardens, and situated not far from the flourishing little town of Boynton. Being an orphan with no brothers or sisters, I set up here a bachelor's hall, in which, for two years, I lived with great satisfaction and comfort, improving my grounds and furnishing my house. When I had made all the improvements which were really needed, and feeling that I now had a most delightful home to come back to, I thought it would be an excellent thing to take a trip to Europe, give my mind a run in fresh fields, and pick up a lot of bric-a-brac and ideas for the adornment and advantage of my house and mind.

It was the custom of the residents in my neighborhood who owned houses and travelled in the summer to let their houses during their absence, and my business agent and myself agreed that this would be an excellent thing for me to do. If the house were let to a suitable family it would yield me a considerable income, and the place would not present on my return that air of retrogression and desolation which I might expect if it were left unoccupied and in charge of a caretaker.

My agent assured me that I would have no trouble whatever in letting my place, for it offered many advantages and I

Frank R. Stockton

expected but a reasonable rent. I desired to leave everything just as it stood, house, furniture, books, horses, cows, and poultry, taking with me only my clothes and personal requisites, and I desired tenants who would come in bringing only their clothes and personal requisites, which they could quietly take away with them when their lease should expire and I should return home.

In spite, however, of the assurances of the agent, it was not easy to let my place. The house was too large for some people, too small for others, and while some applicants had more horses than I had stalls in my stable, others did not want even the horses I would leave. I had engaged my steamer passage, and the day for my departure drew near, and yet no suitable tenants had presented themselves. I had almost come to the conclusion that the whole matter would have to be left in the hands of my agent, for I had no intention whatever of giving up my projected travels, when early one afternoon some people came to look at the house. Fortunately I was at home, and I gave myself the pleasure of personally conducting them about the premises. It was a pleasure, because as soon as I comprehended the fact that these applicants desired to rent my house I wished them to have it.

The family consisted of an elderly gentleman and his wife, with a daughter of twenty or thereabout. This was a family that suited me exactly. Three in number, no children, people of intelligence and position, fond of the country, and anxious for just such a place as I offered them—what could be better?

The more I walked about and talked with these good people and showed them my possessions, the more I desired that the young lady should take my house. Of course her parents were included in this wish, but it was for her ears that all my remarks were intended, although sometimes addressed to the others, and she was the tenant I labored to obtain. I say "labored" advisedly, because I racked my brain to think of inducements which might bring them to a speedy and favorable decision.

Apart from the obvious advantages of the arrangement, it would be a positive delight to me during my summer wanderings in Europe to think that that beautiful girl would be strolling through my grounds, enjoying my flowers, and sitting with her book in the shady nooks I had made so pleasant, lying in my hammocks, spending her evening hours in my study, reading my books, writing at my desk, and perhaps musing in my easy-chair. Before these applicants appeared it had sometimes pained me to imagine strangers in my home; but no such thought crossed my mind in regard to this young lady, who, if charming in the house and on the lawn, grew positively entrancing when she saw my Jersey cows and my two horses, regarding them with an admiration which even surpassed my own.

Long before we had completed the tour of inspection I had made up my mind that this young lady should come to live in my house. If obstacles should show themselves they should be removed. I would tear down, I would build, I would paper and paint, I would put in all sorts of electric bells, I would reduce the rent until it suited their notions exactly, I would have my horses' tails banged if she liked that kind of tails better than long ones—I would do anything to make them definitely decide to take the place before they left me. I trembled to think of her going elsewhere and giving other householders a chance to tempt her. She had looked at a good many country houses, but it was quite plain that none of them had pleased her so well as mine.

I left them in my library to talk the matter over by themselves, and in less than ten minutes the young lady herself came out on the lawn to tell me that her father and mother had decided to take the place and would like to speak with me.

"I am so glad," she said as we went in. "I am sure I shall enjoy every hour of our stay here. It is so different from anything we have yet seen."

When everything had been settled I wanted to take them again over the place and point out a lot of things I had omitted. I particularly wanted to show them some lovely walks in the woods. But there was no time, for they had to catch a train.

Her name was Vincent—Cora Vincent, as I discovered from her mother's remarks.

As soon as they departed I had my mare saddled and rode into town to see my agent. I went into his office exultant.

"I've let my house," I said, "and I want you to make out the lease and have everything fixed and settled as soon as possible. This is the address of my tenants."

The agent asked me a good many questions, being particularly anxious to know what rent had been agreed upon.

"Heavens!" he exclaimed, when I mentioned the sum, "that is ever so much less than I told you you could get. I am in communication now with a party whom I know would pay you considerably more than these people. Have you definitely settled with them? Perhaps it is not too late to withdraw."

"Withdraw!" I cried. "Never! They are the only tenants I want. I was determined to get them, and I think I must have lowered the rent four or five times in the course of the afternoon. I took a big slice out of it before I mentioned the sum at all. You see," said I, very impressively, "these Vincents exactly suit me." And then I went on to state fully the advantages of the arrangement, omitting, however, any references to my visions of Miss Vincent swinging in my hammocks or musing in my study-chair.

It was now May 15, and my steamer would sail on the twenty-first. The intervening days I employed, not in preparing for my travels, but in making every possible arrangement for the comfort and convenience of my incoming tenants. The Vincents did not wish to take possession until June 1, and I was sorry they had not applied before I had engaged my passage, for in that case I would have selected a later date. A very good steamer sailed on June 3, and it would have suited me just as well.

Happening to be in New York one day, I went to the Vincents' city residence to consult with them in regard to some awnings which I proposed putting up at the back of the house. I found no one at home but the old gentleman, and it made no difference to him whether the awnings were black and brown or red and yellow. I cordially invited him to come out before I left, and bring his family, that they might look about the place to see if there was anything they would like to have done which had not already been attended to. It was so much better, I told him, to talk over these matters personally with the owner than with an agent in his absence. Agents were often very unwilling to make changes. Mr. Vincent was a very quiet and exceedingly pleasant elderly gentleman, and thanked me very much for my invitation, but said he did not see how he could find the time to get out to my house before I sailed. I did not like to say that it was not at all necessary for him to neglect his affairs in order to accompany his family to my place, but I assured him that if any of them wished to go out at any time before they took possession they must feel at perfect liberty to do so.

I mentioned this matter to my agent, suggesting that if he happened to be in New York he might call on the Vincents and repeat my invitation. It was not likely that the old gentleman would remember to mention it to his wife and daughter, and it was really important that everything should be made satisfactory before I left.

"It seems to me," he said, smiling a little grimly, "that the Vincents had better be kept away from your house until you have gone. If you do anything more to it you may find out that it would have been more profitable to have shut it up while you are away."

He did call, however, partly because I wished him to and partly because he was curious to see the people I was so anxious to install in my home, and to whom he was to be my legal representative. He reported the next day that he had found no one at home but Miss Vincent, and that she had said that she and her mother would be very glad to come out the next week and go over the place before they took possession.

"Next week!" I exclaimed. "I shall be gone then!"

"But I shall be here," said Mr. Barker, "and I'll show them about and take their suggestions."

This did not suit me at all. It annoyed me very much to think of Barker showing Miss Vincent about my place. He was a good-looking young man and not at all backward in his manners.

"After all," said I, "I suppose that everything that ought to be done has been done. I hope you told her that."

"Of course not," said he. "That would have been running dead against your orders. Besides, it's my business to show people about places. I don't mind it."

This gave me an unpleasant and uneasy feeling. I wondered if Mr. Barker were the agent I ought to have, and if a middle-aged man with a family and more experience might not be better able to manage my affairs.

"Barker," said I, a little later, "there will be no use of your going every month to the Vincents to collect their rent. I shall write to Mr. Vincent to pay as he pleases. He can send a check monthly or at the end of the season, as it may be convenient. He is perfectly responsible, and I would much prefer to have the money in a lump when I come back."

Barker grinned. "All right," said he, "but that's not the way to do business, you know."

I may have been mistaken, but I fancied that I saw in my agent's face an expression which indicated that he intended to call on the first day of each month, on the pretext of telling Vincent that it was not necessary to pay the rent at any particular time, and that he also proposed to make many other intervening visits to inquire if repairs were needed. This might have been a good deal to get out of his expression, but I think I could have got more if I had thought longer.

On the day before that on which I was to sail, my mind was in such a disturbed condition that I could not attend to my packing or anything else. It almost enraged me to think that I was deliberately leaving the country ten days before my tenants would come to my house. There was no reason why I should do this. There were many reasons why I should not. There was Barker. I was now of the opinion that he would personally superintend the removal of the Vincents and their establishment to my home. I remembered that the only suggestion he had made about the improvement of the place had been the construction of a tennis-court. I knew that he was a champion player. Confound it! What a dreadful mistake I had made in selecting such a man for my house-agent. With my mind's eye I could already see Miss Vincent and Barker selecting a spot for tennis and planning the arrangements of the court.

I took the first train to New York and went directly to the steamboat office. It is astonishing how many obstacles can be removed from a man's path if he will make up his mind to give them a good kick. I found that my steamer was crowded. The applications for passage exceeded the accommodations, and the agent was delighted to transfer me to the steamer that sailed on June 3. I went home exultant. Barker drove over in the evening to take his last instructions, and a blank look came over his face when I told him that business had delayed my departure, and that I should not sail the next day. If I had told him that part of that business was the laying out of a tennis-court he might have looked blanker.

Of course the date of my departure did not concern the Vincents, provided the house was vacated by June 1, and I did not inform them of the change in my plans, but when the mother and daughter came out the next week they were much surprised to find me waiting to receive them instead of Barker. I hope that they were also pleased, and I am sure that they had every reason to be so. Mrs. Vincent, having discovered that I was a most complacent landlord, accommodated herself easily to my disposition and made a number of minor requirements, all of which I granted without the slightest hesitation. I was delighted at last to put her into the charge of my housekeeper, and when the two had betaken themselves to the bedrooms I invited Miss Vincent to come out with me to select a spot for a tennis-court. The invitation was accepted with alacrity, for tennis, she declared, was a passion with her.

The selection of that tennis-court took nearly an hour, for there were several good places for one and it was hard to make a selection; besides, I could not lose the opportunity of taking Miss Vincent into the woods and showing her the walks I had made and the rustic seats I had placed in pleasant nooks. Of course she would have discovered these, but it was a great deal better for her to know all about them before she came. At last Mrs. Vincent sent a maid to tell her daughter that it was time to go for the train, and the court had not been definitely planned.

The next day I went to Miss Vincent's house with a plan of the grounds, and she and I talked it over until the matter was settled. It was necessary to be prompt about this, I explained, as there would be a great deal of levelling and rolling to be done.

I also had a talk with the old gentleman about books. There were several large boxes of my books in New York which I had never sent out to my country house. Many of these I thought might be interesting to him, and I offered to have them taken out and left at his disposal. When he heard the titles of some of the books in the collection he was much interested, but insisted that before he made use of them they should be catalogued, as were the rest of my effects. I hesitated a moment, wondering if I could induce Barker to come to New York and catalogue four big boxes of books, when, to my surprise, Miss Vincent incidentally remarked that if they were in any place where she could get at them she would be pleased to help catalogue them; that sort of thing was a great pleasure to her. Instantly I proposed that I should send the books to the Vincent house, that they should there be taken out so that Mr. Vincent could select those he might care to read during the summer, that I would make a list of these, and if Vincent would assist me I would be grateful for the kindness, and those that were not desired could be returned to the storehouse.

What a grand idea was this! I had been internally groaning because I could think of no possible pretence, for further interviews with Miss Vincent, and here was something better than I could have imagined. Her father declared that he could not put me to so much trouble, but I would listen to none of his words, and the next morning my books were spread over his library floor.

The selection and cataloguing of the volumes desired occupied the mornings of three days. The old gentleman's part was soon done, but there were many things in the books which were far more interesting to me than their titles, and to which I desired to draw Miss Vincent's attention. All this greatly protracted our labors. She was not only a beautiful girl, but her intelligence and intellectual grasp were wonderful. I could not help telling her what a great pleasure it would be to me to think, while wandering in foreign lands, that such an appreciative family would be enjoying my books and my place.

"You are so fond of your house and everything you have," said she, "that we shall almost feel as if we were depriving you of your rights. But I suppose that Italian lakes and the Alps will make you forget for a time even your beautiful home."

"Not if you are in it," I longed to say, but I restrained myself. I did not believe that it was possible for me to be more in love with this girl than I was at that moment, but, of course, it would be the rankest stupidity to tell her so. To her I was simply her father's landlord.

I went to that house the next day to see that the boxes were properly repacked, and I actually went the next day to see if the right boxes had gone into the country, and the others back to the storehouse. The first day I saw only the father. The second day it was the mother who assured me that everything had been properly attended to. I began to feel that if I did not wish a decided rebuff I would better not make any more pretences of business at the Vincent house.

There were affairs of my own which should have been attended to, and I ought to have gone home and attended to them, but I could not bear to do so. There was no reason to suppose she would go out there before the first of June.

Thinking over the matter many times, I came to the conclusion that if I could see her once more I would be satisfied. Then I would go away, and carry her image with me into every art-gallery, over every glacier, and under every lovely sky that I should enjoy abroad, hoping all the time that, taking my place, as it were, in my home, and making my possessions, in a measure, her own, she would indirectly become so well acquainted with me that when I returned I might speak to her without shocking her.

To obtain this final interview there was but one way. I had left my house on Saturday, the Vincents would come on the following Monday, and I would sail on Wednesday. I would go on Tuesday to inquire if they found everything to their satisfaction. This would be a very proper attention from a landlord about to leave the country.

When I reached Boynton I determined to walk to my house, for I did not wish to encumber myself with a hired vehicle. I might be asked to stay to luncheon. A very strange feeling came over me as I entered my grounds. They were not mine. For the time being they belonged to somebody else. I was merely a visitor or a trespasser if the Vincents thought proper so to consider me. If they did not like people to walk on the grass I had no right to do it.

None of my servants had been left on the place, and the maid who came to the door informed me that Mr. Vincent had gone to New York that morning, and that Mrs. Vincent and her daughter were out driving. I ventured to ask if she thought they would soon return, and she answered that she did not think they would, as they had gone to Rock Lake, which, from the way they talked about it, must be a long way off.

Rock Lake! When I had driven over there with my friends, we had taken luncheon at the inn and returned in the afternoon. And what did they know of Rock Lake? Who had told them of it? That officious Barker, of course.

"Will you leave a message, sir?" said the maid, who, of course, did not know me.

"No," said I, and as I still stood gazing at the piazza floor, she remarked that if I wished to call again she would go out and speak to the coachman and ask him if anything had been said to him about the time of the party's return.

Worse and worse! Their coachman had not driven them! Some one who knew the country had been their companion. They were not acquainted in the neighborhood, and there could not be a shadow of a doubt that it was that obtrusive Barker who had indecently thrust himself upon them on the very next day after their arrival, and had thus snatched from me this last interview upon which I had counted so earnestly.

I had no right to ask any more questions. I left no message nor any name, and I had no excuse for saying I would call again.

I got back to my hotel without having met any one whom I knew, and that night I received a note from Barker, stating that he had fully intended coming to the steamer to see me off, but that an engagement would prevent him. He sent, however, his best good wishes for my safe passage, and assured me that he would keep me fully informed of the state of my affairs on this side.

"Engagement!" I exclaimed. "Is he going to drive with her again to-morrow?"

My steamer sailed at two o'clock the next day, and after an early breakfast I went to the company's office to see if I could dispose of my ticket. It had become impossible, I told the agent, for me to leave America at present. He said it was a very late hour to sell my ticket, but that he would do what he could, and if an applicant turned up he would give him my room and refund the money. He wanted me to change to another date, but I declined to do this. I was not able to say when I should sail.

I now had no plan of action. All I knew was that I could not leave America without finding out something definite about this Barker business. That is to say, if it should be made known to me that instead of attending to my business, sending a carpenter to make repairs, if such were necessary, or going personally to the plumber to make sure that that erratic personage would give his attention to any pipes in regard to which Mr. Vincent might have written, Barker should mingle in sociable relations with my tenants, and drive or play tennis with the young lady of the house, then would I immediately have done with him. I would withdraw my business from his hands and place it in those of old Mr. Poindexter. More than that, it might be my duty to warn Miss Vincent's parents against Barker. I did not doubt that he was a very good house and land-agent, but in selecting him as such I had no idea of introducing him to the

Vincents in a social way. In fact, the more I thought about it the more I became convinced that if ever I mentioned Barker to my tenants it would be to warn them against him. From certain points of view he was actually a dangerous man.

This, however, I would not do until I found my agent was really culpable. To discover what Barker had done, what he was doing, and what he intended to do, was now my only business in life. Until I had satisfied myself on these points I could not think of starting out upon my travels.

Now that I had determined I would not start for Europe until I had satisfied myself that Mr. Barker was contenting himself with attending to my business, and not endeavoring to force himself into social relations with my tenants, I was anxious that the postponement of my journey should be unknown to my friends and acquaintances, and I was, therefore, very glad to see in a newspaper, published on the afternoon of the day of my intended departure, my name among the list of passengers who had sailed upon the Mnemonic. For the first time I commended the super-enterprise of a reporter who gave more attention to the timeliness of his news than to its accuracy.

I was stopping at a New York hotel, but I did not wish to stay there. Until I felt myself ready to start on my travels the neighborhood of Boynton would suit me better than anywhere else. I did not wish to go to the town itself, for Barker lived there, and I knew many of the townspeople; but there were farmhouses not far away where I might spend a week. After considering the matter, I thought of something that might suit me. About three miles from my house, on an unfrequented road, was a mill which stood at the end of an extensive sheet of water, in reality a mill-pond, but commonly called a lake. The miller, an old man, had recently died, and his house near by was occupied by a newcomer whom I had never seen. If I could get accommodations there it would suit me exactly. I left the train two stations below Boynton and walked over to the mill.

The country-folk in my neighborhood are always pleased to take summer boarders if they can get them, and the miller and his wife were glad to give me a room, not imagining that I was the owner of a good house not far away. The place suited my requirements very well. It was near her, and I might live here for a time unnoticed, but what I was going to do with my opportunity I did not know. Several times the conviction forced itself upon me that I should get up at once and go to Europe by the first steamer, and so show myself that I was a man of sense.

This conviction was banished on the second afternoon of my stay at the mill. I was sitting under a tree in the orchard near the house, thinking and smoking my pipe, when along the road which ran by the side of the lake came Mr. Vincent on my black horse General and his daughter on my mare Sappho. Instinctively I pulled my straw hat over my eyes, but this precaution was not necessary. They were looking at the beautiful lake, with its hills and overhanging trees, and saw me not!

When the very tip of Sappho's tail had melted into the foliage of the road, I arose to my feet and took a deep breath of the happy air. I had seen her, and it was with her father she was riding.

I do not believe I slept a minute that night through thinking of her, and feeling glad that I was near her, and that she had been riding with her father.

When the early dawn began to break an idea brighter than the dawn broke upon me: I would get up and go nearer to her. It is amazing how much we lose by not getting up early on the long summer days. How beautiful the morning might be on this earth I never knew until I found myself wandering by the edge of my woods and over my lawn with the tender gray-blue sky above me and all the freshness of the grass and flowers and trees about me, the birds singing among the branches, and she sleeping sweetly somewhere within that house with its softly defined lights and shadows. How I wished I knew what room she occupied!

The beauties and joys of that hour were lost to every person on the place, who were all, no doubt, in their soundest sleep. I did not even see a dog. Quietly and stealthily stepping from bush to hedge, I went around the house, and as I drew near the barn I fancied I could hear from a little room adjoining it the snores of the coachman. The lazy rascal would probably not awaken for two or three hours yet, but I would ran no risks, and in half an hour I had sped away.

Now I knew exactly why I was staying at the house of the miller. I was doing so in order that I might go early in the mornings to my own home, in which the girl I loved lay dreaming, and that for the rest of the day and much of the night I might think of her.

"What place in Europe," I said to myself, "could be so beautiful, so charming, and so helpful to reflection as this sequestered lake, these noble trees, these stretches of undulating meadow?"

Even if I should care to go abroad, a month or two later would answer all my purposes. Why had I ever thought of spending five months away?

There was a pretty stream which ran from the lake and wended its way through a green and shaded valley, and here, with a rod, I wandered and fished and thought. The miller had boats, and in one of these I rowed far up the lake where it narrowed into a creek, and between the high hills which shut me out from the world I would float and think.

Every morning, soon after break of day, I went to my home and wandered about my grounds. If it rained I did not mind that. I like a summer rain.

Day by day I grew bolder. Nobody in that household thought of getting up until seven o'clock. For two hours, at least, I could ramble undisturbed through my grounds, and much as I had once enjoyed these grounds, they never afforded me the pleasure they gave me now. In these happy mornings I felt all the life and spirits of a boy. I went into my little field and stroked the sleek sides of my cows as they nibbled the dewy grass. I even peeped through the barred window of Sappho's box and fed her, as I had been used to doing, with bunches of clover. I saw that the young chickens were flourishing. I went into the garden and noted the growth of the vegetables, feeling glad that she would have so many fine strawberries and tender peas.

I had not the slightest doubt that she was fond of flowers, and for her sake now, as I used to do for my own sake, I visited the flower beds and borders. Not far from the house there was a cluster of old-fashioned pinks which I was sure were not doing very well. They had been there too long, perhaps, and they looked stunted and weak. In the miller's garden I had noticed great beds of these pinks, and I asked his wife if I might have some, and she, considering them as mere wild flowers, said I might have as many as I liked. She might have thought I wanted simply the blossoms, but the next morning I went over to my house with a basket filled with great matted masses of the plants taken up with the roots and plenty of earth around them, and after twenty minutes' work in my own bed of pinks, I had taken out all the old plants and filled their places with fresh, luxuriant masses of buds and leaves and blossoms. How glad she would be when she saw the fresh life that had come to that flower-bed! With light footsteps I went away, not feeling the weight of the basket filled with the old plants and roots.

The summer grew and strengthened, and the sun rose earlier, but as that had no effect upon the rising of the present inhabitants of my place, it gave me more time for my morning pursuits. Gradually I constituted myself the regular flower-gardener of the premises. How delightful the work was, and how foolish I thought I had been never to think of doing this thing for myself! but no doubt it was because I was doing it for her that I found it so pleasant.

Once again I had seen Miss Vincent. It was in the afternoon, and I had rowed myself to the upper part of the lake, where, with the high hills and the trees on each side of me, I felt as if I were alone in the world. Floating, idly along, with my thoughts about three miles away, I heard the sound of oars, and looking out on the open part of the lake, I saw a boat approaching. The miller was rowing, and in the stern sat an elderly gentleman and a young lady. I knew them in an instant: they were Mr. and Miss Vincent.

With a few vigorous strokes I shot myself into the shadows, and rowed up the stream into the narrow stretches among the lily-pads, under a bridge, and around a little wooded point, where I ran the boat ashore and sprang upon the grassy bank. Although I did not believe the miller would bring them as far as this, I went up to a higher spot and watched for half an hour; but I did not see them again. How relieved I was! It would have been terribly embarrassing had they discovered me. And how disappointed I was that the miller turned back so soon!

I now extended the supervision of my grounds. I walked through the woods, and saw how beautiful they were in the early dawn. I threw aside the fallen twigs and cut away encroaching saplings, which were beginning to encumber the paths I had made, and if I found a bough which hung too low I cut it off. There was a great beech-tree, between which and a dogwood I had the year before suspended a hammock. In passing this, one morning, I was amazed to see a hammock swinging from the hooks I had put in the two trees. This was a retreat which I had supposed no one else would fancy or even think of! In the hammock was a fan—a common Japanese fan. For fifteen minutes I stood looking at that hammock, every nerve a-tingle. Then I glanced around. The spot had been almost unfrequented since last summer. Little bushes, weeds, and vines had sprung up here and there between the two trees. There were dead twigs and limbs lying about, and the short path to the main walk was much overgrown.

I looked at my watch. It was a quarter to six. I had yet a good hour for work, and with nothing but my pocket-knife and my hands I began to clear away the space about that hammock. When I left it, it looked as it used to look when it was my pleasure to lie there and swing and read and reflect.

To approach this spot it was not necessary to go through my grounds, for my bit of woods adjoined a considerable stretch of forest-land, and in my morning walks from the mill I often used a path through these woods. The next morning when I took this path I was late because I had unfortunately overslept myself. When I reached the hammock it wanted fifteen minutes to seven o'clock. It was too late for me to do anything, but I was glad to be able to stay there even for a few minutes, to breathe that air, to stand on that ground, to touch that hammock. I did more than that. Why shouldn't I? I got into it. It was a better one than that I had hung there. It was delightfully comfortable. At this moment, gently swinging in that woodland solitude, with the sweet odors of the morning all about me, I felt myself nearer to her than I had ever been before.

But I knew I must not revel in this place too long. I was on the point of rising to leave when I heard approaching footsteps. My breath stopped. Was I at last to be discovered? This was what came of my reckless security. But perhaps the person, some workman most likely, would pass without noticing me. To remain quiet seemed the best course, and I lay motionless.

But the person approaching turned into the little pathway. The footsteps came nearer. I sprang from the hammock. Before me was Miss Vincent!

What was my aspect I know not, but I have no doubt I turned fiery red. She stopped suddenly, but she did not turn red.

"Oh, Mr. Ripley," she exclaimed, "good morning! You must excuse me. I did not know—"

That she should have had sufficient self-possession to say good morning amazed me. Her whole appearance, in fact, amazed me. There seemed to be something wanting in her manner. I endeavored to get myself into condition.

"You must be surprised," I said, "to see me here. You supposed I was in Europe, but—"

As I spoke I made a couple of steps toward her, but suddenly stopped. One of my coat buttons had caught in the meshes of the hammock. It was confoundedly awkward. I tried to loosen the button, but it was badly entangled. Then I desperately pulled at it to tear it off.

"Oh, don't do that," she said. "Let me unfasten it for you."

And taking the threads of the hammock in one of her little hands and the button in the other, she quickly separated them. "I should think buttons would be very inconvenient things—at least, in hammocks," she said smiling. "You see, girls don't have any such trouble."

I could not understand her manner. She seemed to take my being there as a matter of course.

"I must beg a thousand pardons for this—this trespass," I said.

"Trespass!" said she, with a smile. "People don't trespass on their own land—"

"But it is not my land," said I. "It is your father's for the time being. I have no right here whatever. I do not know how to explain, but you must think it very strange to find me here when you supposed I had started for Europe."

"Oh! I knew you had not started for Europe," said she, "because I have seen you working in the grounds—"

"Seen me!" I interrupted. "Is it possible?"

"Oh, yes," said she. "I don't know how long you had been coming when I first saw you, but when I found that fresh bed of pinks all transplanted from somewhere, and just as lovely as they could be, instead of the old ones, I spoke to the man; but he did not know anything about it, and said he had not had time to do anything to the flowers, whereas I had been giving him credit for ever so much weeding and cleaning up. Then I supposed that Mr. Barker, who is just as kind and attentive as he can be, had done it; but I could hardly believe he was the sort of man to come early in the morning and work out of doors,"—("Oh, how I wish he had come!" I thought. "If I had caught him here working among the flowers!"),—"and when he came that afternoon to play tennis I found that he had been away for two days, and could not have planted the pinks. So I simply got up early one morning and looked out, and there I saw you, with your coat off, working just as hard as ever you could."

I stepped back, my mind for a moment a perfect blank.

"What could you have thought of me?" I exclaimed presently.

"Really, at first I did not know what to think," said she. "Of course I did not know what had detained you in this country, but I remembered that I had heard that you were a very particular person about your flowers and shrubs and grounds, and that most likely you thought they would be better taken care of if you kept an eye on them, and that when you found there was so much to do you just went to work and did it. I did not speak of this to anybody, because if you did not wish it to be known that you were taking care of the grounds it was not my business to tell people about it. But yesterday, when I found this place where I had hung my hammock so beautifully cleared up and made so nice and clean and pleasant in every way, I thought I must come down to tell you how much obliged I am, and also that you ought not to take so much trouble for us. If you think the grounds need more attention, I will persuade my father to hire another man, now and then, to work about the place. Really, Mr. Ripley, you ought not to have to—"

I was humbled, abashed. She had seen me at my morning devotions, and this was the way she interpreted them. She considered me an overnice fellow who was so desperately afraid his place would be injured that he came sneaking around every morning to see if any damage had been done and to put things to rights.

She stood for a moment as if expecting me to speak, brushed a buzzing fly from her sleeve, and then, looking at me with a gentle smile, she turned a little as if she were about to leave.

I could not let her go without telling her something. Her present opinion of me must not rest in her mind another minute. And yet, what story could I devise? How, indeed, could I devise anything with which to deceive a girl who spoke and looked at me as this girl did? I could not do it. I must rush away speechless and never see her again, or I must tell her all. I came a little nearer to her.

"Miss Vincent," said I, "you do not understand at all why I am here—why I have been here so much—why I did not go to Europe. The truth is, I could not leave. I do not wish to be away; I want to come here and live here always—"

"Oh, dear! " she interrupted, "of course it is natural that you should not want to tear yourself away from your lovely home. It would be very hard for us to go away now, especially for father and me, for we have grown to love this place so much. But if you want us to leave, I dare say—"

"I want you to leave!" I exclaimed. "Never! When I say that I want to live here myself, that my heart will not let me go anywhere else, I mean that I want you to live here too—you, your mother and father—that I want—"

"Oh, that would be perfectly splendid!" she said. "I have ever so often thought that it was a shame that you should be deprived of the pleasures you so much enjoy, which I see you can find here and nowhere else. Now, I have a plan which I think will work splendidly. We are a very small family. Why shouldn't you come here and live with us? There is plenty of room, and I know father and mother would be very glad, and you can pay your board, if that

Frank R. Stockton

would please you better. You can have the room at the top of the tower for your study and your smoking den, and the room under it can be your bedroom, so you can be just as independent as you please of the rest of us, and you can be living on your own place without interfering with us in the least. In fact, it would be ever so nice, especially as I am in the habit of going away to the sea-shore with my aunt every summer for six weeks, and I was thinking how lonely it would be this year for father and mother to stay here all by themselves."

The tower and the room under it! For me! What a contemptibly little-minded and insignificant person she must think me. The words with which I strove to tell her that I wished to live here as lord, with her as my queen, would not come. She looked at me for a moment as I stood on the brink of saying something but not saying it, and then she turned suddenly toward the hammock.

"Did you see anything of a fan I left here?" she said. "I know I left it here, but when I came yesterday it was gone. Perhaps you may have noticed it somewhere—"

Now, the morning before, I had taken that fan home with me. It was an awkward thing to carry, but I had concealed it under my coat. It was a contemptible trick, but the fan had her initials on it, and as it was the only thing belonging to her of which I could possess myself, the temptation had been too great to resist. As she stood waiting for my answer there was a light in her eye which illuminated my perceptions.

"Did you see me take that fan?" I asked.

"I did," said she.

"Then you know," I exclaimed, stepping nearer to her, "why

it is I did not leave this country as I intended, why it was impossible for me to tear myself away from this house, why it is that I have been here every morning, hovering around and doing the things I have been doing?"

She looked up at me, and with her eyes she said, "How could I help knowing?" She might have intended to say something with her lips, but I took my answer from her eyes, and with the quick impulse of a lover I stopped her speech.

"You have strange ways," she said presently, blushing and gently pressing back my arm. "I haven't told you a thing."

"Let us tell each other everything now," I cried, and we seated ourselves in the hammock.

It was a quarter of an hour later and we were still sitting together in the hammock.

"You may think," said she, "that, knowing what I did, it was very queer for me to come out to you this morning, but I could not help it. You were getting dreadfully careless, and were staying so late and doing things which people would have been bound to notice, especially as father is always talking about our enjoying the fresh hours of the morning, that I felt I could not let you go on any longer. And when it came to that fan business I saw plainly that you must either immediately start for Europe or—"

"Or what?" I interrupted.

"Or go to my father and regularly engage yourself as a—"

I do not know whether she was going to say "gardener" or not, but it did not matter. I stopped her.

It was perhaps twenty minutes later, and we were standing together at the edge of the woods. She wanted me to come to the house to take breakfast with them.

"Oh, I could not do that!" I said. "They would be so surprised. I should have so much to explain before I could even begin to state my case."

"Well, then, explain," said she. "You will find father on the front piazza. He is always there before breakfast, and there is plenty of time. After all that has been said here, I cannot go to breakfast and look commonplace while you run away."

"But suppose your father objects?" said I.

"Well, then you will have to go back and take breakfast with your miller," said she.

I never saw a family so little affected by surprises as those Vincents. When I appeared on the front piazza the old gentleman did not jump. He shook hands with me and asked me to sit down, and when I told him everything he did not even ejaculate, but simply folded his hands together and looked out over the railing.

"It seemed strange to Mrs. Vincent and myself," he said, "when we first noticed your extraordinary attachment for our daughter, but, after all, it was natural enough."

"Noticed it!" I exclaimed. "When did you do that?"

"Very soon," he said. "When you and Cora were catalo-guing the books at my house in town I noticed it and spoke to Mrs. Vincent, but she said it was nothing new to her, for it was plain enough on the day when we first met you here that you were letting the house to Cora, and that she had not spoken of it to me because she was afraid I might think it wrong to accept the favorable and unusual arrangements you were making with us if I suspected the reason for them. We talked over the matter, but, of course, we could do nothing, because there was nothing to do, and Mrs. Vincent was quite sure you would write to us from Europe. But when my man Ambrose told me he had seen some one working about the place in the very early morning, and that, as it was a gentleman, he supposed it must be the landlord, for nobody else would be doing such things, Mrs. Vincent and I looked out of the window the next day, and when we found it was indeed you who were coming here every day, we felt that the matter was serious and were a good deal troubled. We found, however, that you were conducting affairs in a very honorable way,—that you were not endeavoring to see Cora, and that you did not try to have any secret correspondence with her,—and as we had no right to prevent you from coming on your grounds, we concluded to remain quiet until you should take some step which we would be authorized to notice. Later, when Mr. Barker came and told me that you had not gone to Europe, and were living with a miller not far from here—"

"Barker!" I cried. "The scoundrel!"

"You are mistaken, sir," said Mr. Vincent. "He spoke with the greatest kindness of you, and said that as it was evident you had your own reasons for wishing to stay in the neighborhood, and did not wish the fact to be known, he had spoken of it to no one but me, and he would not have done this had he not thought it would prevent embarrassment in case we should meet."

Would that everlasting Barker ever cease meddling in my affairs?

"Do you suppose," I asked, "that he imagined the reason for my staying here?"

"I do not know," said the old gentleman, "but after the questions I put to him I have no doubt he suspected it. I made many inquiries of him regarding you, your family, habits, and disposition, for this was a very vital matter to me, sir, and I am happy to inform you that he said nothing of you that was not good, so I urged him to keep the matter to himself. I determined, however, that if you continued your morning visits I should take an early opportunity of accosting you and asking an explanation."

"And you never mentioned anything of this to your daughter?" said I.

"Oh, no," he answered. "We carefully kept everything from her."

"But, my dear sir," said I, rising, "you have given me no answer.

You have not told me whether or not you will accept me as a son-in-law."

He smiled. "Truly," he said, "I have not answered you; but the fact is, Mrs. Vincent and I have considered the matter so long, and having come to the conclusion that if you made an honorable and straightforward proposition, and if Cora were willing to accept you, we could see no reason to object to—"

At this moment the front door opened and Cora appeared.

"Are you going to stay to breakfast?" she asked. "Because, if you are, it is ready."

I stayed to breakfast.

I am now living in my own house, not in the two tower

rooms, but in the whole mansion, of which my former tenant, Cora, is now mistress supreme. Mr. and Mrs. Vincent expect to spend the next summer here and take care of the house while we are travelling.

Mr. Barker, an excellent fellow and a most thorough business man, still manages my affairs, and there is nothing on the place that flourishes so vigorously as the bed of pinks which I got from the miller's wife.

By the way, when I went back to my lodging on that eventful day, the miller's wife met me at the door.

"I kept your breakfast waitin' for you for a good while," said she, "but as you didn't come, I supposed you were takin' breakfast in your own house, and I cleared it away."

"Do you know who I am?" I exclaimed.

"Oh, yes, sir," she said. "We did not at first, but when everybody began to talk about it we couldn't help knowin' it."

"Everybody!" I gasped. "And may I ask what you and everybody said about me?"

"I think it was the general opinion, sir," said she, "that you were suspicious of them tenants of yours, and nobody wondered at it, for when city people gets into the country and on other people's property, there's no trustin' them out of your sight for a minute."

I could not let the good woman hold this opinion of my tenants, and I briefly told her the truth. She looked at me with moist admiration in her eyes.

"I am glad to hear that, sir," said she. "I like it very much.

But if I was you I wouldn't be in a hurry to tell my husband and the people in the neighborhood about it. They might be a little disappointed at first, for they had a mighty high opinion of you when they thought that you was layin' low here to keep an eye on them tenants of yours."

THE STAYING POWER OF SIR ROHAN

During the winter in which I reached my twenty fifth year I lived with my mother's brother, Dr. Alfred Morris, in Warburton, a small country town, and I was there beginning the practice of medicine. I had been graduated in the spring, and my uncle earnestly advised me to come to him and act as his assistant, which advice, considering the fact that he was an elderly man, and that I might hope to succeed him in his excellent practice, was considered good advice by myself and my family.

At this time I practised very little, but learned a great deal, for as I often accompanied my uncle on his professional visits, I could not have taken a better postgraduate course.

I had an invitation to spend the Christmas of that year with the Collingwoods, who had opened their country house, about twelve miles from Warburton, for the entertainment of a holiday house party. I had gladly accepted the invitation, and on the day before Christmas I went to the livery stable in the village to hire a horse and sleigh for the trip. At the stable I met Uncle Beamish, who had also come to hire a conveyance.

"Uncle Beamish," as he was generally called in the village, although I am sure he had no nephews or nieces in the place, was an elderly man who had retired from some business, I know not what, and was apparently quite able to live upon whatever income he had. He was a good man, rather illiterate, but very shrewd. Generous in good works, I do not think he was fond of giving away money, but his services were at the call of all who needed them.

I liked Uncle Beamish very much, for he was not only a good story-teller, but he was willing to listen to my stories, and when I found he wanted to hire a horse and sleigh to go to the house of his married sister, with whom he intended to spend Christmas, and that his sister lived on Upper Hill turnpike, on which road the Collingwood house was situated, I proposed that we should hire a sleigh together.

"That will suit me," said Uncle Beamish. "There couldn't have been a better fit if I had been measured for it. Less than half a mile after you turn into the turnpike, you pass my sister's house. Then you can drop me and go on to the Collingwoods', which I should say isn't more than three miles further."

The arrangement was made, a horse and sleigh ordered, and early in the afternoon we started from Warburton.

The sleighing was good, but the same could not be said of the horse. He was a big roan, powerful and steady, but entirely too deliberate in action. Uncle Beamish, however, was quite satisfied with him.

"What you want when you are goin' to take a journey with a horse," said he, "is stayin' power. Your fast trotter is all very well for a mile or two, but if I have got to go into the country in winter, give me a horse like this."

I did not agree with him, but we jogged along quite pleasantly until the afternoon grew prematurely dark and it began to snow.

"Now," said I, giving the roan a useless cut, "what we ought to have is a fast horse, so that we may get there before there is a storm."

"No, doctor, you're wrong," said Uncle Beamish. "What we want is a strong horse that will take us there whether it storms or not, and we have got him. And who cares for a little snow that won't hurt nobody?"

I did not care for snow, and we turned up our collars and went as merrily as people can go to the music of slowly jingling sleigh-bells.

The snow began to fall rapidly, and, what was worse, the wind blew directly in our faces, so that sometimes my eyes were so plastered up with snowflakes that I could scarcely see how to drive. I never knew snow to fall with such violence. The roadway in front of us, as far as I could see it, was soon one unbroken stretch of white from fence to fence.

"This is the big storm of the season," said Uncle Beamish, "and it is a good thing we started in time, for if the wind keeps blowin', this road will be pretty hard to travel in a couple of hours."

In about half an hour the wind lulled a little and I could get a better view of our surroundings, although I could not see very far through the swiftly descending snow.

"I was thinkin'," said Uncle Beamish, "that it might be a good idee, when we get to Crocker's place, to stop a little, and let you warm your fingers and nose. Crocker's is ruther more than half-way to the pike."

"Oh, I do not want to stop anywhere," I replied quickly. "I am all right."

Nothing was said for some time, and then Uncle Beamish remarked:

"I don't want to stop any more than you do, but it does seem strange that we ain't passed Crocker's yit. We could hardly miss his house, it is so close to the road. This horse is slow, but I tell you one thing, doctor, he's improvin'. He is goin' better than he did. That's the way with this kind. It takes them a good while to get warmed up, but they keep on gettin' fresher instead of tireder."

The big roan was going better, but still we did not reach Crocker's, which disappointed Uncle Beamish, who wanted to be assured that the greater part of his journey was over.

"We must have passed it," he said, "when the snow was so blindin'."

I did not wish to discourage him by saying that I did not think we had yet reached Crocker's, but I believed I had a much better appreciation of our horse's slowness than he had.

Again the wind began to blow in our faces, and the snow fell faster, but the violence of the storm seemed to encourage our horse, for his pace was now greatly increased.

"That's the sort of beast to have," exclaimed Uncle Beamish, spluttering as the snow blew in his mouth. "He is gettin' his spirits up just when they are most wanted. We must have passed Crocker's a good while ago, and it can't be long before we get to the pike. And it's time we was there, for it's darkenin'."

On and on we went, but still we did not reach the pike. We had lost a great deal of time during the first part of the journey, and although the horse was travelling so much better now, his pace was below the average of good roadsters.

"When we get to the pike," said Uncle Beamish, "you can't miss it, for this road doesn't cross it. All you've got to do is to turn to the left, and in ten minutes you will see the lights in my sister's house. And I'll tell you, doctor, if you would like to stop there for the night, she'd be mighty glad to have you."

"Much obliged," replied I, "but I shall go on. It's not late yet, and I can reach the Collingwoods' in good time."

We now drove on in silence, our horse actually arching his neck as he thumped through the snow. Drifts had begun to form across the road, but through these he bravely plunged.

"Stayin' power is what we want, doctor!" exclaimed Uncle Beamish. "Where would your fast trotter be in drifts like these, I'd like to know? We got the right horse when we got this one, but I wish we had been goin' this fast all the time."

It grew darker and darker, but at last we saw, not far in front of us, a light.

"That beats me," said Uncle Beamish. "I don't remember no other house so near the road. It can't be we ain't passed Crocker's yit! If we ain't got no further than that, I'm in favor of stoppin'. I'm not afraid of a snow-storm, but I ain't a fool nuther, and if we haven't got further than Crocker's it will be foolhardy to try to push on through the dark and these big drifts, which will be gettin' bigger."

I did not give it up so easily. I greatly wished to' reach my destination that night. But there were three wills in the party, and one of them belonged to the horse. Before I had any idea of such a thing, the animal made a sudden turn,—too sudden for safety,—passed through a wide gateway, and after a few rapid bounds which, to my surprise, I could not restrain, he stopped suddenly.

"Hello!" exclaimed Uncle Beamish, peering forward, "here's a barn door." And he immediately began to throw off the far robe that covered our knees.

"What are you going to do?" I asked.

"I'm goin' to open the barn door and let the horse go in," said he. "He seems to want to. I don't know whether this is Crocker's barn or not. It don't look like it, but I may be mistaken. Anyway, we will let the horse in, and then go to the house. This ain't no night to be travellin' any further, doctor, and that is the long and the short of it. If the people here ain't Crockers, I guess they are Christians!"

I had not much time to consider the situation, for while he had been speaking, Uncle Beamish had waded through the snow, and finding the barn door unfastened, had slid it to one side. Instantly the horse entered the dark barn, fortunately finding nothing in his way.

"Now," said Uncle Beamish, "if we can get somethin' to tie him with, so that he don't do no mischief, we can leave him here and go up to the house." I carried a pocket lantern, and quickly lighted it. "By George!" said Uncle Beamish, as I held up the lantern, "this ain't much of a barn—it's no more than a wagon-house. It ain't Crocker's—but no matter; we'll go up to the house. Here is a hitchin'-rope."

We fastened the horse, threw a robe over him, shut the barn door behind us, and slowly made our way to the back of the house, in which there was a lighted window. Mounting a little portico, we reached a door, and were about to knock when it was opened for us. A woman, plainly a servant, stood in a kitchen, light and warm.

"Come right in," she said. "I heard your bells. Did you put your horse in the barn?"

"Yes," said Uncle Beamish, "and now we would like to see—"

"All right," interrupted the woman, moving toward an inner door. "Just wait here for a minute. I'm going up to tell her."

"I don't know this place," said Uncle Beamish, as we stood by the kitchen stove, "but I expect it belongs to a widow woman."

"What makes you think that?" I asked.

"'Cause she said she was goin' to tell HER. If there had been a man in the house, she would have gone to tell HIM."

In a few moments the woman returned.

"She says you are to take off your wet things and then go into the sitting-room. She'll be down in a minute."

I looked at Uncle Beamish, thinking it was his right to make explanations, but, giving me a little wink, he began to take off his overcoat. It was plain to perceive that Uncle Beamish desired to assume that a place of refuge would be offered us.

"It's an awful bad night," he said to the woman, as he sat down to take off his arctic overshoes.

"It's all that," said she. "You may hang your coats over them chairs. It won't matter if they do drip on this bare floor.

Now, then, come right into the sitting-room."

In spite of my disappointment, I was glad to be in a warm house, and hoped we might be able to stay there. I could hear the storm beating furiously against the window-panes behind the drawn shades. There was a stove in the sitting-room, and a large lamp.

"Sit down," said the woman. "She will be here in a minute."

"It strikes me," said Uncle Beamish, when we were left alone, "that somebody is expected in this house, most likely to spend Christmas, and that we are mistook for them, whoever they are."

"I have the same idea," I replied, "and we must explain as soon as possible."

"Of course we will do that," said he, "but I can tell you one thing: whoever is expected ain't comin', for he can't get here. But we've got to stay here tonight, no matter who comes or doesn't come, and we've got to be keerful in speakin' to the woman of the house. If she is one kind of a person, we can offer to pay for lodgin's and horse-feed; but if she is another kind, we must steer clear of mentionin' pay, for it will make her angry. You had better leave the explainin' business to me."

I was about to reply that I was more than willing to do so when the door opened and a person entered—evidently the mistress of the house. She was tall and thin, past middle age, and plainly dressed. Her pale countenance wore a defiant look, and behind her spectacles blazed a pair of dark eyes, which, after an instant's survey of her visitors, were fixed steadily upon me. She made but a step into the room, and stood holding the door. We both rose from our chairs.

"You can sit down again," she said sharply to me. "I don't want you. Now, sir," she continued, turning to Uncle

Beamish, "please come with me."

Uncle Beamish gave a glance of surprise at me, but he immediately followed the old lady out of the room, and the door was closed behind them.

For ten minutes, at least, I sat quietly waiting to see what would happen next—very much surprised at the remark that had been made to me, and wondering at Uncle Beamish's protracted absence. Suddenly he entered the room and closed the door.

"Here's a go!" said he, slapping his leg, but very gently. "We're mistook the worst kind. We're mistook for doctors." "That is only half a mistake," said I. "What is the matter, and what can I do?"

"Nothin'," said he, quickly,—"that is, nothin' your own self. Just the minute she got me outside that door she began pitchin' into you. 'I suppose that's young Dr. Glover,' said she. I told her it was, and then she went on to say, givin' me no chance to explain nothin', that she didn't want to have anything to do with you; that she thought it was a shame to turn people's houses into paupers' hospitals for the purpose of teachin' medical students; that she had heard of you, and what she had heard she hadn't liked. All this time she kept goin' up-stairs, and I follerin' her, and the fust thing I knowed she opened a door and went into a room, and I went in after her, and there, in a bed, was a patient of some kind. I was took back dreadful, for the state of the case came to me like a flash.

Your uncle had been sent for, and I was mistook for him. Now, what to say was a puzzle to me, and I began to think pretty fast.

It was an awkward business to have to explain things to that sharp-set old woman. The fact is, I didn't know how to begin, and was a good deal afraid, besides, but she didn't give me no time for considerin'. 'I think it's her brain,' said she, 'but perhaps you'll know better. Catherine, uncover your head!' And with that the patient turned over a little and uncovered her head, which she had had the sheet over. It was a young woman, and she gave me a good look, but she didn't say nothin'. Now I WAS in a state of mind."

"Of course you must have been," I answered. "Why didn't you tell her that you were not a doctor, but that I was. It would have been easy enough to explain matters. She might have thought my uncle could not come and he had sent me, and that you had come along for company. The patient ought to be attended to without delay."

"She's got to be-attended to," said Uncle Beamish, "or else there will be a row and we'll have to travel—storm or no storm. But if you had heard what that old woman said about young doctors, and you in particular, you would know that you wasn't goin' to have anything to do with this case—at least, you wouldn't show in it. But I've got no more time for talkin'. I came down here on business. When the old lady said, 'Catherine, hold out your hand!' and she held it out, I had nothin' to do but step up and feel her pulse. I know how to do that, for I have done a lot of nussin' in my life. And then it seemed nat'ral to ask her to put out her tongue, and when she did it I gave a look at it and nodded my head. 'Do you think it is her brain?' said the old woman, half whisperin'. 'Can't say anything about that yit,' said I. 'I must go down-stairs and get the medicine-case. The fust thing to do is to give her a draught, and I will bring it up to her as soon as it is mixed.' You have got a pocket medicine-case with you, haven't you?"

"Oh, yes," said I. "It is in my overcoat."

"I knowed it," said Uncle Beamish. "An old doctor might go visitin' without his medicine-case, but a young one would be sure to take it along, no matter where he was goin'. Now you get it, please, quick."

"My notion is," said he, when I returned from the kitchen with the case, "that you mix somethin' that might soothe her a little, if she has got anything the matter with her brain, and which won't hurt her if she hasn't. And then, when I take it up to her, you tell me what symptoms to look for. I can do it—I have spent nights lookin' for symptoms. Then, when I come down and report, you might send her up somethin' that would keep her from gettin' any wuss till the doctor can come in the mornin', for he ain't comin' here to-night."

"A very good plan," said I. "Now, what can I give her? What is the patient's age?"

"Oh, her age don't matter much," said Uncle Beamish, impatiently. "She may be twenty, more or less, and any mild stuff will do to begin with."

"I will give her some sweet spirits of nitre," said I, taking out a little vial. "Will you ask the servant for a glass of water and a teaspoon?"

"Now," said I, when I had quickly prepared the mixture, "she can have a teaspoonful of this, and another in ten minutes, and then we will see whether we will go on with it or not."

"And what am I to look for?" said he.

"In the first place," said I, producing a clinical thermometer, "you must take her temperature. You know how to do that?"

Frank R. Stockton

"Oh, yes," said he. "I have done it hundreds of times. She must hold it in her mouth five minutes."

"Yes, and while you are waiting," I continued, "you must try to find out, in the first place, if there are, or have been, any signs of delirium. You might ask the old lady, and besides, you may be able to judge for yourself."

"I can do that," said he. "I have seen lots of it."

"Then, again," said I, "you must observe whether or not her pupils are dilated. You might also inquire whether there had been any partial paralysis or numbness in any part of the body. These things must be looked for in brain trouble. Then you can come down, ostensibly to prepare another prescription, and when you have reported, I have no doubt I can give you something which will modify, or I should say—"

"Hold her where she is till mornin'," said Uncle Beamish. "That's what you mean. Be quick. Give me that thermometer and the tumbler, and when I come down again, I reckon you can fit her out with a prescription just as good as anybody."

He hurried away, and I sat down to consider. I was full of ambition, full of enthusiasm for the practice of my profession. I would have been willing to pay largely for the privilege of undertaking an important case by myself, in which it would depend upon me whether or not I should call in a consulting brother. So far, in the cases I had undertaken, a consulting brother had always called himself in—that is, I had practised in hospitals or with my uncle. Perhaps it might be found necessary, notwithstanding all that had been said against me, that I should go up to take charge of this case. I wished I had not forgotten to ask the old man how he had found the tongue and pulse.

In less than a quarter of an hour Uncle Beamish returned.

"Well," said I, quickly, "what are the symptoms?"

"I'll give them to you," said he, taking his seat. "I'm not in such a hurry now, because I told the old woman I would like to wait a little and see how that fust medicine acted. The patient spoke to me this time. When I took the thermometer out of her mouth she says, 'You are comin' up ag'in, doctor?' speakin' low and quickish, as if she wanted nobody but me to hear."

"But how about the symptoms?" said I, impatiently.

"Well," he answered, "in the fust place her temperature is ninety-eight and a half, and that's about nat'ral, I take it."

"Yes," I said, "but you didn't tell me about her tongue and pulse."

"There wasn't nothin' remarkable about them," said he.

"All of which means," I remarked, "that there is no fever. But that is not at all a necessary accompaniment of brain derangements. How about the dilatation of her pupils?"

"There isn't none," said Uncle Beamish; "they are ruther squinched up, if anything. And as to delirium, I couldn't see no signs of it, and when I asked the old lady about the numbness, she said she didn't believe there had been any."

"No tendency to shiver, no disposition to stretch?"

"No," said the old man, "no chance for quinine."

"The trouble is," said I, standing before the stove and fixing my mind upon the case with earnest intensity, "that there are so few symptoms in brain derangement. If I could only get hold of something tangible—"

"If I was you," interrupted Uncle Beamish, "I wouldn't try to get hold of nothin'. I would just give her somethin' to keep her where she is till mornin'. If you can do that, I'll guarantee that any good doctor can take her up and go on with her to-morrow."

Without noticing the implication contained in these remarks, I continued my consideration of the case.

"If I could get a drop of her blood," said I.

"No, no!" exclaimed Uncle Beamish, "I'm not goin' to do anything of that sort. What in the name of common sense would you do with her blood?"

"I would examine it microscopically," I said. "I might find out all I want to know."

Uncle Beamish did not sympathize with this method of diagnosis.

"If you did find out there was the wrong kind of germs, you couldn't do anything with them to-night, and it would just worry you," said the old man. "I believe that nature will get along fust-rate without any help, at least till mornin'. But you've got to give her some medicine—not so much for her good as for our good. If she's not treated we're bounced. Can't you give her somethin' that would do anybody good, no matter what's the matter with 'em? If it was the spring of the year I would say sarsaparilla. If you could mix her up somethin' and put into it some of them benevolent microbes the doctors talk about, it would be a good deed to do to anybody."

"The benign bacilli," said I. "Unfortunately I haven't any of them with me."

"And if you had," he remarked, "I'd be in favor of givin' 'em to the old woman. I take it they would do, her more good than anybody else. Come along now, doctor; it is about time for me to go up-stairs and see how the other stuff acted—not on the patient, I don't mean, but on the old woman. The fact is, you know, it's her we're dosin'."

"Not at all," said I, speaking a little severely. "I am trying to do my very best for the patient, but I fear I cannot do it without seeing her. Don't you think that if you told the old lady how absolutely necessary—"

"Don't say anything more about that!" exclaimed Uncle Beamish. "I hoped I wouldn't have to mention it, but she told me ag'in that she would never have one of those unfledged medical students, just out of the egg-shell, experimentin' on any of her family, and from what she said about you in particular, I should say she considered you as a medical chick without even down on you."

"What can she know of me?" I asked indignantly.

"Give it up," said he. "Can't guess it. But that ain't the p'int. The p'int is, what are you goin' to give her? When I was young the doctors used to say, When you are in doubt, give calomel—as if you were playin' trumps."

"Nonsense, nonsense," said I, my eyes earnestly fixed upon my open medical case.

"I suppose a mustard-plaster on the back of her neck—"

"Wouldn't do at all," I interrupted. "Wait a minute, now— yes—I know what I will do: I will give her sodium bromide

Frank R. Stockton

—ten grains."

"'Which will hit if it's a deer and miss if it's a calf' as the hunter said?" inquired Uncle Beamish.

"It will certainly not injure her," said I, "and I am quite sure it will be a positive advantage. If there has been cerebral disturbance, which has subsided temporarily, it will assist her to tide over the interim before its recurrence."

"All right," said Uncle Beamish, "give it to me, and I'll be off. It's time I showed up ag'in."

He did not stay up-stairs very long this time.

"No symptoms yit, but the patient looked at me as if she wanted to say somethin'; but she didn't git no chance, for the old lady set herself down as if she was planted in a garden-bed and intended to stay there. But the patient took the medicine as mild as a lamb."

"That is very good," said I. "It may be that she appreciates the seriousness of her ewe better than we do."

"I should say she wants to git well," he replied. "She looks like that sort of a person to me. The old woman said she thought we would have to stay awhile till the storm slackened, and I said, yes, indeed, and there wasn't any chance of its slackenin' to-night; besides, I wanted to see the patient before bedtime."

At this moment the door opened and the servant-woman came in.

"She says you are to have supper, and it will be ready in about half an hour. One of you had better go out and attend to your horse, for the man is not coming back to-night."

"I will go to the barn," said I, rising. Uncle Beamish also rose and said he would go with me.

"I guess you can find some hay and oats," said the woman, as we were putting on our coats and overshoes in the kitchen, "and here's a lantern. We don't keep no horse now, but there's feed left."

As we pushed through the deep snow into the barn, Uncle Beamish said:

"I've been tryin' my best to think where we are without askin' any questions, and I'm dead beat. I don't remember no such house as this on the road."

"Perhaps we got off the road," said I.

"That may be," said he, as we entered the barn. "It's a straight road from Warburton to the pike near my sister's house, but there's two other roads that branch off to the right and strike the pike further off to the east. Perhaps we got on one of them in all that darkness and perplexin' whiteness, when it wasn't easy to see whether we were keepin' a straight road or not."

The horse neighed as we approached with a light.

"I would not be at all surprised," said I, "if this horse had once belonged here and that was the reason why, as soon as he got a chance, he turned and made straight for his old home."

"That isn't unlikely," said Uncle Beamish, "and that's the reason we did not pass Crocker's. But here we are, wherever it is, and here we've got to stay till mornin'."

We found hay and oats and a pump in the corner of the wagon-house, and having put the horse in the stall and made him as comfortable as possible with some old blankets, we returned to the house, bringing our valises with us.

Our supper was served in the sitting-room because there was a good fire there, and the servant told us we would have to eat by ourselves, as "she" was not coming down.

"We'll excuse her," said Uncle Beamish, with an alacrity of expression that might have caused suspicion.

We had a good supper, and were then shown a room on the first floor on the other side of the hall, where the servant said we were to sleep.

We sat by the stove awhile, waiting for developments, but as Uncle Beamish's bedtime was rapidly approaching, he sent word to the sick-chamber that he was coming up for his final visit.

This time he stayed up-stairs but a few minutes.

"She's fast asleep," said he, "and the old woman says she'll call me if I'm needed in the night, and you'll have to jump up sharp and overhaul that medicine-case if that happens."

The next morning, and very early in the morning, I was awaked by Uncle Beamish, who stood at my side.

"Look here," said he, "I've been outside. It's stopped snowin' and it's clearin' off. I've been to the barn and I've fed the horse, and I tell you what I'm in favor of doin'. There's nobody up yit, and I don't want to stay here and make no explanations to that old woman. I don't fancy gittin' into rows on Christmas mornin'. We've done all the good we can here, and the best thing we can do now is to git away before anybody is up, and leave a note sayin' that we've got to go on without losin' time, and that we will send another doctor as soon as possible. My sister's doctor don't live fur away from her, and I know she will be willin' to send for him. Then our duty will be done, and what the old woman thinks of us won't make no, difference to nobody."

"That plan suits me," said I, rising. "I don't want to stay here, and as I am not to be allowed to see the patient, there is no reason why I should stay. What we have done will more than pay for our supper and lodgings, so that our consciences are clear."

"But you must write a note," said Uncle Beamish. "Got any paper?"

I tore a leaf from my note-book, and went to the window, where it was barely light enough for me to see how to write.

"Make it short," said the old man. "I'm awful fidgety to git off."

I made it very short, and then, valises in hand, we quietly took our way to the kitchen.

"How this floor does creak!" said Uncle Beamish. "Git on your overcoat and shoes as quick as you can, and we'll leave the note on this table."

I had just shaken myself into my overcoat when Uncle Beamish gave a subdued exclamation, and quickly turning, I saw entering the kitchen a female figure in winter wraps and carrying a hand-bag.

"By George!" whispered the old man, "it's the patient!"

The figure advanced directly toward me.

"Oh, Dr. Glover!" she whispered, "I am so glad to get down before you went away!"

I stared in amazement at the speaker, but even in the dim light I recognized her. This was the human being whose expected presence at the Collingwood mansion was taking me there to spend Christmas.

"Kitty!" I exclaimed—"Miss Burroughs, I mean,—what is the meaning of this?"

"Don't ask me for any meanings now," she said. "I want you and your uncle to take me to the Collingwoods'. I suppose you are on your way there, for they wrote you were coming. And oh! let us be quick, for I'm afraid Jane will come down, and she will be sure to wake up aunty. I saw one of you go out to the barn, and knew you intended to leave, so I got ready just as fast as I could. But I must leave some word for aunty."

"I have written a note," said I. "But are you well enough to travel?"

"Just let me add a line to it," said she. "I am as well as I ever was."

I gave her a pencil, and she hurriedly wrote something on the paper which I had left on the kitchen table. Then, quickly glancing around, she picked up a large carving-fork, and sticking it through the paper into the soft wood of the table, she left it standing there.

"Now it won't blow away when we open the door," she whispered. "Come on."

"You cannot go out to the barn," I said; "we will bring up the sleigh."

"Oh, no, no, no," she answered, "I must not wait here. If I once get out of the house I shall feel safe. Of course I shall go anyway, but I don't want any quarrelling on this Christmas morning."

"I'm with you there," said Uncle Beamish, approvingly. "Doctor, we can take her to the barn without her touching the snow. Let her sit in this arm-chair, and we can carry her between us. She's no weight."

In half a minute the kitchen door was softly closed behind us, and we were carrying Miss Burroughs to the barn. My soul was in a wild tumult. Dozens of questions were on my tongue, but I had no chance to ask any of them.

Uncle Beamish and I returned to the porch for the valises, and then, closing the back door, we rapidly began to make preparations for leaving.

"I suppose," said Uncle Beamish, as we went into the stable, leaving Miss Burroughs in the wagon-house, "that this business is all right? You seem to know the young woman, and she is of age to act for herself."

 "Whatever she wants to do," I answered, "is perfectly right. You may trust to that. I do not understand the matter any more than you do, but I know she is expected at the Collingwoods', and wants to go there."

"Very good," said Uncle Beamish. "We'll git away fust and ask explanations afterwards."

"Dr. Glover," said Miss Burroughs, as we led the horse into the wagon-house, "don't put the bells on him. Stuff them gently under the seat—as softly as you can. But how are we all to go away? I have been looking at that sleigh, and it is intended only for two."

"It's rather late to think of that, miss," said Uncle Beamish, "but there's one thing that's certain. We're both very polite to ladies, but neither of us is willin' to be left behind on this trip. But it's a good-sized sleigh, and we'll all pack in, well enough. You and me can sit on the seat, and the doctor can stand up in front of us and drive. In old times it was considered the right thing for the driver of the sleigh to stand up and do his drivin'."

The baggage was carefully stowed away, and, after a look around the dimly lighted wagon-house, Miss Burroughs and Uncle Beamish got into the sleigh, and I tucked the big fur robe around them.

"I hate to make a journey before breakfast," said Uncle Beamish, as I was doing this, "especially on Christmas mornin', but somehow or other there seems to be somethin' jolly about this business, and we won't have to wait so long for breakfast, nuther. It can't be far from my sister's, and we'll all stop there and have breakfast. Then you two can leave me and go on. She'll be as glad to see any friends of mine as if they were her own. And she'll be pretty sure, on a mornin' like this, to have buckwheat cakes and sausages."

Miss Burroughs looked at the old man with a puzzled air, but she asked him no questions.

"How are you going to keep yourself warm, Dr. Glover?" she said.

"Oh, this long ulster will be enough for me," I replied, "and as I shall stand up, I could not use a robe, if we had another."

In fact, the thought of being with Miss Burroughs and the anticipation of a sleigh-ride alone with her after we had left Uncle Beamish with his sister, had put me into such a glow that I scarcely knew it was cold weather.

"You'd better be keerful, doctor," said Uncle Beamish. "You don't want to git rheumatism in your j'ints on this Christmas mornin'. Here's this horse-blanket that we are settin' on. We don't need it, and you'd better wrap it round you, after you git in, to keep your legs warm."

"Oh, do! " said Miss Burroughs. "It may look funny, but we will not meet anybody so early as this."

"All right!" said I, "and now we are ready to start."

I slid back the barn door and then led the horse outside. Closing the door, and making as little noise as possible in doing it, I got into the sleigh, finding plenty of room to stand up in front of my companions. Now I wrapped the horse-blanket about the lower part of my body, and as I had no belt with which to secure it, Miss Burroughs kindly offered to fasten it round my waist by means of a long pin which she took from her hat. It is impossible to describe the exhilaration that pervaded me as she performed this kindly office. After thanking her warmly, I took the reins and we started.

"It is so lucky," whispered Miss Burroughs, "that I happened to think about the bells. We don't make any noise at all."

This was true. The slowly uplifted hoofs of the horse descended quietly into the soft snow, and the sleigh-runners slipped along without a sound.

"Drive straight for the gate, doctor," whispered Uncle

Beamish. "It don't matter nothin' about goin' over flower-beds and grass-plats in such weather."

I followed his advice, for no roadway could be seen. But we had gone but a short distance when the horse suddenly stopped.

"What's the matter?" asked Miss Burroughs, in a low voice. "Is it too deep for him?"

"We're in a drift," said Uncle Beamish. "But it's not too deep. Make him go ahead, doctor."

I clicked gently and tapped the horse with the whip, but he did not move.

"What a dreadful thing," whispered Miss Burroughs, leaning forward, "for him to stop so near the house! Dr. Glover, what does this mean?" And, as she spoke, she half rose behind me. "Where did Sir Rohan come from?"

"Who's he?" asked Uncle Beamish, quickly.

"That horse," she answered. "That's my aunt's horse. She sold him a few days ago."

"By George! " ejaculated Uncle Beamish, unconsciously raising his voice a little. "Wilson bought him, and his bringin' us here is as plain as A B C. And now he don't want to leave home."

"But he has got to do it," said I, jerking the horse's head to one side and giving him a cut with the whip.

"Don't whip him," whispered Miss Burroughs; "it always makes him more stubborn. How glad I am I thought of the bells! The only way to get him to go is to mollify him."

"But how is that to be done?" I asked anxiously.

"You must give him sugar and pat his neck. If I had some sugar and could get out—"

"But you haven't it, and you can't git out," said Uncle Beamish. "Try him again doctor!"

I jerked the reins impatiently. "Go along!" said I. But he did not go along.

"Haven't you got somethin' in your medicine-case you could mollify him with?" said Uncle Beamish. "Somethin' sweet that he might like?"

For an instant I caught at this absurd suggestion, and my mind ran over the contents of my little bottles. If I had known his character, some sodium bromide in his morning feed might, by this time, have mollified his obstinacy.

"If I could be free of this blanket," said I, fumbling at the pin behind me, "I would get out and lead him into the road."

"You could not do it," said Miss Burroughs. "You might pull his head off, but he wouldn't move. I have seen him tried."

At this moment a window-sash in the second story of the house was raised, and there, not thirty feet from us, stood an elderly female, wrapped in a gray shawl, with piercing eyes shining through great spectacles.

"You seem to be stuck," said she, sarcastically. "You are worse stuck than the fork was in my kitchen table."

We made no answer. I do not know how Miss Burroughs

looked or felt, or what was the appearance of Uncle Beamish, but I know I must have been very red in the face. I gave the horse a powerful crack and shouted to him to go on. There was no need for low speaking now.

"You needn't be cruel to dumb animals," said the old lady, "and you can't budge him. He never did like snow, especially in going away from home. You cut a powerful queer figure, young man, with that horse-blanket around you. You don't look much like a practising physician."

"Miss Burroughs," I exclaimed, "please take that pin out of this blanket. If I can get at his head I know I can pull him around and make him go."

But she did not seem to hear me. "Aunty," she cried, "it's a shame to stand there and make fun of us. We have got a perfect right to go away if we want to, and we ought not to be laughed at."

The old lady paid no attention to this remark.

"And there's that false doctor," she said. "I wonder how he feels just now."

"False doctor!" exclaimed Miss Burroughs. "I don't understand."

"Young lady," said Uncle Beamish, "I'm no false doctor. I intended to tell you all about it as soon as I got a chance, but I haven't had one. And, old lady, I'd like you to know that I don't say I'm a doctor, but I do say I'm a nuss, and a good nuss, and you can't deny it."

To this challenge the figure at the window made no answer.

"Catherine," said she, "I can't stand here and take cold, but

I just want to know one thing: Have you positively made up your mind to marry that young doctor in the horse-blanket?"

This question fell like a bomb-shell into the middle of the stationary sleigh.

I had never asked Kitty to marry me. I loved her with all my heart and soul, and I hoped, almost believed, that she loved me. It had been my intention, when we should be left together in the sleigh this morning, after dropping Uncle Beamish at his sister's house, to ask her to marry me.

The old woman's question pierced me as if it had been a flash of lightning coming through the frosty air of a winter morning. I dropped the useless reins and turned. Kitty's face was ablaze. She made a movement as if she was about to jump out of the sleigh and flee.

"Oh, Kitty!" said I, bending down toward her, "tell her yes! I beg I entreat, I implore you to tell her yes! Oh, Kitty! if you don't say yes I shall never know another happy day."

For one moment Kitty looked up into my face, and then said she:

"It is my positive intention to marry him!"

With the agility of a youth, Uncle Beamish threw the robe from him and sprang out into the deep snow. Then, turning toward us, he took off his hat.

"By George!" said he, "you're a pair of trumps. I never did see any human bein's step up to the mark more prompt. Madam," he cried, addressing the old lady, "you ought to be the proudest woman in this county at seein' such a thing as this happen under your window of a Christmas mornin'.

And now the best thing that you can do is to invite us all in to have breakfast." "You'll have to come in," said she, "or else stay out there and freeze to death, for that horse isn't going to take you away.

And if my niece really intends to marry the young man, and has gone so far as to start to run away with him,—and with a false doctor,—of course I've got no more to say about it, and you can come in and have breakfast." And with that she shut down the window. "That's talkin'," said Uncle Beamish. "Sit still, doctor, and I'll lead him around to the back door. I guess he'll move quick enough when you want him to turn back."

Without the slightest objection Sir Rohan permitted himself to be turned back and led up to the kitchen porch.

"Now you two sparklin' angels get out," said Uncle Beamish, "and go in. I'll attend to the horse."

Jane, with a broad grin on her face, opened the kitchen door.

"Merry Christmas to you both!" said she.

"Merry Christmas!" we cried, and each of us shook her by the hand.

"Go in the sitting-room and get warm," said Jane. "She'll be down pretty soon."

I do not know how long we were together in that sitting-room. We had thousands of things to say, and we said most of them. Among other things, we managed to get in some explanations of the occurrences of the previous night. Kitty told her tale briefly. She and her aunt, to whom she was making a visit, and who wanted her to make her house her home, had had a quarrel two days before. Kitty was wild to go to the Collingwoods', and the old lady, who, for some reason, hated the family, was determined she should not go. But Kitty was immovable, and never gave up until she found that her aunt had gone so far as to dispose of her horse, thus making it impossible to travel in such weather, there being no public conveyances passing the house. Kitty was an orphan, and had a guardian who would have come to her aid, but she could not write to him in time, and, in utter despair, she went to bed. She would not eat or drink, she would not speak, and she covered up her head.

"After a day and a night," said Kitty, "aunty got dreadfully frightened and thought something was the matter with my brain. Her family are awfully anxious about their brains. I knew she had sent for the doctor and I was glad of it, for I thought he would help me. I must say I was surprised when I first saw that Mr. Beamish, for I thought he was Dr. Morris. Now tell me about your coming here."

"And so," she said, when I had finished, "you had no idea that you were prescribing for me! Please do tell me what were those medicines you sent up to me and which I took like a truly good girl."

"I didn't know it at the time," said I, "but I sent you sixty drops of the deepest, strongest love in a glass of water, and ten grains of perfect adoration."

"Nonsense!" said Kitty, with a blush, and at that moment Uncle Beamish knocked at the door.

"I thought I'd just step in and tell you," said he, "that breakfast will be comin' along in a minute. I found they were goin' to have buckwheat cakes, anyway, and I prevailed on Jane to put sausages in the bill of fare. Merry Christmas to you both! I would like to say more, but here comes the old lady and Jane."

The breakfast was a strange meal, but a very happy one. The old lady was very dignified. She made no allusion to Christmas or to what had happened, but talked to Uncle Beamish about people in Warburton.

I have a practical mind, and, in spite of the present joy, I could not help feeling a little anxiety about what was to be done when breakfast was over. But just as we were about to rise from the table we were all startled by a great jingle of sleigh-bells outside. The old lady arose and stopped to the window.

"There!" said she, turning toward us. "Here's a pretty kettle of fish! There's a two-horse sleigh outside, with a man driving, and a gentleman in the back seat who I am sure is Dr. Morris, and he has come all the way on this bitter cold morning to see the patient I sent for him to come to. Now, who is going to tell him he has come on a fool's errand?"

"Fool's errand!" I cried. "Every one of you wait in here and I'll go out and tell him."

When I dashed out of doors and stood by the side of my uncle's sleigh, he was truly an amazed man.

"I will get in, uncle," said I, "and if you will let John drive the horses slowly around the yard, I will tell you how I happen to be here."

The story was a much longer one than I expected it to be, and John must have driven those horses backward and forward for half an hour.

"Well," said my uncle, at last, "I never saw your Kitty, but I knew her father and her mother, and I will go in and take a look at her. If I like her, I will take you all on to the Collingwoods', and drop Uncle Beamish at his sister's house."

"I'll tell you what it is, young doctor," said Uncle Beamish, at parting, "you ought to buy that big roan horse. He has been a regular guardian angel to us this Christmas."

"Oh, that would never do at all," cried Kitty. "His patients would all die before he got there."

"That is, if they had anything the matter with them," added my uncle.

A PIECE OF RED CALICO

Before beginning the relation of the following incidents, I wish to state that I am a young married man, doing business in a large city, in the suburbs of which I live.

I was going into town the other morning, when my wife handed me a little piece of red calico, and asked me if I would have time, during the day, to buy her two yards and a half of calico like it. I assured her that it would be no trouble at all, and putting the piece of calico in my pocket, I took the train for the city.

At lunch-time I stopped in at a large dry-goods store to attend to my wife's commission. I saw a well-dressed man walking the floor between the counters, where long lines of girls were waiting on much longer lines of customers, and asked him where I could see some red calico.

"This way, sir," and he led me up the store. "Miss Stone," said he to a young lady, "show this gentleman some red calico."

"What shade do you want!" asked Miss Stone.

I showed her the little piece of calico that my wife had given me. She looked at it and handed it back to me. Then she took down a great roll of red calico and spread it out on the counter.

"Why, that isn't the shade!" said I.

"No, not exactly," said she. "But it is prettier than your sample."

"That may be," said I. "But, you see, I want to match this piece. There is something already in my house, made of this kind of calico, which needs to be made larger, or mended, or something. I want some calico of the same shade."

The girl made no answer, but took down another roll.

"That's the shade," said she.

"Yes," I replied, "but it's striped."

"Stripes are more worn than anything else in calicoes," said she.

"Yes. But this isn't to be worn. It's for furniture, I think. At any rate, I want perfectly plain stuff, to match something already in use."

"Well, I don't think you can find it perfectly plain, unless you get Turkey red."

"What is Turkey red?" I asked.

"Turkey red is perfectly plain in calicoes," she answered.

"Well, let me see some."

"We haven't any Turkey red calico left," she said, "but we have some very nice plain calicoes in other colors."

"I don't want any other color. I want stuff to match this."

"It's hard to match cheap calico like that," she said, and so I left her.

I next went into a store a few doors farther up Broadway. When I entered I approached the "floorwalker," and handing him my sample, said:

"Have you any calico like this?"

"Yes, sir," said he. "Third counter to the right." I went to the third counter to the right, and showed my sample to the salesman in attendance there. He looked at it on both sides. Then he said:

"We haven't any of this."

"The floorwalker said you had," said I.

"We had it, but we're out of it now. You'll get that goods at an upholsterers."

I went across the street to an upholsterer's.

"Have you any stuff like this?" I asked.

"No," said the salesman, "we haven't. Is it for furniture?"

"Yes," I replied.

"Then Turkey red is what you want."

"Is Turkey red just like this?" I asked.

"No," said he, "but it's much better."

"That makes no difference to me," I replied. "I want something just like this."

"But they don't use that for furniture," he said.

"I should think people could use anything they wanted for furniture," I remarked, somewhat sharply.

"They can, but they don't," he said quite calmly. "They don't use red like that. They use Turkey red."

I said no more, but left. The next place I visited was a very large dry-goods store. Of the first salesman I saw I inquired if they kept red calico like my sample.

"You'll find that on the second story," said he.

I went up-stairs. There I asked a man:

"Where shall I find red calico?"

"In the far room to the left," and he pointed to a distant corner.

I walked through the crowds of purchasers and salespeople, around the counters and tables filled with goods, to the far room to the left. When I got there I asked for red calico.

"The second counter down this side," said the man. I went there and produced my sample. "Calicoes down-stairs," said the man.

"They told me they were up here," I said.

"Not these plain goods. You'll find them downstairs at the back of the store, over on that side."

I went down-stairs to the back of the store.

"Where can I find red calico like this?" I asked.

"Next counter but one, " said the man addressed, walking with me in the direction pointed out. "Dunn, show red calicoes."

Mr. Dunn took my sample and looked at it. "We haven't this shade in that quality of goods," he said.

"Well, have you it in any quality of goods?" I asked.

"Yes. We've got it finer." He took down a piece of calico, and unrolled a yard or two of it.

"That's not this shade," I said.

"No," said he. "The goods is finer and the color's better."

"I want it to match this," I said.

"I thought you weren't particular about the match," said the salesman. "You said you didn't care for the quality of the goods, and you know you can't match without you take into consideration quality and color both. If you want that quality of goods in red, you ought to get Turkey red."

I did not think it necessary to answer this remark, but said:

"Then you've got nothing to match this?"

"No, sir. But perhaps they may have it in the upholstery department, in the sixth story."

I got into the elevator and went up to the top of the house.

"Have you any red stuff like this?" I said to a young man.

"Red stuff? Upholstery department—other end of this floor."

I went to the other end of the floor.

"I want some red calico," I said to a man.

"Furniture goods?" he asked.

"Yes," said I.

"Fourth counter to the left."

I went to the fourth counter to the left, and showed my sample to a salesman. He looked at it, and said: "You'll get this down on the first floor—calico department."

I turned on my heel, descended in the elevator, and went out on Broadway. I was thoroughly sick of red calico. But I determined to make one more trial. My wife had bought her red calico not long before, and there must be some to be had somewhere. I ought to have asked her where she bought it, but I thought a simple little thing like that could be procured anywhere.

I went into another large dry-goods store. As I entered the door a sudden tremor seized me. I could not bear to take out that piece of red calico. If I had had any other kind of a rag about me—a pen-wiper or anything of the sort—I think I would have asked them if they could match that.

But I stepped up to a young woman and presented my sample, with the usual question.

"Back room, counter on the left," she said.

I went there.

"Have you any red calico like this?" I asked of the lady behind the counter.

"No, sir," she said, "but we have it in Turkey red."

Turkey red again! I surrendered.

"All right," I said. "Give me Turkey red."

"How much, sir?" she asked.

"I don't know—say five yards."

The lady looked at me rather strangely, but measured off five yards of Turkey red calico. Then she rapped on the counter and called out, "Cash!" A little girl, with yellow hair in two long plaits, came slowly up. The lady wrote the number of yards; the name of the goods; her own number; the price; the amount of the bank-note I handed her; and some other matters—probably the color of my eyes and the direction and velocity of the wind—on a slip of paper. She then copied all this in a little book which she kept by her. Then she handed the slip of paper, the money, and the Turkey red to the yellow-haired girl. This young girl copied the slip in a little book she carried, and then she went away with the calico, the paper slip, and the money.

After a very long time—during which the little girl probably took the goods, the money, and the slip to some central desk, where the note was received, its amount and number entered in a book; change given to the girl; a copy of the slip made and entered; girl's entry examined and approved; goods wrapped up; girl registered; plaits counted and entered on a slip of paper and copied by the girl in her book; girl taken to a hydrant and washed; number of towel entered on a paper slip and copied by the girl in her book; value of my note and amount of change branded somewhere on the child, and said process noted on a slip of paper and copied in her book—the girl came to me, bringing my change and the package of Turkey red calico. I had time for but very little work at the office that afternoon, and when I reached home I handed the package of calico to my wife. She unrolled it and exclaimed:

"Why, this doesn't match the piece I gave you!"

"Match it!" I cried. "Oh no! it doesn't match it. You didn't want that matched. You were mistaken. What you wanted was Turkey red—third counter to the left. I mean, Turkey red is what they use!"

My wife looked at me in amazement, and then I detailed to her my troubles.

"Well," said she, "this Turkey red is a great deal prettier than what I had, and you've bought so much of it that I needn't use the other at all. I wish I had thought of Turkey red before."

"I wish from my heart you had!" said I.

THE CHRISTMAS WRECK

"Well, sir," said old Silas, as he gave a preliminary puff to the pipe he had just lighted, and so satisfied himself that the draught was all right, "the wind's a-comin', an' so's Christmas. But it's no use bein' in a hurry fur either of 'em, fur sometimes they come afore you want 'em, anyway."

Silas was sitting in the stern of a small sailing-boat which he owned, and in which he sometimes took the Sandport visitors out for a sail, and at other times applied to its more legitimate but less profitable use, that of fishing. That afternoon he had taken young Mr. Nugent for a brief excursion on that portion of the Atlantic Ocean which sends its breakers up on the beach of Sandport. But he had found it difficult, nay, impossible, just now, to bring him back, for the wind had gradually died away until there was not a breath of it left. Mr. Nugent, to whom nautical experiences were as new as the very nautical suit of blue flannel which he wore, rather liked the calm. It was such a relief to the monotony of rolling waves. He took out a cigar and lighted it, and then he remarked:

"I can easily imagine how a wind might come before you sailors might want it, but I don't see how Christmas could come too soon."

"It come wunst on me when things couldn't 'a' looked

more onready fur it," said Silas.

"How was that?" asked Mr. Nugent, settling himself a little more comfortably on the hard thwart. "If it's a story, let's have it. This is a good time to spin a yarn."

"Very well," said old Silas. "I'll spin her."

The bare-legged boy whose duty it was to stay forward and mind the jib came aft as soon as he smelt a story, and took a nautical position, which was duly studied by Mr. Nugent, on a bag of ballast in the bottom of the boat.

"It's nigh on to fifteen year ago," said Silas, "that I was on the bark Mary Auguster, bound for Sydney, New South Wales, with a cargo of canned goods. We was somewhere about longitood a hundred an' seventy, latitood nothin', an' it was the twenty-second o' December, when we was ketched by a reg'lar typhoon which blew straight along, end on, fur a day an' a half. It blew away the storm-sails. It blew away every yard, spar, shroud, an' every strand o' riggin', an' snapped the masts off close to the deck. It blew away all the boats. It blew away the cook's caboose, an' everythin' else on deck. It blew off the hatches, an' sent 'em spinnin' in the air about a mile to leeward. An' afore it got through, it washed away the cap'n an' all the crew 'cept me an' two others. These was Tom Simmons, the second mate, an' Andy Boyle, a chap from the Adirondack Mount'ins, who'd never been to sea afore. As he was a landsman, he ought, by rights, to 'a' been swep' off by the wind an' water, consid'rin' that the cap'n an' sixteen good seamen had gone a'ready. But he had hands eleven inches long, an' that give him a grip which no typhoon could git the better of. Andy had let out that his father was a miller up there in York State, an' a story had got round among the crew that his granfather an' great-gran'father was millers, too; an' the way the fam'ly got such big hands come from their habit of scoopin' up a extry quart or two of meal or flour fur themselves when they was levellin' off their customers' measures. He was a good-natered feller, though, an' never got riled when I'd tell him to clap his flour-scoops onter a halyard. "We was all soaked, an' washed, an' beat, an' battered. We held on some way or other till the wind blowed itself out, an' then we got on our legs an' began to look about us to see how things stood. The sea had washed into the open hatches till the vessel was more'n half full of water, an' that had sunk her, so deep that she must 'a' looked like a canal-boat loaded with gravel. We hadn't had a thing to eat or drink durin' that whole blow, an' we was pretty ravenous. We found a keg of water which was all right, and a box of biscuit which was what you might call softtack, fur they was soaked through an' through with sea-water.

We eat a lot of them so, fur we couldn't wait, an' the rest we spread on the deck to dry, fur the sun was now shinin' hot enough to bake bread. We couldn't go below much, fur there was a pretty good swell on the sea, an' things was floatin' about so's to make it dangerous. But we fished out a piece of canvas, which we rigged up ag'in' the stump of the mainmast so that we could have somethin' that we could sit down an' grumble under. What struck us all the hardest was that the bark was loaded with a whole cargo of jolly things to eat, which was just as good as ever they was, fur the water couldn't git through the tin cans in which they was all put up, an' here we was with nothin' to live on but them salted biscuit. There wasn't no way of gittin' at any of the ship's stores, or any of the fancy prog, fur everythin' was stowed away tight under six or seven feet of water, an' pretty nigh all the room that was left between decks was filled up with extry spars, lumber, boxes, an' other floatin' stuff. All was shiftin', an' bumpin', an' bangin' every time the vessel rolled.

"As I said afore, Tom was second mate, an' I was bo's'n.

Says I to Tom, 'The thing we've got to do is to put up some kind of a spar with a rag on it fur a distress flag, so that we'll lose no time bein' took off.' 'There's no use a-slavin' at anythin' like that,' says Tom, 'fur we've been blowed off the track of traders, an' the more we work the hungrier we'll git, an' the sooner will them biscuit be gone.'

"Now when I heared Tom say this I sot still an' began to consider. Bein' second mate, Tom was, by rights, in command of this craft. But it was easy enough to see that if he commanded there'd never be nothin' fur Andy an' me to do. All the grit he had in him he'd used up in holdin' on durin' that typhoon. What he wanted to do now was to make himself comfortable till the time come for him to go to Davy Jones's locker—an' thinkin', most likely, that Davy couldn't make it any hotter fur him than it was on that deck, still in latitood nothin' at all, fur we'd been blowed along the line pretty nigh due west. So I calls to Andy, who was busy turnin' over the biscuits on the deck. 'Andy,' says I, when he had got under the canvas, 'we's goin' to have a 'lection fur skipper. Tom, here, is about played out. He's one candydate, an' I'm another. Now, who do you vote fur? An' mind yer eye, youngster, that you don't make no mistake.' 'I vote fur you' says Andy. 'Carried unanermous!' says I. 'An' I want you to take notice that I'm cap'n of what's left of the Mary Auguster, an' you two has got to keep your minds on that, an' obey orders.' If Davy Jones was to do all that Tom Simmons said when he heared this, the old chap would be kept busier than he ever was yit. But I let him growl his growl out, knowin' he'd come round all right, fur there wasn't no help fur it, consid'rin' Andy an' me was two to his one. Pretty soon we all went to work, an' got up a spar from below, which we rigged to the stump of the foremast, with Andy's shirt atop of it.

"Them sea-soaked, sun-dried biscuit was pretty mean prog, as you might think, but we eat so many of 'em that afternoon, an' 'cordingly drank so much water, that I was obliged to put us all on short rations the next day. 'This is the day afore Christmas,' says Andy Boyle, 'an' to-night will be Christmas eve, an' it's pretty tough fur us to be sittin' here with not even so much hardtack as we want, an' all the time thinkin' that the hold of this ship is packed full of the gayest kind of good things to eat.' 'Shut up about Christmas!' says Tom Simmons. 'Them two youngsters of mine, up in Bangor, is havin' their toes and noses pretty nigh froze, I 'spect, but they'll hang up their stockin's all the same to-night, never thinkin' that their dad's bein' cooked alive on a empty stomach.' 'Of course they wouldn't hang 'em up,' says I, if they knowed what a fix you was in, but they don't know it, an' what's the use of grumblin' at 'em fur bein' a little jolly?' 'Well,' says Andy 'they couldn't be more jollier than I'd be if I could git at some of them fancy fixin's down in the hold. I worked well on to a week at 'Frisco puttin' in them boxes, an' the names of the things was on the outside of most of 'em; an' I tell you what it is, mates, it made my mouth water, even then, to read 'em, an' I wasn't hungry, nuther, havin' plenty to eat three times a day. There was roast beef, an' roast mutton, an' duck, an' chicken, an' soup, an' peas, an' beans, an' termaters, an' plum-puddin',an' mince-pie—' 'Shut up with your mince-pie!' sung out Tom Simmons. 'Isn't it enough to have to gnaw on these salt chips, without hearin' about mince-pie?' 'An' more'n that' says Andy, 'there was canned peaches, an' pears, an' plums, an' cherries.'

"Now these things did sound so cool an' good to me on that br'ilin' deck that I couldn't stand it, an' I leans over to Andy, an' I says: 'Now look-a here; if you don't shut up talkin' about them things what's stowed below, an' what we can't git at nohow, overboard you go!' 'That would make you short-handed,' says Andy, with a grin. 'Which is more'n you could say,' says I, 'if you'd chuck Tom an, me over'— alludin' to his eleven-inch grip. Andy didn't say no more then, but after a while he comes to me, as I was lookin' round to see if anything was in sight, an' says he, 'I spose you ain't got nothin' to say ag'in' my divin' into the hold just aft of the foremast, where there seems to be a bit of pretty clear water, an' see if I can't git up somethin'?' 'You kin do it, if you like,' says I, 'but it's at your own risk.

You can't take out no insurance at this office.' 'All right, then,' says Andy; 'an' if I git stove in by floatin' boxes, you an' Tom'll have to eat the rest of them salt crackers.' 'Now, boy,' says I,—an' he wasn't much more, bein' only nineteen year old,— 'you'd better keep out o' that hold. You'll just git yourself smashed. An' as to movin' any of them there heavy boxes, which must be swelled up as tight as if they was part of the ship, you might as well try to pull out one of the Mary Auguster's ribs.' 'I'll try it,' says Andy, 'fur to-morrer is Christmas, an' if I kin help it I ain't goin' to be floatin' atop of a Christmas dinner without eatin' any on it.' I let him go, fur he was a good swimmer an' diver, an' I did hope he might root out somethin' or other, fur Christmas is about the worst day in the year fur men to be starvin' on, an' that's what we was a-comin' to.

"Well, fur about two hours Andy swum, an' dove, an' come up blubberin', an' dodged all sorts of floatin' an' pitchin' stuff, fur the swell was still on. But he couldn't even be so much as sartin that he'd found the canned vittles. To dive down through hatchways, an' among broken bulkheads, to hunt fur any partiklar kind o' boxes under seven foot of sea-water, ain't no easy job. An' though Andy said he got hold of the end of a box that felt to him like the big uns he'd noticed as havin' the meat-pies in, he couldn't move it no more'n if it had been the stump of the foremast. If we could have pumped the water out of the hold we could have got at any part of the cargo we wanted, but as it was, we couldn't even reach the ship's stores, which, of course, must have been mostly sp'iled anyway, whereas the canned vittles was just as good as new. The pumps was all smashed or stopped up, for we tried 'em, but if they hadn't 'a' been we three couldn't never have pumped out that ship on three biscuit a day, an' only about two days' rations at that.

"So Andy he come up, so fagged out that it was as much as he could do to get his clothes on, though they wasn't much, an' then he stretched himself out under the canvas an' went to sleep, an' it wasn't long afore he was talkin' about roast turkey an' cranberry sass, an' punkin-pie, an' sech stuff, most of which we knowed was under our feet that present minnit. Tom Simmons he just b'iled over, an' sung out: 'Roll him out in the sun an' let him cook! I can't stand no more of this!' But I wasn't goin' to have Andy treated no sech way as that, fur if it hadn't been fur Tom Simmons' wife an' young uns, Andy'd been worth two of him to anybody who was consid'rin' savin' life. But I give the boy a good punch in the ribs to stop his dreamin', fur I was as hungry as Tom was, an' couldn't stand no nonsense about Christmas dinners.

"It was a little arter noon when Andy woke up, an' he went outside to stretch himself. In about a minute he give a yell that made Tom an' me jump. 'A sail!' he hollered. 'A sail!' An' you may bet your life, young man, that 'twasn't more'n half a second afore us two had scuffled out from under that canvas, an' was standin' by Andy. 'There she is!' he shouted, 'not a mile to win'ard.' I give one look, an' then I sings out: ''Tain't a sail! It's a flag of distress! Can't you see, you landlubber, that that's the Stars and Stripes upside down?' 'Why, so it is,' says Andy, with a couple of reefs in the joyfulness of his voice. An' Tom he began to growl as if somebody had cheated him out of half a year's wages.

"The flag that we saw was on the hull of a steamer that had been driftin' down on us while we was sittin' under our canvas. It was plain to see she'd been caught in the typhoon, too, fur there wasn't a mast or a smoke-stack on her. But her hull was high enough out of the water to catch what wind there was, while we was so low sunk that we didn't make no way at all. There was people aboard, and they saw us, an' waved their hats an' arms, an' Andy an' me waved ours; but all we could do was to wait till they drifted nearer, fur we hadn't no boats to go to 'em if we'd wanted to.

"'I'd like to know what good that old hulk is to us,' says Tom Simmons. 'She can't take us off.' It did look to me somethin' like the blind leadin' the blind. But Andy he sings out: 'We'd be better off aboard of her, fur she ain't water-logged, an', more'n that, I don't s'pose her stores are all soaked up in salt water.' There was some sense in that, an' when the steamer had got to within half a mile of us, we was glad to see a boat put out from her with three men in it. It was a queer boat, very low an' flat, an' not like any ship's boat I ever see.

But the two fellers at the oars pulled stiddy, an' pretty soon the boat was 'longside of us, an' the three men on our deck. One of 'em was the first mate of the other wreck, an' when he found out what was the matter with us, he spun his yarn, which was a longer one than ours. His vessel was the Water Crescent, nine hundred tons, from 'Frisco to Melbourne, an' they had sailed about six weeks afore we did. They was about two weeks out when some of their machinery broke down, an' when they got it patched up it broke ag'in, worse than afore, so that they couldn't do nothin' with it. They kep' along under sail for about a month, makin' mighty poor headway till the typhoon struck 'em, an' that cleaned their decks off about as slick as it did ours, but their hatches wasn't blowed off, an' they didn't ship no water wuth mentionin', an' the crew havin' kep' below, none of 'em was lost. But now they was clean out of provisions an' water, havin' been short when the breakdown happened, fur they had sold all the stores they could spare to a French brig in distress that they overhauled when about a week out. When they sighted us they felt pretty sure they'd git some provisions out of us. But when I told the mate what a fix we was in his jaw dropped till his face was as long as one of Andy's hands. Howsomdever, he said he'd send the boat back fur as many men as it could bring over, an' see if they couldn't git up some of our stores. Even if they was soaked with salt water, they'd be better than nothin'. Part of the cargo of the Water Crescent was tools an, things fur some railway contractors out in Australier, an' the mate told the men to bring over some of them irons that might be used to fish out the stores. All their ship's boats had been blowed away, an' the one they had was a kind of shore boat for fresh water, that had been shipped as part of the cargo, an' stowed below. It couldn't stand no kind of a sea, but there wasn't nothin' but a swell on, an' when it come back it had the cap'n in it, an' five men, besides a lot of chains an' tools.

"Them fellers an' us worked pretty nigh the rest of the day, an' we got out a couple of bar'ls of water, which was all right, havin' been tight bunged, an' a lot of sea-biscuit, all soaked an sloppy, but we only got a half-bar'l of meat, though three or four of the men stripped an' dove fur more'n an hour. We cut up some of the meat an' eat it raw, an' the cap'n sent some over to the other wreck, which had drifted past us to leeward, an' would have gone clean away from us if the cap'n hadn't had a line got out an' made us fast to it while we was a-workin' at the stores.

"That night the cap'n took us three, as well as the provisions we'd got out, on board his hull, where the 'commodations was consid'able better than they was on the half-sunk Mary Auguster. An' afore we turned in he took me aft an' had a talk with me as commandin' off'cer of my vessel. 'That wreck o' yourn,' says he, 'has got a vallyble cargo in it, which isn't sp'iled by bein' under water. Now, if you could get that cargo into port it would put a lot of money in your pocket, fur the owners couldn't git out of payin' you fur takin' charge of it an' havin' it brung in. Now I'll tell you what I'll do. I'll lie by you, an' I've got carpenters aboard that'll put your pumps in order, an' I'll set my men to work to pump out your vessel. An' then, when she's afloat all right, I'll go to work ag'in at my vessel—which I didn't s'pose there was any use o' doin', but whilst I was huntin' round amongst our cargo to-day I found that some of the machinery we carried might be worked up so's to take the place of what is broke in our engine. We've got a forge aboard, an' I believe we can make these pieces of machinery fit, an' git goin' ag'in. Then I'll tow you into Sydney, an' we'll divide the salvage money. I won't git nothin' fur savin' my vessel, coz that's my business, but you wasn't cap'n o' yourn, an' took charge of her a-purpose to save her, which is another thing.'

"I wasn't at all sure that I didn't take charge of the Mary Auguster to save myself an' not the vessel, but I didn't mention that, an' asked the cap'n how he expected to live all this time.

"'Oh, we kin git at your stores easy enough,' says he, when the water's pumped out.' 'They'll be mostly sp'iled,' says I. 'That don't matter' says he. 'Men'll eat anything when they can't git nothin' else.' An' with that he left me to think it over.

"I must say, young man, an' you kin b'lieve me if you know anything about sech things, that the idee of a pile of money was mighty temptin' to a feller like me, who had a girl at home ready to marry him, and who would like nothin' better'n to have a little house of his own, an' a little vessel of his own, an' give up the other side of the world altogether. But while I was goin' over all this in my mind, an' wonderin' if the cap'n ever could git us into port, along comes Andy Boyle, an' sits down beside me. 'It drives me pretty nigh crazy,' says he, 'to think that to-morrer's Christmas, an' we've got to feed on that sloppy stuff we fished out of our stores, an' not much of it, nuther, while there's all that roast turkey an' plum-puddin' an' mince-pie a-floatin' out there just afore our eyes, an' we can't have none of it.' 'You hadn't oughter think so much about eatin', Andy,' says I, 'but if I was talkin' about them things I wouldn't leave out canned peaches. By George! On a hot Christmas like this is goin' to be, I'd be the jolliest Jack on the ocean if I could git at that canned fruit.' 'Well, there's a way,' says Andy, 'that we might git some of 'em. A part of the cargo of this ship is stuff far blastin' rocks—ca'tridges, 'lectric bat'ries, an' that sort of thing; an' there's a man aboard who's goin' out to take charge of 'em. I've been talkin' to this bat'ry man, an' I've made up my mind it'll be easy enough to lower a little ca'tridge down among our cargo an' blow out a part of it.' 'What 'u'd be the good of it,' says I, 'blowed into chips?' 'It might smash some,' says he, 'but others would be only loosened, an' they'd float up to the top, where we could git 'em, specially them as was packed with pies, which must be pretty light.' 'Git out, Andy,' says I, 'with all that stuff!' An' he got out.

"But the idees he'd put into my head didn't git out, an' as I laid on my back on the deck, lookin' up at the stars, they sometimes seemed to put themselves into the shape of a little house, with a little woman cookin' at the kitchin fire, an' a little schooner layin' at anchor just off shore. An' then ag'in they'd hump themselves up till they looked like a lot of new tin cans with their tops off, an' all kinds of good things to eat inside, specially canned peaches—the big white kind, soft an' cool, each one split in half, with a holler in the middle filled with juice. By George, sir! the very thought of a tin can like that made me beat my heels ag'in the deck. I'd been mighty hungry, an' had eat a lot of salt pork, wet an' raw, an' now the very idee of it, even cooked, turned my stomach. I looked up to the stars ag'in, an' the little house an' the little schooner was clean gone, an' the whole sky was filled with nothin' but bright new tin cans.

"In the mornin' Andy he come to me ag'in. 'Have you made up your mind,' says he, 'about gittin' some of them good things fur Christmas dinner?' 'Confound you!' says I, 'you talk as if all we had to do was to go an' git 'em.' 'An' that's what I b'lieve we kin do,' says he, 'with the help of that bat'ry man.' 'Yes,' says I, 'an' blow a lot of the cargo into flinders, an' damage the Mary Auguster so's she couldn't never be took into port.' An' then I told him what the cap'n had said to me, an' what I was goin' to do with the money. 'A little ca'tridge,' says Andy, 'would do all we want, an' wouldn't hurt the vessel, nuther. Besides that, I don't b'lieve what this cap'n says about tinkerin' up his engine. 'Tain't likely he'll ever git her runnin' ag'in, nor pump out the Mary Auguster, nuther. If I was you I'd a durned sight ruther have a Christmas dinner in hand than a house an' wife in the bush.' 'I ain't thinkin' o' marryin' a girl in Australier,' says I. An' Andy he grinned, an' said I wouldn't marry nobody if I had to live on sp'iled vittles till I got her.

"A little arter that I went to the cap'n an' I told him about Andy's idee, but he was down on it. 'It's your vessel, an' not mine,' says he, 'an' if you want to try to git a dinner out of her I'll not stand in your way. But it's my 'pinion you'll just damage the ship, an' do nothin'.' Howsomdever, I talked to the bat'ry man about it, an' he thought it could be done, an' not hurt the ship, nuther. The men was all in favor of it, fur none of 'em had forgot it was Christmas day. But Tom Simmons he was ag'in' it strong, fur he was thinkin' he'd git some of the money if we got the Mary Auguster into port. He was a selfish-minded man, was Tom, but it was his nater, an' I s'pose he couldn't help it.

"Well, it wasn't long afore I began to feel pretty empty an' mean, an' if I'd wanted any of the prog we got out the day afore, I couldn't have found much, fur the men had eat it up nearly all in the night. An' so I just made up my mind without any more foolin', an' me an' Andy Boyle an' the bat'ry man, with some ca'tridges an' a coil of wire, got into the little shore boat, an' pulled over to the Mary Auguster. There we lowered a small ca'tridge down the main hatchway, an' let it rest down among the cargo. Then we rowed back to the steamer, uncoilin' the wire as. we went. The bat'ry man clumb up on deck, an' fixed his wire to a 'lectric machine, which he'd got all ready afore we started. Andy an' me didn't git out of the boat. We had too much sense fur that, with all them hungry fellers waitin' to jump in her. But we just pushed a little off, an' sot waitin', with our mouths awaterin', fur him to touch her off. He seemed to be a long time about it, but at last he did it, an' that instant there was a bang on board the Mary Auguster that made my heart jump. Andy an' me pulled fur her like mad, the others a-hollerin' arter us, an' we was on deck in no time. The deck was all covered with the water that had been throwed up. But I tell you, sir, that we poked an' fished about, an' Andy stripped an' went down an' swum all round, an' we couldn't find one floatin' box of canned goods. There was a lot of splinters, but where they come from we didn't know. By this time my dander was up, an' I just pitched around savage. That little ca'tridge wasn't no good, an' I didn't intend to stand any more foolin'. We just rowed back to the other wreck, an' I called to the ba'try man to come down, an' bring some bigger ca'tridges with him, fur if we was goin' to do anything we might as well do it right. So he got down with a package of bigger ones, an' jumped into the boat.

The cap'n he called out to us to be keerful, an' Tom Simmons leaned over the rail an' swored; but I didn't pay no 'tention to nuther of 'em, an' we pulled away.

"When I got aboard the Mary Auguster, I says to the bat'ry man: 'We don't want no nonsense this time, an' I want you to put in enough ca'tridges to heave up somethin' that'll do fur a Christmas dinner. I don't know how the cargo is stored, but you kin put one big ca'tridge 'midship, another for'ard, an' another aft, an' one or nuther of 'em oughter fetch up somethin'.' Well, we got the three ca'tridges into place. They was a good deal bigger than the one we fust used, an' we j'ined 'em all to one wire, an' then we rowed back, carryin' the long wire with us. When we reached the steamer, me an' Andy was a-goin' to stay in the boat as we did afore, but the cap'n sung out that he wouldn't allow the bat'ry to be touched off till we come aboard. 'Ther's got to be fair play,' says he. 'It's your vittles, but it's my side that's doin' the work. After we've blasted her this time you two can go in the boat an' see what there is to git hold of, but two of my men must go along.' So me an' Andy had to go on deck, an' two big fellers was detailed to go with us in the little boat when the time come, an' then the bat'ry man he teched her off.

"Well, sir, the pop that followed that tech was somethin' to remember. It shuck the water, it shuck the air, an' it shuck the hull we was on. A reg'lar cloud of smoke an' flyin' bits of things rose up out of the Mary Auguster; an' when that smoke cleared away, an' the water was all b'ilin' with the splash of various-sized hunks that come rainin' down from the sky, what was left of the Mary Auguster was sprinkled over the sea like a wooden carpet fur water-birds to walk on.

"Some of the men sung out one thing, an' some another, an' I could hear Tom Simmons swear; but Andy an' me said never a word, but scuttled down into the boat, follered close by the two men who was to go with us. Then we rowed like devils fur the lot of stuff that was bobbin' about on the water, out where the Mary Auguster had been. In we went among the floatin' spars and ship's timbers, I keepin' the

Frank R. Stockton

things off with an oar, the two men rowin', an' Andy in the bow.

"Suddenly Andy give a yell, an' then he reached himself for'ard with sech a bounce that I thought he'd go overboard. But up he come in a minnit, his two 'leven-inch hands gripped round a box. He sot down in the bottom of the boat with the box on his lap an' his eyes screwed on some letters that was stamped on one end. 'Pidjin-pies!' he sings out. "Tain't turkeys, nor 'tain't cranberries but, by the Lord Harry, it's Christmas pies all the same!' After that Andy didn't do no more work, but sot holdin' that box as if it had been his fust baby. But we kep' pushin' on to see what else there was. It's my 'pinion that the biggest part of that bark's cargo was blowed into mince-meat, an' the most of the rest of it was so heavy that it sunk. But it wasn't all busted up, an' it didn't all sink. There was a big piece of wreck with a lot of boxes stove into the timbers, and some of these had in 'em beef ready b'iled an' packed into cans, an' there was other kinds of meat, an' dif'rent sorts of vegetables, an' one box of turtle soup. I looked at every one of 'em as we took 'em in, an' when we got the little boat pretty well loaded I wanted to still keep on searchin'; but the men they said that shore boat 'u'd sink if we took in any more cargo, an' so we put back, I feelin' glummer'n I oughter felt, fur I had begun to be afeared that canned fruit, sech as peaches, was heavy, an' li'ble to sink.

"As soon as we had got our boxes aboard, four fresh men put out in the boat, an' after a while they come back with another load. An' I was mighty keerful to read the names on all the boxes. Some was meat-pies, an' some was salmon, an' some was potted herrin's, an' some was lobsters. But nary a thing could I see that ever had growed on a tree.

"Well, sir, there was three loads brought in altogether, an' the Christmas dinner we had on the for'ard deck of that steamer's hull was about the jolliest one that was ever seen of a hot day aboard of a wreck in the Pacific Ocean. The cap'n kept good order, an' when all was ready the tops was jerked off the boxes, and each man grabbed a can an' opened it with his knife. When he had cleaned it out, he tuk another without doin' much questionin' as to the bill of fare. Whether anybody got pidjin-pie 'cept Andy, I can't say, but the way we piled in Delmoniker prog would 'a' made people open their eyes as was eatin' their Christmas dinners on shore that day. Some of the things would 'a' been better cooked a little more, or het up, but we was too fearful hungry to wait fur that, an' they was tiptop as they was.

"The cap'n went out afterwards, an' towed in a couple of bar'ls of flour that was only part soaked through, an' he got some other plain prog that would do fur future use. But none of us give our minds to stuff like this arter the glorious Christmas dinner that we'd quarried out of the Mary Auguster. Every man that wasn't on duty went below and turned in fur a snooze—all 'cept me, an' I didn't feel just altogether satisfied. To be sure, I'd had an A1 dinner, an', though a little mixed, I'd never eat a jollier one on any Christmas that I kin look back at. But, fur all that, there was a hanker inside o' me. I hadn't got all I'd laid out to git when we teched off the Mary Auguster. The day was blazin' hot, an' a lot of the things I'd eat was pretty peppery. 'Now,' thinks I, 'if there had been just one can o' peaches sech as I seen shinin' in the stars last night!' An' just then, as I was walkin' aft, all by myself, I seed lodged on the stump of the mizzenmast a box with one corner druv down among the splinters. It was half split open, an' I could see the tin cans shinin' through the crack. I give one jump at it, an' wrenched the side off. On the top of the first can I seed was a picture of a big white peach with green leaves. That box had been blowed up so high that if it had come down

Frank R. Stockton

anywhere 'cept among them splinters it would 'a' smashed itself to flinders, or killed somebody. So fur as I know, it was the only thing that fell nigh us, an' by George, sir, I got it! When I had finished a can of 'em I hunted up Andy, an' then we went aft an' eat some more. 'Well,' says Andy, as we was a-eatin', 'how d'ye feel now about blowin' up your wife, an' your house, an' that little schooner you was goin' to own?'

"'Andy,' says I, 'this is the joyfulest Christmas I've had yit, an' if I was to live till twenty hundred I don't b'lieve I'd have no joyfuler, with things comin' in so pat; so don't you throw no shadders.'"

"'Shadders!' says Andy. 'That ain't me. I leave that sort of thing fur Tom Simmons.'"

"'Shadders is cool,' says I, 'an' I kin go to sleep under all he throws.'"

"Well, sir," continued old Silas, putting his hand on the tiller and turning his face seaward, "if Tom Simmons had kept command of that wreck, we all would 'a' laid there an' waited an' waited till some of us was starved, an' the others got nothin' fur it, fur the cap'n never mended his engine, an' it wasn't more'n a week afore we was took off, an' then it was by a sailin' vessel, which left the hull of the Water Crescent behind her, just as she would 'a' had to leave the Mary Auguster if that jolly old Christmas wreck had been there.

"An' now, sir," said Silas, "d'ye see that stretch o' little ripples over yander, lookin' as if it was a lot o' herrin' turnin' over to dry their sides? Do you know what that is? That's the supper wind. That means coffee, an' hot cakes, an' a bit of br'iled fish, an' pertaters, an' p'r'aps, if the old woman feels in a partiklar good humor, some canned peaches—big white uns, cut in half, with a holler place in the middle filled with cool, sweet juice."

Frank R. Stockton

MY WELL AND WHAT CAME OUT OF IT

Early in my married life I bought a small country estate which my wife and I looked upon as a paradise. After enjoying its delight for a little more than a year our souls were saddened by the discovery that our Eden contained a serpent. This was an insufficient water-supply.

It had been a rainy season when we first went there, and for a long time our cisterns gave us full aqueous satisfaction, but early this year a drought had set in, and we were obliged to be exceedingly careful of our water.

It was quite natural that the scarcity of water for domestic purposes should affect my wife much more than it did me, and perceiving the discontent which was growing in her mind, I determined to dig a well. The very next day I began to look for a well-digger. Such an individual was not easy to find, for in the region in which I lived wells had become unfashionable; but I determined to persevere in my search, and in about a week I found a well-digger.

He was a man of somewhat rough exterior, but of an ingratiating turn of mind. It was easy to see that it was his earnest desire to serve me.

"And now, then," said he, when we had had a little conversation about terms, "the first thing to do is to find out where there is water. Have you a peach-tree on the place?" We walked to such a tree, and he cut therefrom a forked twig.

"I thought," said I, "that divining-rods were always of hazel wood."

"A peach twig will do quite as well," said he, and I have since found that he was right. Divining-rods of peach will turn and find water quite as well as those of hazel or any other kind of wood.

He took an end of the twig in each hand, and, with the point projecting in front of him, he slowly walked along over the grass in my little orchard. Presently the point of the twig seemed to bend itself downward toward the ground.

"There," said he, stopping, "you will find water here."

"I do not want a well here," said I. "This is at the bottom of a hill, and my barn-yard is at the top. Besides, it is too far from the house."

"Very good," said he. "We will try somewhere else."

His rod turned at several other places, but I had objections to all of them. A sanitary engineer had once visited me, and he had given me a great deal of advice about drainage, and I knew what to avoid.

We crossed the ridge of the hill into the low ground on the other side. Here were no buildings, nothing which would interfere with the purity of a well. My well-digger walked slowly over the ground with his divining-rod. Very soon he exclaimed: "Here is water!" And picking up a stick, he sharpened one end of it and drove it into the ground. Then he took a string from his pocket, and making a loop in one end, he put it over the stick.

"What are you going to do?" I asked.

"I am going to make a circle four feet in diameter," he said. "We have to dig the well as wide as that, you know."

"But I do not want a well here," said I. "It's too close to the wall. I could not build a house over it. It would not do at all."

He stood up and looked at me. "Well, sir," said he, "will you tell me where you would like to have a well?"

"Yes," said I. "I would like to have it over there in the corner of the hedge. It would be near enough to the house; it would have a warm exposure, which will be desirable in winter; and the little house which I intend to build over it would look better there than anywhere else."

He took his divining-rod and went to the spot I had indicated. "Is this the place?" he asked wishing to be sure he had understood me.

"Yes," I replied.

He put his twig in position, and in a few seconds it turned in the direction of the ground. Then he drove down a stick, marked out a circle, and the next day he came with two men and a derrick, and began to dig my well.

When they had gone down twenty-five feet they found water, and when they had progressed a few feet deeper they began to be afraid of drowning. I thought they ought to go deeper, but the well-digger said that they could not dig without first taking out the water, and that the water came in as fast as they bailed it out, and he asked me to put it to myself and tell him how they could dig it deeper. I put the question to myself, but could find no answer. I also laid the matter before some specialists, and it was generally agreed that if water came in as fast as it was taken out, nothing more could be desired. The well was, therefore, pronounced deep enough. It was lined with great tiles, nearly a yard in diameter, and my well-digger, after congratulating me on finding water so easily, bade me good-by and departed with his men and his derrick.

On the other side of the wall which bounded my grounds, and near which my well had been dug, there ran a country lane, leading nowhere in particular, which seemed to be there for the purpose of allowing people to pass my house, who might otherwise be obliged to stop.

Along this lane my neighbors would pass, and often strangers drove by, and as my well could easily be seen over the low stone wall, its construction had excited a great deal of interest. Some of the people who drove by were summer folks from the city, and I am sure, from remarks I overheard, that it was thought a very queer thing to dig for water. Of course they must have known that people used to do this in the olden times, even as far back as the time of Jacob and Rebecca, but the expressions of some of their faces indicated that they remembered that this was the nineteenth century.

My neighbors, however, were all rural people, and much more intelligent in regard to water-supplies. One of them, Phineas Colwell by name, took a more lively interest in my operations than did any one else. He was a man of about fifty years of age, who had been a soldier. This fact was kept alive in the minds of his associates by his dress, a part of which was always military. If he did not wear an old fatigue-jacket with brass buttons, he wore his blue trousers, or, perhaps, a waistcoat that belonged to his uniform, and if he wore none of these, his military hat would appear upon his head. I think he must also have been a sailor, judging from the little gold rings in his ears. But when I first knew him he was a carpenter, who did mason-work whenever any of the neighbors had any jobs of the sort. He also worked in gardens by the day, and had told me that he understood the care of horses and was a very good driver. He sometimes worked on farms, especially at harvest-time, and I know he could paint, for he once showed me a fence which he said he had painted. I frequently saw him, because he always seemed to be either going to his work or coming from it. In fact, he appeared to consider actual labor in the light of a bad habit which he wished to conceal, and which he was continually endeavoring to reform.

Phineas walked along our lane at least once a day, and whenever he saw me he told me something about the well. He did not approve of the place I had selected for it. If he had been digging a well he would have put it in a very different place. When I had talked with him for some time and explained why I had chosen this spot, he would say that perhaps I was right, and begin to talk of something else. But the next time I saw him he would again assert that if he had been digging that well he would not have put it there.

About a quarter of a mile from my house, at a turn of the lane, lived Mrs. Betty Perch. She was a widow with about twelve children. A few of these were her own, and the others she had inherited from two sisters who had married and died, and whose husbands, having proved their disloyalty by marrying again, were not allowed by the indignant Mrs. Perch to resume possession of their offspring. The casual observer might have supposed the number of these children to be very great,—fifteen or perhaps even twenty,—for if he happened to see a group of them on the door-step, he would see a lot more if he looked into the little garden; and under some cedar-trees at the back of the house there were always some of them on fine days. But perhaps they sought to increase their apparent number, and ran from one place to another to be ready to meet observation, like the famous clown Grimaldi, who used to go through his performances at one London theatre, and then dash off in his paint and motley to another, so that perambulating theatre-going men might imagine that there were two greatest clowns in the world.

When Mrs. Perch had time she sewed for the neighbors, and, whether she had time or not, she was always ready to supply them with news. From the moment she heard I was going to dig a well she took a vital interest in it. Her own water-supply was unsatisfactory, as she depended upon a little spring which sometimes dried up in summer, and should my well turn out to be a good one, she knew I would not object to her sending the children for pails of water on occasions.

"It will be fun for them," she said, "and if your water really is good it will often come in very well for me. Mr. Colwell tells me," she continued, "that you put your well in the wrong place. He is a practical man and knows all about wells, and I do hope that for your sake he may be wrong."

My neighbors were generally pessimists. Country people are proverbially prudent, and pessimism is prudence. We feel safe when we doubt the success of another, because if he should succeed we can say we were glad we were mistaken, and so step from a position of good judgment to one of generous disposition without feeling that we have changed our plane of merit. But the optimist often gets himself into terrible scrapes, for if he is wrong he cannot say he is glad of it.

But, whatever else he may be, a pessimist is depressing, and it was, therefore, a great pleasure to me to have a friend who was an out-and-out optimist. In fact, he might be called a working optimist. He lived about six miles from my house, and had a hobby, which was natural phenomena. He was always on the lookout for that sort of thing, and when he found it he would study its nature and effect. He was a man in the maturity of youth, and if the estate on which he lived had not belonged to his mother, he would have spent much time and money in investigating its natural phenomena. He often drove over to see me, and always told me how glad he would be if he had an opportunity of digging a well.

"I have the wildest desire," he said, "to know what is in the earth under our place, and if it should so happen in the course of time that the limits of earthly existence should be reached by—I mean if the estate should come into my hands—I would go down, down, down, until I had found out all that could be discovered. To own a plug of earth four thousand miles long and only to know what is on the surface of the upper end of it is unmanly. We might as well be grazing beasts."

He was sorry that I was digging only for water, because water is a very commonplace thing, but he was quite sure I would get it, and when my well was finished he was one of the first to congratulate me.

"But if I had been in your place," said he, "with full right to do as I pleased, I would not have let those men go away. I would have set them to work in some place where there would be no danger of getting water,—at least, for a long time,—and then you would have found out what are the deeper treasures of your land."

Having finished my well, I now set about getting the water into my residence near by. I built a house over the well and put in it a little engine, and by means of a system of pipes, like the arteries and veins of the human body, I proposed to distribute the water to the various desirable points in my house.

The engine was the heart, which should start the circulation, which should keep it going, and which should send throbbing through every pipe the water which, if it were not our life, was very necessary to it.

When all was ready we started the engine, and in a very short time we discovered that something was wrong. For fifteen or twenty minutes water flowed into the tank at the top of the house, with a sound that was grander in the ears of my wife and myself than the roar of Niagara, and then it stopped. Investigation proved that the flow had stopped because there was no more water in the well.

It is needless to detail the examinations, investigations, and the multitude of counsels and opinions with which our minds were filled for the next few days. It was plain to see that although this well was fully able to meet the demands of a hand-pump or of bailing buckets, the water did not flow into it as fast as it could be pumped out by an engine. Therefore, for the purposes of supplying the circulation of my domestic water system, the well was declared a failure.

My non-success was much talked about in the neighborhood, and we received a great deal of sympathy and condolence. Phineas Colwell was not surprised at the outcome of the affair. He had said that the well had been put in the wrong place. Mrs. Betty was not only surprised, but disgusted.

"It is all very well for you," she said, "who could afford to buy water if it was necessary, but it is very different with the widow and the orphan. If I had not supposed you were going to have a real well, I would have had my spring cleaned out and deepened. I could have had it done in the early summer, but it is of no use now. The spring has dried up."

She told a neighbor that she believed the digging of my well had dried up her spring, and that that was the way of this world, where the widow and the orphan were sure to come out at the little end.

Of course I did not submit to defeat—at least, not without a struggle. I had a well, and if anything could be done to make that well supply me with water, I was going to do it. I consulted specialists, and, after careful consideration of the matter, they agreed that it would be unadvisable for me to attempt to deepen my present well, as there was reason to suppose there was very little water in the place where I had dug it, and that the very best thing I could do would be to try a driven well. As I had already excavated about thirty feet, that was so much gain to me, and if I should have a six-inch pipe put into my present well and then driven down and down until it came to a place where there was plenty of water, I would have all I wanted.

How far down the pipe would have to be driven, of course they did not know, but they all agreed that if I drove deep enough I would get all the water I wanted. This was the only kind of a well, they said, which one could sink as deep as he pleased without being interfered with by the water at the bottom. My wife and I then considered the matter, and ultimately decided that it would be a waste of the money which we had already spent upon the engine, the pipes, and the little house, and, as there was nothing else to be done but to drive a well, we would have a well driven.

Of course we were both very sorry that the work must be begun again, but I was especially dissatisfied, for the weather was getting cold, there was already snow upon the ground, and I was told that work could not be carried on in winter weather. I lost no time, however, in making a contract with a well-driver, who assured me that as soon as the working season should open, which probably would be very early in the spring, he would come to my place and begin to drive my well.

The season did open, and so did the pea-blossoms, and the pods actually began to fill before I saw that well-driver again. I had had a good deal of correspondence with him in the meantime, urging him to prompt action, but he always had some good reason for delay. (I found out afterwards that he was busy fulfilling a contract made before mine, in which he promised to drive a well as soon as the season should open.)

At last—it was early in the summer—he came with his derricks, a steam-engine, a trip-hammer, and a lot of men. They took off the roof of my house, removed the engine, and set to work.

For many a long day, and I am sorry to say for many a longer night, that trip-hammer hammered and banged. On the next day after the night-work began, one of my neighbors came to me to know what they did that for. I told him they were anxious to get through.

"Get through what?" said he. "The earth? If they do that, and your six-inch pipe comes out in a Chinaman's back yard, he will sue you for damages."

When the pipe had been driven through the soft stratum under the old well, and began to reach firmer ground, the pounding and shaking of the earth became worse and worse. My wife was obliged to leave home with our child.

"If he is to do without both water and sleep," said she, "he cannot long survive." And I agreed with her.

She departed for a pleasant summer resort where her married sister with her child was staying, and from week to week I received very pleasant letters from her, telling me of the charms of the place, and dwelling particularly upon the abundance of cool spring water with which the house was supplied.

While this terrible pounding was going on I heard various reports of its effect upon my neighbors. One of them, an agriculturist, with whom I had always been on the best of terms, came with a clouded brow.

"When I first felt those shakes," he said, "I thought they were the effects of seismic disturbances, and I did not mind, but when I found it was your well I thought I ought to come over to speak about it. I do not object to the shaking of my barn, because my man tells me the continual jolting is thrashing out the oats and wheat, but I do not like to have all my apples and pears shaken off my trees. And then," said he, "I have a late brood of chickens, and they cannot walk, because every time they try to make a step they are jolted into the air about a foot. And again, we have had to give up having soup. We like soup, but we do not care to have it spout up like a fountain whenever that hammer comes down."

I was grieved to trouble this friend, and I asked him what I should do. "Do you want me to stop the work on the well?" said I.

"Oh, no," said he, heartily. "Go on with the work. You must have water, and we will try to stand the bumping. I dare say it is good for dyspepsia, and the cows are getting used to having the grass jammed up against their noses. Go ahead; we can stand it in the daytime, but if you could stop the night-work we would be very glad. Some people may think it a well-spring of pleasure to be bounced out of bed, but I don't."

Mrs. Perch came to me with a face like a squeezed lemon, and asked me if I could lend her five nails.

"What sort? " said I.

"The kind you nail clapboards on with," said she. "There is one of them been shook entirely off my house by your well. I am in hopes that before the rest are all shook off I shall get in some money that is owing me and can afford to buy nails for myself."

I stopped the night-work, but this was all I could do for these neighbors.

My optimist friend was delighted when he heard of my driven well. He lived so far away that he and his mother were not disturbed by the jarring of the ground. Now he was sure that some of the internal secrets of the earth would be laid bare, and he rode or drove over every day to see what we were getting out of the well. I know that he was afraid we would soon get water, but was too kind-hearted to say so.

One day the pipe refused to go deeper. No matter how hard it was struck, it bounced up again. When some of the substance it had struck was brought up it looked like French chalk, and my optimist eagerly examined it.

"A French-chalk mine," said he, "would not be a bad thing, but I hoped that you had struck a bed of mineral gutta-percha. That would be a grand find."

But the chalk-bed was at last passed, and we began again to bring up nothing but common earth.

"I suppose," said my optimist to me, one morning, "that you must soon come to water, and if you do I hope it will be hot water."

"Hot water!" I exclaimed. "I do not want that."

"Oh, yes, you would, if you had thought about it as much as I have," he replied. "I lay awake for hours last night, thinking what would happen if you struck hot water. In the first place, it would be absolutely pure, because, even if it were possible for germs and bacilli to get down so deep, they would be boiled before you got them, and then you could cool that water for drinking. When fresh it would be already heated for cooking and hot baths. And then—just think of it!—you could introduce the hot-water system of heating into your house, and there would be the hot water always ready. But the great thing would be your garden. Think of the refuse hot water circulating in pipes up and down and under all your beds! That garden would bloom in the winter as others do in the summer; at least, you could begin to have Lima-beans and tomatoes as soon as the frost was out of the air."

I laughed. "It would take a lot of pumping," I said, "to do all that with the hot water."

"Oh, I forgot to say," he cried, with sparkling eyes, "that I do not believe you would ever have any more pumping to do. You have now gone down so far that I am sure whatever you find will force itself up. It will spout high into the air or through all your pipes, and run always."

Phineas Colwell was by when this was said, and he must have gone down to Mrs. Betty Perch's house to talk it over with her, for in the afternoon she came to see me.

"I understand," said she, "that you are trying to get hot

water out of your well, and that there is likely to be a lot more than you need, so that it will run down by the side of the road. I just want to say that if a stream of hot water comes down past my house some of the children will be bound to get into it and be scalded to death, and I came to say that if that well is going to squirt b'iling water I'd like to have notice so that I can move, though where a widow with so many orphans is going to move to nobody knows. Mr. Colwell says that if you had got him to tell you where to put that well there would have been no danger of this sort of thing."

The next day the optimist came to me, his face fairly blazing with a new idea. "I rode over on purpose to urge you," he cried, "if you should strike hot water, not to stop there. Go on, and, by George! you may strike fire."

"Heavens!" I cried.

"Oh, quite the opposite," said he. "But do not let us joke. I think that would be the grandest thing of this age. Think of a fire well, with the flames shooting up perhaps a hundred feet into the air!"

I wish Phineas Colwell had not been there. As it was, he turned pale and sat down on the wall.

"You look astonished!" exclaimed the optimist, "but listen to me. You have not thought of this thing as I have. If you should strike fire your fortune would be made. By a system of reflectors you could light up the whole country. By means of tiles and pipes this region could be made tropical. You could warm all the houses in the neighborhood with hot air. And then the power you could generate—just think of it! Heat is power; the cost of power is the fuel. You could furnish power to all who wanted it. You could fill this region with industries. My dear sir, you must excuse my agitation, but if you should strike fire there is no limit to the possibilities of achievement."

"But I want water," said I. "Fire would not take the place of that."

"Oh, water is a trifle," said he. "You could have pipes laid from town; it is only about two miles. But fire! Nobody has yet gone down deep enough for that. You have your future in your hands."

As I did not care to connect my future with fire, this idea did not strike me very forcibly, but it struck Phineas Colwell. He did not say anything to me, but after I had gone he went to the well-drivers.

"If you feel them pipes getting hot," he said to them, "I warn you to stop. I have been in countries where there are volcanoes, and I know what they are. There's enough of them in this world, and there's no need of making new ones."

In the afternoon a wagoner, who happened to be passing, brought me a note from Mrs. Perch, very badly spelled, asking if I would let one of my men bring her a pail of water, for she could not think of coming herself or letting any of the children come near my place if spouting fires were expected.

The well-driving had gone on and on, with intermissions on account of sickness in the families of the various workmen, until it had reached the limit which I had fixed, and we had not found water in sufficient quantity, hot or cold, nor had we struck fire, or anything else worth having.

The well-drivers and some specialists were of the opinion that if I were to go ten, twenty, or perhaps a hundred feet deeper, I would be very likely to get all the water I wanted. But, of course, they could not tell how deep they must go, for some wells were over a thousand feet deep. I shook my head at this. There seemed to be only one thing certain about this drilling business, and that was the expense. I declined to go any deeper.

"I think," a facetious neighbor said to me, "it would be cheaper for you to buy a lot of Apollinaris water,—at wholesale rates, of course,—and let your men open so many bottles a day and empty them into your tank. You would find that would pay better in the long run."

Phineas Colwell told me that when he had informed Mrs. Perch that I was going to stop operations, she was in a dreadful state of mind. After all she had undergone, she said, it was simply cruel to think of my stopping before I got water, and that after having dried up her spring!

This is what Phineas said she said, but when next I met her she told me that he had declared that if I had put the well where he thought it ought to be, I should have been having all the water I wanted before now.

My optimist was dreadfully cast down when he heard that I would drive no deeper.

"I have been afraid of this," he said. "I have, been afraid of it. And if circumstances had so arranged themselves that I should have command of money, I should have been glad to assume the expense of deeper explorations. I have been thinking a great deal about the matter, and I feel quite sure that even if you did not get water or anything else that might prove of value to you, it would be a great advantage to have a pipe sunk into the earth to the depth of, say, one thousand feet."

"What possible advantage could that be?" I asked.

"I will tell you," he said. "You would then have one of the grandest opportunities ever offered to man of constructing a gravity-engine. This would be an engine which would be of no expense at all to run. It would need no fuel. Gravity would be the power. It would work a pump splendidly. You could start it when you liked and stop it when you liked."

"Pump!" said I. "What is the good of a pump without water?"

"Oh, of course you would have to have water," he answered. "But, no matter how you get it, you will have to pump it up to your tank so as to make it circulate over your house. Now, my gravity-pump would do this beautifully. You see, the pump would be arranged with cog-wheels and all that sort of thing, and the power would be supplied by a weight, which would be a cylinder of lead or iron, fastened to a rope and run down inside your pipe. Just think of it! It would run down a thousand feet, and where is there anything worked by weight that has such a fall as that?"

I laughed. "That is all very well," said I. "But how about the power required to wind that weight up again when it got to the bottom? I should have to have an engine to do that."

"Oh, no," said he. "I have planned the thing better than that. You see, the greater the weight the greater the power and the velocity. Now, if you take a solid cylinder of lead about four inches in diameter, so that it would slip easily down your pipe,—you might grease it, for that matter,— and twenty feet in length, it would be an enormous weight, and in slowly descending for about an hour a day—for that would be long enough for your pumping—and going down a thousand feet, it would run your engine for a year. Now, then, at the end of the year you could not expect to haul that weight up again. You would have a trigger arrangement which would detach it from the rope when it got to the bottom. Then you would wind up your rope,—a man could do that in a short time,—and you would attach another cylinder of lead, and that would run your engine for another year, minus a few days, because it would only go down nine hundred and eighty feet. The next year you would put on another cylinder, and so on. I have not worked out the figures exactly, but I think that in this way your engine would run for thirty years before the pipe became entirely filled with cylinders. That would be probably as long as you would care to have water forced into the house."

"Yes"' said I, "I think that is likely."

He saw that his scheme did not strike me favorably. Suddenly a light flashed across his face.

"I tell you what you can do with your pipe," he said, "just as it is. You can set up a clock over it which would run for forty years without winding."

I smiled, and he turned sadly away to his horse; but he had not ridden ten yards before he came back and called to me over the wall.

"If the earth at the bottom of your pipe should ever yield to pressure and give way, and if water or gas, or—anything, should be squirted out of it, I beg you will let me know as soon as possible."

I promised to do so.

When the pounding was at an end my wife and child came home. But the season continued dry, and even their presence could not counteract the feeling of aridity which seemed to permeate everything which belonged to us, material or immaterial. We had a great deal of commiseration from our neighbors. I think even Mrs. Betty Perch began to pity us a little, for her spring had begun to trickle again in a small way, and she sent word to me that if we were really in need of water she would be willing to divide with us. Phineas Colwell was sorry for us, of course, but he could not help feeling and saying that if I had consulted him the misfortune would have been prevented.

It was late in the summer when my wife returned, and when she made her first visit of inspection to the grounds and gardens, her eyes, of course, fell upon the unfinished well. She was shocked.

"I never saw such a scene of wreckage," she said. "It looks like a Western town after a cyclone. I think the best thing you can do is to have this dreadful litter cleared up, the ground smoothed and raked, the wall mended, and the roof put back on that little house, and then if we can make anybody believe it is an ice-house, so much the better."

This was good advice, and I sent for a man to put the vicinity of the well in order and give it the air of neatness which characterizes the rest of our home.

The man who came was named Mr. Barnet. He was a contemplative fellow with a pipe in his mouth. After having worked at the place for half a day he sent for me and said:

"I'll tell you what I would do if I was in your place. I'd put that pump-house in order, and I'd set up the engine, and put the pump down into that thirty-foot well you first dug, and I'd pump water into my house."

I looked at him in amazement.

"There's lots of water in that well," he continued, "and if

there's that much now in this drought, you will surely have ever so much more when the weather isn't so dry. I have measured the water, and I know."

I could not understand him. It seemed to me that he was talking wildly. He filled his pipe and lighted it and sat upon the wall.

"Now," said he, after he had taken a few puffs, "I'll tell you where the trouble's been with your well. People are always in too big a hurry in this world about all sorts of things as well as wells. I am a well-digger and I know all about them. We know if there is any water in the ground it will always find its way to the deepest hole there is, and we dig a well so as to give it a deep hole to go to in the place where we want it. But you can't expect the water to come to that hole just the very day it's finished. Of course you will get some, because it's right there in the neighborhood, but there is always a lot more that will come if you give it time. It's got to make little channels and passages for itself, and of course it takes time to do that. It's like settling up a new country. Only a few pioneers come at first, and you have to wait for the population to flow in. This being a dry season, and the water in the ground a little sluggish on that account, it was a good while finding out where your well was. If I had happened along when you was talking about a well, I think I should have said to you that I knew a proverb which would about fit your case, and that is: 'Let well enough alone.'"

I felt like taking this good man by the hand, but I did not. I only told him to go ahead and do everything that was proper.

The next morning, as I was going to the well, I saw Phineas Colwell coming down the lane and Mrs. Betty Perch coming up it. I did not wish them to question me, so I stepped behind some bushes. When they met they stopped.

"Upon my word!" exclaimed Mrs. Betty, "if he isn't going to work again on that everlasting well! If he's got so much money he don't know what to do with it, I could tell him that there's people in this world, and not far away either, who would be the better for some of it. It's a sin and a shame and an abomination. Do you believe, Mr. Colwell, that there is the least chance in the world of his ever getting water enough out of that well to shave himself with?"

"Mrs. Perch," said Phineas, "it ain't no use talking about that well. It ain't no use, and it never can be no use, because it's in the wrong place. If he ever pumps water out of that well into his house I'll do—"

"What will you do?" asked Mr. Barnet, who just then appeared from the recesses of the engine-house.

"I'll do anything on this earth that you choose to name," said Phineas. "I am safe, whatever it is."

"Well, then," said Mr. Barnet, knocking the ashes from his pipe preparatory to filling it again, "will you marry Mrs. Perch?"

Phineas laughed. "Yes," he said. "I promised I would do anything, and I'll promise that."

"A slim chance for me," said Mrs. Betty, "even if I'd have you." And she marched on with her nose in the air.

When Mr. Barnet got fairly to work with his derrick, his men, and his buckets, he found that there was a good deal more to do than he had expected. The well-drivers had injured the original well by breaking some of the tiles which lined it, and these had to be taken out and others put in, and in the course of this work other improvements suggested themselves and were made. Several times operations were delayed by sickness in the family of Mr. Barnet, and also in the families of his workmen, but still the work went on in a very fair manner, although much more slowly than had been supposed by any one. But in the course of time—I will not say how much time—the work was finished, the engine was in its place, and it pumped water into my house, and every day since then it has pumped all the water we need, pure, cold, and delicious.

Knowing the promise Phineas Colwell had made, and feeling desirous of having everything which concerned my well settled and finished, I went to look for him to remind him of his duty toward Mrs. Perch, but I could not find that naval and military mechanical agriculturist. He had gone away to take a job or a contract,—I could not discover which,—and he has not since appeared in our neighborhood. Mrs. Perch is very severe on me about this.

"There's plenty of bad things come out of that well," she said, "but I never thought anything bad enough would come out of it to make Mr. Colwell go away and leave me to keep on being a widow with all them orphans."

MR.TOLMAN

Mr. Tolman was a gentleman whose apparent age was of a varying character. At times, when deep in thought on business matters or other affairs, one might have thought him fifty-five or fifty-seven, or even sixty. Ordinarily, however, when things were running along in a satisfactory and commonplace way, he appeared to be about fifty years old, while upon some extraordinary occasions, when the world assumed an unusually attractive aspect, his age seemed to run down to forty-five or less.

He was the head of a business firm. In fact, he was the only member of it. The firm was known as Pusey and Co. But Pusey had long been dead and the "Co.," of which Mr. Tolman had been a member, was dissolved. Our elderly hero, having bought out the business, firm-name and all, for many years had carried it on with success and profit. His counting-house was a small and quiet place, but a great deal of money had been made in it. Mr. Tolman was rich—very rich indeed.

And yet, as he sat in his counting-room one winter evening, he looked his oldest. He had on his hat and his overcoat, his gloves and his fur collar. Every one else in the establishment had gone home, and he, with the keys in his hand, was ready to lock up and leave also. He often stayed later than any one else, and left the keys with Mr. Canterfield, the head clerk, as he passed his house on his way home.

Mr. Tolman seemed in no hurry to go. He simply sat and thought, and increased his apparent age. The truth was, he did not want to go home. He was tired of going home. This was not because his home was not a pleasant one. No single gentleman in the city had a handsomer or more comfortable suite of rooms. It was not because he felt lonely, or regretted that a wife and children did not brighten and enliven his home. He was perfectly satisfied to be a bachelor. The conditions suited him exactly. But, in spite of all this, he was tired of going home.

"I wish," said Mr. Tolman to himself, "that I could feel some interest in going home." Then he rose and took a turn or two up and down the room. But as that did not seem to give him any more interest in the matter, he sat down again. "I wish it were necessary for me to go home," said he, "but it isn't." So then he fell again to thinking. "What I need," he said, after a while, "is to depend more upon myself—to feel that I am necessary to myself. Just now I'm not. I'll stop going home—at least, in this way. Where's the sense in envying other men, when I can have all that they have just as well as not? And I'll have it, too," said Mr. Tolman, as he went out and locked the doors. Once in the streets, and walking rapidly, his ideas shaped themselves easily and readily into a plan which, by the time he reached the house of his head clerk, was quite matured. Mr. Canterfield was just going down to dinner as his employer rang the bell, so he opened the door himself. "I will detain you but a minute or two," said Mr. Tolman, handing the keys to Mr. Canterfield. "Shall we step into the parlor?"

When his employer had gone, and Mr. Canterfield had joined his family at the dinner-table, his wife immediately asked him what Mr. Tolman wanted. "Only to say that he is going away to-morrow, and that I am to attend to the business, and send his personal letters to—," naming a city not a hundred miles away.

"How long is he going to stay?"

"He didn't say," answered Mr. Canterfield.

"I'll tell you what he ought to do," said the lady. "He ought to make you a partner in the firm, and then he could go away and stay as long as he pleased."

"He can do that now," returned her husband. "He has made a good many trips since I have been with him, and things have gone on very much in the same way as when he is here. He knows that."

"But still you'd like to be a partner?"

"Oh, yes," said Mr. Canterfield.

"And common gratitude ought to prompt him to make you one," said his wife.

Mr. Tolman went home and wrote a will. He left all his property, with the exception of a few legacies, to the richest and most powerful charitable organization in the country.

"People will think I am crazy," said he to himself, "and if I should die while I am carrying out my plan, I will leave the task of defending my sanity to people who are able to make a good fight for me." And before he went to bed his will was signed and witnessed.

The next day he packed a trunk and left for the neighboring city. His apartments were to be kept in readiness for his return at any time. If you had seen him walking over to the railroad depot, you would have taken him for a man of forty-five.

When he arrived at his destination, Mr. Tolman established himself temporarily at a hotel, and spent the next three or four days in walking about the city looking for what he wanted. What he wanted was rather difficult to define, but the way in which he put the matter to himself was something like this:

"I would like to find a snug little place where, I can live, and carry on some business which I can attend to myself, and which will bring me into contact with people of all sorts— people who will interest me. It must be a small business, because I don't want to have to work very hard, and it must be snug and comfortable, because I want to enjoy it. I would like a shop of some sort, because that brings a man face to face with his fellow-creatures."

The city in which he was walking about was one of the best places in the country in which to find the place of business he desired. It was full of independent little shops. But Mr. Tolman could not readily find one which resembled his ideal. A small dry-goods establishment seemed to presuppose a female proprietor. A grocery store would give him many interesting customers; but he did not know much about groceries, and the business did not appear to him to possess any aesthetic features.

He was much pleased by a small shop belonging to a taxidermist. It was exceedingly cosey, and the business was probably not so great as to overwork any one. He might send the birds and beasts which were brought to be stuffed to some practical operator, and have him put them in proper condition for the customers. He might—But no. It would be very unsatisfactory to engage in a business of which he knew absolutely nothing. A taxidermist ought not to blush with ignorance when asked some simple question about a little dead bird or a defunct fish. And so he tore himself from the window of this fascinating place, where, he fancied, had his education been differently managed, he could in time have shown the world the spectacle of a cheerful and unblighted Mr. Venus.

The shop which at last appeared to suit him best was one which he had passed and looked at several times before it struck him favorably. It was in a small brick house in a side street, but not far from one of the main business avenues of the city. The shop seemed devoted to articles of stationery and small notions of various kinds not easy to be classified. He had stopped to look at three penknives fastened to a card, which was propped up in the little show-window, supported on one side by a chess-board with "History of Asia" in gilt letters on the back, and on the other by a small violin labelled "1 dollar." And as he gazed past these articles into the interior of the shop, which was now lighted up, it gradually dawned upon him that it was something like his ideal of an attractive and interesting business place. At any rate, he would go in and look at it. He did not care for a violin, even at the low price marked on the one in the window, but a new pocket-knife might be useful. So he walked in and asked to look at pocket-knives.

The shop was in charge of a very pleasant old lady of about sixty, who sat sewing behind the little counter. While she went to the window and very carefully reached over the articles displayed therein to get the card of penknives, Mr. Tolman looked about him. The shop was quite small, but there seemed to be a good deal in it. There were shelves behind the counter, and there were shelves on the opposite wall, and they all seemed well filled with something or other. In the corner near the old lady's chair was a little coal stove with a bright fire in it, and at the back of the shop, at the top of two steps, was a glass door partly open, through which he saw a small room, with a red carpet on the floor, and a little table apparently set for a meal.

Mr. Tolman looked at the knives when the old lady showed them to him, and after a good deal of consideration he selected one which he thought would be a good knife to give to a boy. Then he looked over some things in the way of paper-cutters, whist-markers, and such small matters, which were in a glass case on the counter. And while he looked at them he talked to the old lady.

She was a friendly, sociable body, very glad to have any one to talk to, and so it was not at all difficult for Mr. Tolman, by some general remarks, to draw from her a great many points about herself and her shop. She was a widow, with a son who, from her remarks, must have been forty years old. He was connected with a mercantile establishment, and they had lived here for a long time. While her son was a salesman, and came home every evening, this was very pleasant. But after he became a commercial traveller, and was away from the city for months at a time, she did not like it at all. It was very lonely for her.

Mr. Tolman's heart rose within him, but he did not interrupt her.

"If I could do it," said she, "I would give up this place, and go and live with my sister in the country. It would be better for both of us, and Henry could come there just as well as here when he gets back from his trips."

"Why don't you sell out?" asked Mr. Tolman, a little fearfully, for he began to think that all this was too easy sailing to be entirely safe.

"That would not be easy," said she, with a smile. "It might be a long time before we could find any one who would want to take the place. We have a fair trade in the store, but

Frank R. Stockton

it isn't what it used to be when times were better. And the library is falling off, too. Most of the books are getting pretty old, and it don't pay to spend much money for new ones now."

"The library!" said Mr. Tolman. "Have you a library?"

"Oh, yes," replied the old lady. "I've had a circulating library here for nearly fifteen years. There it is on those two upper shelves behind you."

Mr. Tolman turned, and beheld two long rows of books in brown-paper covers, with a short step-ladder, standing near the door of the inner room, by which these shelves might be reached. This pleased him greatly. He had had no idea that there was a library here.

"I declare!" said he. "It must be very pleasant to manage a circulating library—a small one like this, I mean. I shouldn't mind going into a business of the kind myself."

The old lady looked up, surprised. Did he wish to go into business? She had not supposed that, just from looking at him.

Mr. Tolman explained his views to her. He did not tell what he had been doing in the way of business, or what Mr. Canterfield was doing for him now. He merely stated his present wishes, and acknowledged to her that it was the attractiveness of her establishment that had led him to come in.

"Then you do not want the penknife?" she said quickly.

"Oh, yes, I do," said he. "And I really believe, if we can come to terms, that I would like the two other knives, together with the rest of your stock in trade."

The old lady laughed a little nervously. She hoped very much indeed that they could come to terms. She brought a chair from the back room, and Mr. Tolman sat down with her by the stove to talk it over. Few customers came in to interrupt them, and they talked the matter over very thoroughly. They both came to the conclusion that there would be no difficulty about terms, nor about Mr. Tolman's ability to carry on the business after a very little instruction from the present proprietress. When Mr. Tolman left, it was with the understanding that he was to call again in a couple of days, when the son Henry would be at home, and matters could be definitely arranged.

When the three met, the bargain was soon struck. As each party was so desirous of making it, few difficulties were interposed. The old lady, indeed, was in favor of some delay in the transfer of the establishment, as she would like to clean and dust every shelf and corner and every article in the place. But Mr. Tolman was in a hurry to take possession; and as the son Henry would have to start off on another trip in a short time, he wanted to see his mother moved and settled before he left. There was not much to move but trunks and bandboxes, and some antiquated pieces of furniture of special value to the old lady, for Mr. Tolman insisted on buying everything in the house, just as it stood. The whole thing did not cost him, he said to himself, as much as some of his acquaintances would pay for a horse. The methodical son Henry took an account of stock, and Mr. Tolman took several lessons from the old lady, in which she explained to him how to find out the selling prices of the various articles from the marks on the little tags attached to them. And she particularly instructed him in the management of the circulating library. She informed him of the character of the books, and, as far as possible, of the character of the regular patrons. She told him whom he might trust to take out a book without paying for the one brought in, if they didn't happen to have the change with them, and she indicated with little crosses opposite their names those persons who should be required to pay cash down for what they had had, before receiving further benefits.

It was astonishing to see what interest Mr. Tolman took in all this. He was really anxious to meet some of the people about whom the old lady discoursed. He tried, too, to remember a few of the many things she told him of her methods of buying and selling, and the general management of her shop; and he probably did not forget more than three fourths of what she told him.

Finally everything was settled to the satisfaction of the two male parties to the bargain,—although the old lady thought of a hundred things she would yet like to do,—and one fine frosty afternoon a cart-load of furniture and baggage left the door, the old lady and her son took leave of the old place, and Mr. Tolman was left sitting behind the little counter, the sole manager and proprietor of a circulating library and a stationery and notion shop. He laughed when he thought of it, but he rubbed his hands and felt very well satisfied.

"There is nothing really crazy about it," he said to himself. "If there is a thing that I think I would like, and I can afford to have it, and there's no harm in it, why not have it?"

There was nobody there to say anything against this, so Mr. Tolman rubbed his hands again before the fire, and rose to walk up and down his shop, and wonder who would be his first customer.

In the course of twenty minutes a little boy opened the door and came in. Mr. Tolman hastened behind the counter to receive his commands. The little boy wanted two sheets of note-paper and an envelope.

"Any particular kind!" asked Mr. Tolman.

The boy didn't know of any particular variety being desired. He thought the same kind she always got would do. And he looked very hard at Mr. Tolman, evidently wondering at the change in the shopkeeper, but asking no questions.

"You are a regular customer, I suppose," said Mr. Tolman, opening several boxes of paper which he had taken down from the shelves. "I have just begun business here, and don't know what kind of paper you have been in the habit of buying. But I suppose this will do." And he took out a couple of sheets of the best, with an envelope to match. These he carefully tied up in a piece of thin brown paper, and gave to the boy, who handed him three cents. Mr. Tolman took them, smiled, and then, having made a rapid calculation, he called to the boy, who was just opening the door, and gave him back one cent.

"You have paid me too much," he said.

The boy took the cent, looked at Mr. Tolman, and then got out of the store as quickly as he could.

"Such profits as that are enormous," said Mr. Tolman, "but I suppose the small sales balance them." This Mr. Tolman subsequently found to be the case.

One or two other customers came in in the course of the afternoon, and about dark the people who took out books began to arrive. These kept Mr. Tolman very busy. He not only had to do a good deal of entering and cancelling, but he had to answer a great many questions about the change in proprietorship, and the probability of his getting in some new books, with suggestions as to the quantity and character of these, mingled with a few dissatisfied remarks in regard to the volumes already on hand.

Frank R. Stockton

Every one seemed sorry that the old lady had gone away. But Mr. Tolman was so pleasant and anxious to please, and took such an interest in their selection of books, that only one of the subscribers appeared to take the change very much to heart. This was a young man who was forty-three cents in arrears. He was a long time selecting a book, and when at last he brought it to Mr. Tolman to be entered, he told him in a low voice that he hoped there would be no objection to letting his account run on for a little while longer. On the first of the month he would settle it, and then he hoped to be able to pay cash whenever he brought in a book.

Mr. Tolman looked for his name on the old lady's list, and, finding no cross against it, told him that it was all right, and that the first of the month would do very well. The young man went away perfectly satisfied with the new librarian. Thus did Mr. Tolman begin to build up his popularity. As the evening grew on he found himself becoming very hungry. But he did not like to shut up the shop, for every now and then some one dropped in, sometimes to ask what time it was, and sometimes to make a little purchase, while there were still some library patrons coming in at intervals.

However, taking courage during a short rest from customers, he put up the shutters, locked the door, and hurried off to a hotel, where he partook of a meal such as few keepers of little shops ever think of indulging in.

The next morning Mr. Tolman got his own breakfast. This was delightful. He had seen how cosily the old lady had spread her table in the little back room, where there was a stove suitable for any cooking he might wish to indulge in, and he longed for such a cosey meal. There were plenty of stock provisions in the house, which he had purchased with the rest of the goods, and he went out and bought himself a fresh loaf of bread. Then he broiled a piece of ham, made some good strong tea, boiled some eggs, and had a breakfast on the little round table which, though plain enough, he enjoyed more than any breakfast at his club which he could remember. He had opened the shop, and sat facing the glass door, hoping, almost, that there would be some interruption to his meal. It would seem so much more proper in that sort of business if he had to get up and go attend to a customer.

Before the evening of that day Mr. Tolman became convinced that he would soon be obliged to employ a boy or some one to attend to the establishment during his absence. After breakfast, a woman recommended by the old lady came to make his bed and clean up generally, but when she had gone he was left alone with his shop. He determined not to allow this responsibility to injure his health, and so at one o'clock boldly locked the shop door and went out to his lunch. He hoped that no one would call during his absence, but when he returned he found a little girl with a pitcher standing at the door. She came to borrow half a pint of milk.

"Milk!" exclaimed Mr. Tolman, in surprise. "Why, my child, I have no milk. I don't even use it in my tea."

The little girl looked very much disappointed. "Is Mrs. Walker gone away for good?" said she.

"Yes," replied Mr. Tolman. "But I would be just as willing to lend you the milk as she would be, if I had any. Is there any place near here where you can buy milk?"

"Oh, yes," said the girl. "You can get it round in the market-house."

"How much would half a pint cost?" he asked.

"Three cents," replied the girl.

"Well, then," said Mr. Tolman, "here are three cents. You can go and buy the milk for me, and then you can borrow it. Will that suit?"

The girl thought it would suit very well, and away she went.

Even this little incident pleased Mr. Tolman. It was so very novel. When he came back from his dinner in the evening, he found two circulating library subscribers stamping their feet on the door-step, and he afterwards heard that several others had called and gone away. It would certainly injure the library if he suspended business at meal-times. He could easily have his choice of a hundred boys if he chose to advertise for one, but he shrank from having a youngster in the place. It would interfere greatly with his cosiness and his experiences. He might possibly find a boy who went to school, and who would be willing to come at noon and in the evening if he were paid enough. But it would have to be a very steady and responsible boy. He would think it over before taking any steps.

He thought it over for a day or two, but he did not spend his whole time in doing so. When he had no customers, he sauntered about in the little parlor over the shop, with its odd old furniture, its quaint prints on the walls, and its absurd ornaments on the mantelpiece. The other little rooms seemed almost as funny to him, and he was sorry when the bell on the shop door called him down from their contemplation. It was pleasant to him to think that he owned all these odd things. The ownership of the varied goods in the shop also gave him an agreeable feeling which none of his other possessions had ever afforded him. It was all so odd and novel.

He liked much to look over the books in the library. Many of them were old novels, the names of which were familiar enough to him, but which he had never read. He determined to read some of them as soon as he felt fixed and settled.

In looking over the book in which the names and accounts of the subscribers were entered, he amused himself by wondering what sort of persons they were who had out certain books. Who, for instance, wanted to read "The Book of Cats," and who could possibly care for "The Mysteries of Udolpho"? But the unknown person in regard to whom Mr. Tolman felt the greatest curiosity was the subscriber who now had in his possession a volume entitled "Dormstock's Logarithms of the Diapason."

"How on earth," exclaimed Mr. Tolman, "did such a book get into this library? And where on earth did the person spring from who would want to take it out? And not only want to take it," he continued, as he examined the entry regarding the volume, "but come and have it renewed one, two, three, four—nine times! He has had that book for eighteen weeks!"

Without exactly making up his mind to do so, Mr. Tolman deferred taking steps toward getting an assistant until P. Glascow, the person in question, should make an appearance, and it was nearly time for the book to be brought in again.

"If I get a boy now," thought Mr. Tolman, "Glascow will be sure to come and bring the book while I am out."

In almost exactly two weeks from the date of the last renewal of the book, P. Glascow came in. It was the middle of the afternoon, and Mr. Tolman was alone. This investigator of musical philosophy was a quiet young man of about thirty, wearing a light-brown cloak, and carrying under one arm a large book.

P. Glascow was surprised when he heard of the change in the proprietorship of the library. Still, he hoped that there would be no objection to his renewing the book which he had with him, and which he had taken out some time ago.

"Oh, no," said Mr. Tolman, "none in the world. In fact, I don't suppose there are any other subscribers who would want it. I have had the curiosity to look to see if it had ever been taken out before, and I find it has not."

The young man smiled quietly. "No," said he, "I suppose not. It is not every one who would care to study the higher mathematics of music, especially when treated as Dormstock treats the subject."

"He seems to go into it pretty deeply," remarked Mr. Tolman, who had taken up the book. "At least, I should think so, judging from all these calculations, and problems, and squares, and cubes."

"Indeed he does," said Glascow. "And although I have had the book some months, and have more reading time at my disposal than most persons, I have only reached the fifty-sixth page, and doubt if I shall not have to review some of that before I can feel that I thoroughly understand it."

"And there are three hundred and forty pages in all!" said Mr. Tolman, compassionately.

"Yes," replied the other. "But I am quite sure that the matter will grow easier as I proceed. I have found that out from what I have already done."

"You say you have a good deal of leisure?" remarked Mr. Tolman. "Is the musical business dull at present?"

"Oh, I'm not in the musical business," said Glascow. "I have a great love for music, and wish to thoroughly understand it. But my business is quite different. I am a night druggist, and that is the reason I have so much leisure for reading."

"A night druggist?" repeated Mr. Tolman, inquiringly.

"Yes, sir," said the other. "I am in a large downtown drug store which is kept open all night, and I go on duty after the day clerks leave."

"And does that give you more leisure?" asked Mr. Tolman.

"It seems to," answered Glascow. "I sleep until about noon, and then I have the rest of the day, until seven o'clock, to myself. I think that people who work at night can make a more satisfactory use of their own time than those who work in the daytime. In the summer I can take a trip on the river, or go somewhere out of town, every day, if I like."

"Daylight is more available for many things, that is true," said Mr. Tolman. "But is it not dreadfully lonely sitting in a drug store all night? There can't be many people to come to buy medicine at night. I thought there was generally a night-bell to drug stores, by which a clerk could be awakened if anybody wanted anything."

"It's not very lonely in our store at night," said Glascow. "In fact, it's often more lively then than in the daytime. You see, we are right down among the newspaper offices, and there's always somebody coming in for soda-water, or cigars, or something or other. The store is a bright, warm place for the night editors and reporters to meet together and talk and drink hot soda, and there's always a knot of 'em around the stove about the time the papers begin to go to press. And they're a lively set, I can tell you, sir. I've heard some of the best stories I ever heard in my life told in our place after three o'clock in the morning."

Frank R. Stockton

"A strange life!" said Mr. Tolman. "Do you know, I never thought that people amused themselves in that way—and night after night, I suppose."

"Yes, sir, night after night, Sundays and all."

The night druggist now took up his book.

"Going home to read?" asked Mr. Tolman.

"Well, no," said the other. "It's rather cold this afternoon to read. I think I'll take a brisk walk."

"Can't you leave your book until you return!" asked Mr. Tolman. "That is, if you will come back this way. It's an awkward book to carry about."

"Thank you, I will," said Glascow. "I shall come back this way."

When he had gone, Mr. Tolman took up the book, and began to look over it more carefully than he had done before. But his examination did not last long.

"How anybody of common sense can take any interest in this stuff is beyond my comprehension," said Mr. Tolman, as he closed the book and put it on a little shelf behind the counter.

When Glascow came back, Mr. Tolman asked him to stay and warm himself. And then, after they had talked for a short time, Mr. Tolman began to feel hungry. He had his winter appetite, and had lunched early. So said he to the night druggist, who had opened his "Dormstock," "How would you like to sit here and read awhile, while I go and get my dinner? I will light the gas, and you can be very comfortable here, if you are not in a hurry."

P. Glascow was in no hurry at all, and was very glad to have some quiet reading by a warm fire; and so Mr. Tolman left him, feeling perfectly confident that a man who had been allowed by the old lady to renew a book nine times must be perfectly trustworthy.

When Mr. Tolman returned, the two had some further conversation in the corner by the little stove.

"It must be rather annoying," said the night druggist, "not to be able to go out to your meals without shutting up your shop. If you like," said he, rather hesitatingly, "I will stop in about this time in the afternoon, and stay here while you go to dinner. I'll be glad to do this until you get an assistant. I can easily attend to most people who come in, and others can wait."

Mr. Tolman jumped at this proposition. It was exactly what he wanted.

So P. Glascow came every afternoon and read "Dormstock" while Mr. Tolman went to dinner; and before long he came at lunch-time also. It was just as convenient as not, he said. He had finished his breakfast, and would like to read awhile. Mr. Tolman fancied that the night druggist's lodgings were, perhaps, not very well warmed, which idea explained the desire to walk rather than read on a cold afternoon. Glascow's name was entered on the free list, and he always took away the "Dormstock" at night, because he might have a chance of looking into it at the store, when custom began to grow slack in the latter part of the early morning.

One afternoon there came into the shop a young lady, who brought back two books which she had had for more than a month. She made no excuses for keeping the books longer than the prescribed time, but simply handed them in and paid her fine. Mr. Tolman did not like to take this money, for it was the first of the kind he had received; but the young lady looked as if she were well able to afford the luxury of keeping books over their time, and business was business. So he gravely gave her her change. Then she said she would like to take out "Dormstock's Logarithms of the Diapason."

Mr. Tolman stared at her. She was a bright, handsome young lady, and looked as if she had very good sense. He could not understand it. But he told her the book was out.

"Out!" she said. "Why, it's always out. It seems strange to me that there should be such a demand for that book. I have been trying to get it for ever so long."

"It IS strange," said Mr. Tolman, "but it is certainly in demand. Did Mrs. Walker ever make you any promises about it?"

"No," said she, "but I thought my turn would come around some time. And I particularly want the book just now."

Mr. Tolman felt somewhat troubled. He knew that the night druggist ought not to monopolize the volume, and yet he did not wish to disoblige one who was so useful to him, and who took such an earnest interest in the book. And he could not temporize with the young lady, and say that he thought the book would soon be in. He knew it would not. There were three hundred and forty pages of it. So he merely remarked that he was sorry.

"So am I, " said the young lady, "very sorry. It so happens that just now I have a peculiar opportunity for studying that book which may not occur again."

There was something in Mr. Tolman's sympathetic face which seemed to invite her confidence, and she continued.

"I am a teacher," she said, "and on account of certain circumstances I have a holiday for a month, which I intended to give up almost entirely to the study of music, and I particularly wanted "Dormstock." Do you think there is any chance of its early return, and will you reserve it for me?"

"Reserve it!" said Mr. Tolman. "Most certainly I will." And then he reflected a second or two. "If you will come here the day after to-morrow, I will be able to tell you something definite."

She said she would come.

Mr. Tolman was out a long time at lunch-time the next day. He went to all the leading book-stores to see if he could buy a copy of Dormstock's great work. But he was unsuccessful. The booksellers told him that there was no probability that he could get a copy in the country, unless, indeed, he found it in the stock of some second-hand dealer, and that even if he sent to England for it, where it was published, it was not likely he could get it, for it had been long out of print. There was no demand at all for it. The next day he went to several second-hand stores, but no "Dormstock" could he find.

When he came back he spoke to Glasgow on the subject. He was sorry to do so, but thought that simple justice compelled him to mention the matter. The night druggist was thrown into a perturbed state of mind by the information that some one wanted his beloved book.

"A woman!" he exclaimed. "Why, she would not understand two pages out of the whole of it. It is too bad. I didn't suppose any one would want this book."

"Do not disturb yourself too much," said Mr. Tolman. "I

Frank R. Stockton

am not sure that you ought to give it up."

"I am very glad to hear you say so," said Glascow. "I have no doubt it is only a passing fancy with her. I dare say she would really rather have a good new novel." And then, having heard that the lady was expected that afternoon, he went out to walk, with the "Dormstock" under his arm.

When the young lady arrived, an hour or so later, she was not at all satisfied to take out a new novel, and was very sorry indeed not to find the "Logarithms of the Diapason" waiting for her. Mr. Tolman told her that he had tried to buy another copy of the work, and for this she expressed herself gratefully. He also found himself compelled to say that the book was in the possession of a gentleman who had had it for some time—all the time it had been out, in fact—and had not yet finished it.

At this the young lady seemed somewhat nettled.

"Is it not against the rules for any person to keep one book out so long?" she asked.

"No," said Mr. Tolman. "I have looked into that. Our rules are very simple, and merely say that a book may be renewed by the payment of a certain sum."

"Then I am never to have it?" remarked the young lady.

"Oh, I wouldn't despair about it," said Mr. Tolman. "He has not had time to reflect upon the matter. He is a reasonable young man, and I believe that he will be willing to give up his study of the book for a time and let you take it."

"No," said she, "I don't wish that. If he is studying, as you say he is, day and night, I do not wish to interrupt him. I should want the book at least a month, and that, I suppose, would upset his course of study entirely. But I do not think any one should begin in a circulating library to study a book that will take him a year to finish; for, from what you say, it will take this gentleman at least that time to finish Dormstock's book." So she went her way.

When P. Glascow heard all this in the evening, he was very grave. He had evidently been reflecting.

"It is not fair," said he. "I ought not to keep the book so long. I now give it up for a while. You may let her have it when she comes." And he put the "Dormstock" on the counter, and went and sat down by the stove.

Mr. Tolman was grieved. He knew the night druggist had done right, but still he was sorry for him. "What will you do?" he asked. "Will you stop your studies?"

"Oh, no," said Glascow, gazing solemnly into the stove. "I will take up some other books on the diapason which I have, and so will keep my ideas fresh on the subject until this lady is done with the book. I do not really believe she will study it very long." Then he added: "If it is all the same to you, I will come around here and read, as I have been doing, until you shall get a regular assistant."

Mr. Tolman would be delighted to have him come, he said. He had entirely given up the idea of getting an assistant, but this he did not say.

It was some time before the lady came back, and Mr. Tolman was afraid she was not coming at all. But she did come, and asked for Mrs. Burney's "Evelina." She smiled when she named the book, and said that she believed she would have to take a novel, after all, and she had always wanted to read that one.

"I wouldn't take a novel if I were you," said Mr. Tolman; and he triumphantly took down the "Dormstock" and laid it before her.

She was evidently much pleased, but when he told her of Mr. Glascow's gentlemanly conduct in the matter, her countenance instantly changed.

"Not at all," said she, laying down the book. "I will not break up his study. I will take the 'Evelina' if you please."

And as no persuasion from Mr. Tolman had any effect upon her, she went away with Mrs. Burney's novel in her muff.

"Now, then," said Mr. Tolman to Glascow, in the evening, "you may as well take the book along with you. She won't have it."

But Glascow would do nothing of the kind. "No," he remarked, as he sat looking into the stove. "When I said I would let her have it, I meant it. She'll take it when she sees that it continues to remain in the library."

Glascow was mistaken: she did not take it, having the idea that he would soon conclude that it would be wiser for him to read it than to let it stand idly on the shelf.

"It would serve them both right," said Mr. Tolman to himself, "if somebody else should come and take it." But there was no one else among his subscribers who would even think of such a thing.

One day, however, the young lady came in and asked to look at the book. "Don't think that I am going to take it out," she said, noticing Mr. Tolman's look of pleasure as he handed her the volume. "I only wish to see what he says on a certain subject which I am studying now." And so she sat down by the stove on the chair which Mr. Tolman placed for her, and opened "Dormstock."

She sat earnestly poring over the book for half an hour or more, and then she looked up and said: "I really cannot make out what this part means. Excuse my troubling you, but I would be very glad if you would explain the latter part of this passage."

"Me!" exclaimed Mr. Tolman. "Why, my good madam,—miss, I mean,—I couldn't explain it to you if it were to save my life. But what page is it?" said he, looking at his watch.

"Page twenty-four," answered the young lady.

"Oh, well, then," said he, "if you can wait ten or fifteen minutes, the gentleman who has had the book will be here, and I think he can explain anything in the first part of the work."

The young lady seemed to hesitate whether to wait or not; but as she had a certain curiosity to see what sort of a person he was who had been so absorbed in the book, she concluded to sit a little longer and look into some other parts of the volume.

The night druggist soon came in, and when Mr. Tolman introduced him to the lady, he readily agreed to explain the passage to her if he could. So Mr. Tolman got him a chair from the inner room, and he also sat down by the stove.

The explanation was difficult, but it was achieved at last, and then the young lady broached the subject of leaving the book unused. This was discussed for some time, but came to nothing, although Mr. Tolman put down his afternoon paper and joined in the argument, urging, among other points, that as the matter now stood he was deprived by the dead-lock of all income from the book. But even this strong argument proved of no avail.

"Then I will tell you what I wish you would do," said Mr. Tolman, as the young lady rose to go: "come here and look at the book whenever you wish to do so. I would like to make this more of a reading-room, anyway. It would give me more company."

After this the young lady looked into "Dormstock" when she came in; and as her holidays had been extended by the continued absence of the family in which she taught, she had plenty of time for study, and came quite frequently. She often met Glascow in the shop, and on such occasions they generally consulted "Dormstock," and sometimes had quite lengthy talks on musical matters. One afternoon they came in together, having met on their way to the library, and entered into a conversation on diapasonic logarithms, which continued during the lady's stay in the shop.

"The proper thing," thought Mr. Tolman, "would be for these two people to get married. Then they could take the book and study it to their heart's content. And they would certainly suit each other, for they are both greatly attached to musical mathematics and philosophy, and neither of them either plays or sings, as they have told me. It would be an admirable match."

Mr. Tolman thought over this matter a good deal, and at last determined to mention it to Glascow. When he did so, the young man colored, and expressed the opinion that it would be of no use to think of such a thing. But it was evident from his manner and subsequent discourse that he had thought of it.

Mr. Tolman gradually became quite anxious on the subject, especially as the night druggist did not seem inclined to take any steps in the matter. The weather was now beginning to be warmer, and Mr. Tolman reflected that the little house and the little shop were probably much more cosey and comfortable in winter than in summer. There were higher buildings all about the house, and even now he began to feel that the circulation of air would be quite as agreeable as the circulation of books. He thought a good deal about his airy rooms in the neighboring city.

"Mr. Glascow," said he, one afternoon, "I have made up my mind to sell out this business shortly."

"What!" exclaimed the other. "Do you mean you will give it up and go away—leave the place altogether?"

"Yes," replied Mr. Tolman, "I shall give up the place entirely, and leave the city."

The night druggist was shocked. He had spent many happy hours in that shop, and his hours there were now becoming pleasanter than ever. If Mr. Tolman went away, all this must end. Nothing of the kind could be expected of any new proprietor.

"And considering this," continued Mr. Tolman, "I think it would be well for you to bring your love matters to a conclusion while I am here to help you."

"My love matters!" exclaimed Mr. Glascow, with a flush.

"Yes, certainly," said Mr. Tolman. "I have eyes, and I know all about it. Now let me tell you what I think. When a thing is to be done, it ought to be done the first time there is a good chance. That's the way I do business. Now you might as well come around here to-morrow afternoon prepared to propose to Miss Edwards. She is due to-morrow, for she has been two days away. If she doesn't come, we will postpone the matter until the next day. But you should be ready to-morrow. I don't believe you can see her much when you don't meet her here, for that family is expected back very soon, and from what I infer from her account of her employers, you won't care to visit her at their house."

The night druggist wanted to think about it.

"There is nothing to think," said Mr. Tolman. "We know all about the lady." (He spoke truly, for he had informed himself about both parties to the affair.) "Take my advice, and be here to-morrow afternoon—and come rather early."

The next morning Mr. Tolman went up to his parlor on the second floor, and brought down two blue stuffed chairs, the best he had, and put them in the little room back of the shop. He also brought down one or two knickknacks and put them on the mantelpiece, and he dusted and brightened up the room as well as he could. He even covered the table with a red cloth from the parlor.

When the young lady arrived, he invited her to walk into the back room to look over some new books he had just got in. If she had known he proposed to give up the business, she would have thought it rather strange that he should be buying new books. But she knew nothing of his intentions. When she was seated at the table whereon the new books were spread, Mr. Tolman stepped outside of the shop door to watch for Glascow's approach. He soon appeared.

"Walk right in," said Mr. Tolman. "She's in the back room looking over books. I'll wait here, and keep out customers as far as possible. It's pleasant, and I want a little fresh air. I'll give you twenty minutes."

Glascow was pale, but he went in without a word, and Mr. Tolman, with his hands under his coat-tail, and his feet rather far apart, established a blockade on the doorstep. He stood there for some time, looking at the people outside, and wondering what the people inside were doing. The little girl who had borrowed the milk of him, and who had never returned it, was about to pass the door; but seeing him standing there, she crossed over to the other side of the street. But he did not notice her. He was wondering if it was time to go in. A boy came up to the door, and wanted to know if he kept Easter eggs. Mr. Tolman was happy to say he did not. When he had allowed the night druggist a very liberal twenty minutes, he went in. As he entered the shop door, giving the bell a very decided ring as he did so, P. Glascow came down the two steps that led from the inner room. His face showed that it was all right with him.

A few days after this Mr. Tolman sold out his stock, good will, and fixtures, together with the furniture and lease of the house. And who should he sell out to but to Mr. Glascow! This piece of business was one of the happiest points in the whole affair. There was no reason why the happy couple should not be married very soon, and the young lady was charmed to give up her position as teacher and governess in a family, and come and take charge of that delightful little store and that cunning little house, with almost everything in it that they wanted.

One thing in the establishment Mr. Tolman refused to sell. That was Dormstock's great work. He made the couple a present of the volume, and between two of the earlier pages he placed a bank-note which in value was very much more than that of the ordinary wedding gift.

"What are YOU going to do?" they asked of him, when all these things were settled. And then he told them how he was going back to his business in the neighboring city, and he told them what it was, and how he had come to manage a circulating library. They did not think him crazy. People

Frank R. Stockton

who studied the logarithms of the diapason would not be apt to think a man crazy for such a little thing as that.

When Mr. Tolman returned to the establishment of Pusey & Co., he found everything going on very satisfactorily.

"You look ten years younger, sir," said Mr. Canterfield. "You must have had a very pleasant time. I did not think there was enough to interest you in—for so long a time."

"Interest me!" exclaimed Mr. Tolman. "Why, objects of interest crowded on me. I never had a more enjoyable holiday in my life."

When he went home that evening (and he found himself quite willing to go), he tore up the will he had made. He now felt that there was no necessity for proving his sanity.

MY UNWILLING NEIGHBOR

I was about twenty-five years old when I began life as the owner of a vineyard in western Virginia. I bought a large tract of land, the greater part of which lay upon the sloping side of one of the foot-hills of the Blue Ridge, the exposure being that most favorable to the growth of the vine. I am an enthusiastic lover of the country and of country life, and believed that I should derive more pleasure as well as profit from the culture of my far-stretching vineyard than I would from ordinary farm operations.

I built myself a good house of moderate size upon a little plateau on the higher part of my estate. Sitting in my porch, smoking my pipe after the labors of the day, I could look down over my vineyard into a beautiful valley, with here and there a little curling smoke arising from some of the few dwellings which were scattered about among the groves and spreading fields, and above this beauty I could imagine all my hillside clothed in green and purple.

My family consisted of myself alone. It is true that I expected some day that there would be others in my house besides myself, but I was not ready for this yet.

During the summer I found it very pleasant to live by myself. It was a novelty, and I could arrange and manage everything in my own fashion, which was a pleasure I had

Frank R. Stockton

not enjoyed when I lived in my father's house. But when winter came I found it very lonely. Even my servants lived in a cabin at some little distance, and there were many dark and stormy evenings when the company even of a bore would have been welcome to me. Sometimes I walked over to the town and visited my friends there, but this was not feasible on stormy nights, and the winter seemed to me a very long one.

But spring came, outdoor operations began, and for a few weeks I felt again that I was all-sufficient for my own pleasure and comfort. Then came a change. One of those seasons of bad and stormy weather which so frequently follow an early spring settled down upon my spirits and my hillside. It rained, it was cold, fierce winds blew, and I became more anxious for somebody to talk to than I had been at any time during the winter.

One night, when a very bad storm was raging, I went to bed early, and as I lay awake I revolved in my mind a scheme of which I had frequently thought before. I would build a neat little house on my grounds, not very far away from my house, but not too near, and I would ask Jack Brandiger to come there and live. Jack was a friend of mine who was reading law in the town, and it seemed to me that it would be much more pleasant, and even more profitable, to read law on a pretty hillside overlooking a charming valley, with woods and mountains behind and above him, where he could ramble to his heart's content.

I had thought of asking Jack to come and live with me, but this idea I soon dismissed. I am a very particular person, and Jack was not. He left his pipes about in all sorts of places— sometimes when they were still lighted. When he came to see me he was quite as likely to put his hat over the inkstand as to put it anywhere else. But if Jack lived at a little distance, and we could go backward and forward to see each other whenever we pleased, that would be quite another thing. He could do as he pleased in his own house, and I could do as I pleased in mine, and we might have many pleasant evenings together. This was a cheering idea, and I was planning how we might arrange with the negro woman who managed my household affairs to attend also to those of Jack when I fell asleep.

I did not sleep long before I was awakened by the increased violence of the storm. My house shook with the fury of the wind.

The rain seemed to be pouring on its roof and northern side as if there were a waterfall above us, and every now and then I could hear a shower of hailstones rattling against the shutters. My bedroom was one of the rooms on the lower floor, and even there I could hear the pounding of the deluge and the hailstones upon the roof.

All this was very doleful, and had a tendency to depress the spirits of a man awake and alone in a good-sized house. But I shook off this depression. It was, not agreeable to be up here by myself in such a terrible storm, but there was nothing to be afraid of, as my house was new and very strongly built, being constructed of logs, weather-boarded outside and ceiled within. It would require a hurricane to blow off the roof, and I believed my shutters to be hail-proof. So, as there was no reason to stay awake, I turned over and went to sleep.

I do not know how long it was before I was awakened again, this time not by the noise of the storm, but by a curious movement of my bedstead. I had once felt the slight shock of an earthquake, and it seemed to me that this must be something of the kind. Certainly my bed moved under me. I sat up. The room was pitchy dark. In a moment I felt another movement, but this time it did not seem to me to resemble an earthquake shock. Such motion, I think, is generally in horizontal directions, while that which I felt was more like the movement of a ship upon the water. The storm was at its height; the wind raged and roared, and the rain seemed to be pouring down as heavily as ever.

I was about to get up and light the lamp, for even the faintest candle-flame would be some sort of company at such a grewsome moment, when my bedstead gave another movement, more shiplike than before. It actually lurched forward as if it were descending into the trough of the sea, but, unlike a ship, it did not rise again, but remained in such a slanting position that I began to slide down toward the foot. I believe that if it had not been a bedstead provided with a footboard, I should have slipped out upon the floor.

I did not jump out of bed. I did not do anything. I was trying to think, to understand the situation, to find out whether I was asleep or awake, when I became aware of noises in the room and all over the house which even through the din of the storm made themselves noticed by their peculiarity. Tables, everything in the room, seemed to be grating and grinding on the floor, and in a moment there was a crash. I knew what that meant; my lamp had slipped off the table. Any doubt on that point would have been dispelled by the smell of kerosene which soon filled the air of the room.

The motion of the bed, which I now believe must have been the motion of the whole house, still continued; but the grating noises in the room gradually ceased, from which I inferred that the furniture had brought up against the front wall of the room.

It now was impossible for me to get up and strike a light, for to do so with kerosene oil all over the floor and its vapor diffused through the room would probably result in setting the house on fire. So I must stay in darkness and wait. I do not think I was very much frightened—I was so astonished that there was no room in my mind for fear. In fact, all my mental energies were occupied in trying to find out what had happened. It required, however, only a few more minutes of reflection, and a few more minutes of the grating, bumping, trembling of my house, to enable me to make up my mind what was happening. My house was sliding downhill!

The wind must have blown the building from its foundations, and upon the slippery surface of the hillside, probably lashed into liquid mud by the pouring rain, it was making its way down toward the valley! In a flash my mind's eye ran over the whole surface of the country beneath me as far as I knew it. I was almost positive that there was no precipice, no terrible chasm into which my house might fall. There was nothing but sloping hillside, and beneath that a wide stretch of fields.

Now there was a new and sudden noise of heavy objects falling upon the roof, and I knew what that meant: my chimney had been wrenched from its foundations, and the upper part of it had now toppled over. I could hear, through the storm, the bricks banging and sliding upon the slanting roof. Continuous sounds of cracking and snapping came to me through the closed front windows, and these were caused, I supposed, by the destruction of the stakes of my vines as the heavy house moved over them.

Of course, when I thoroughly understood the state of the case, my first impulse was to spring out of bed, and, as quickly as possible, to get out of that thumping and sliding house. But I restrained myself. The floor might be covered with broken glass, I might not be able to find my clothes in the darkness and in the jumble of furniture at the end of the room, and even if I could dress myself, it would be folly to jump out in the midst of that raging storm into a probable mass of wreckage which I could not see. It would be far better to remain dry and warm under my roof. There was no reason whatever to suppose that the house would go to pieces, or that it would turn over. It must stop some time or other, and, until it did so, I would be safer in my bed than anywhere else. Therefore in my bed I stayed.

Sitting upright, with my feet pressed against the footboard, I listened and felt. The noises of the storm, and the cracking and the snapping and grinding before me and under me, still continued, although I sometimes thought that the wind was moderating a little, and that the strange motion was becoming more regular. I believed the house was moving faster than when it first began its strange career, but that it was sliding over a smooth surface. Now I noticed a succession of loud cracks and snaps at the front of the house, and, from the character of the sounds, I concluded that my little front porch, which had been acting as a cutwater at the bow of my shiplike house, had yielded at last to the rough contact with the ground, and would probably soon be torn away. This did not disturb me, for the house must still be firm.

It was not long before I perceived that the slanting of my bed was becoming less and less, and also I was quite sure that the house was moving more slowly. Then the crackings and snappings before my front wall ceased altogether. The bed resumed its ordinary horizontal position, and although I did not know at what moment the house had ceased sliding and had come to a standstill, I was sure that it had done so. It was now resting upon a level surface. The room was still perfectly dark, and the storm continued. It was useless for me to get up until daylight came,—I could not see what had happened,—so I lay back upon my pillow and tried to imagine upon what level portion of my farm I had stranded. While doing this I fell asleep.

When I woke, a little light was stealing into the room through the blinds of my shutters. I quickly slipped out of bed, opened a window, and looked out. Day was just breaking, the rain and wind had ceased, and I could discern objects. But it seemed as if I needed some light in my brain to enable me to comprehend what I saw. My eyes fell upon nothing familiar.

I did not stop to investigate, however, from my window. I found my clothes huddled together with the furniture at the front end of the room, and as soon as I was dressed I went into the hall and then to my front door. I quickly jerked this open and was about to step outside when, suddenly, I stopped. I was positive that my front porch had been destroyed. But there I saw a porch a little lower than mine and a great deal wider, and on the other side of it, not more than eight feet from me, was a window—the window of a house, and on the other side of the window was a face—the face of a young girl! As I stood staring in blank amazement at the house which presented itself at my front door, the face at the window disappeared, and I was left to contemplate the scene by myself. I ran to my back door and threw it open. There I saw, stretching up the fields and far up the hillside, the wide path which my house had made as it came down from its elevated position to the valley beneath, where it had ended its onward career by stopping up against another house. As I looked from the back porch I saw that the ground still continued to slope, so that if my house had not found in its path another building, it would probably have proceeded somewhat farther on its course. It was lighter, and I saw bushes and fences and outbuildings— I was in a back yard.

Almost breathless with amazement and consternation, I ran again to the front door. When I reached it I found a young woman standing on the porch of the house before me. I was about to say something—I know not what—when she put her finger on her lips and stepped forward.

"Please don't speak loudly," she said. "I am afraid it will frighten mother. She is asleep yet. I suppose you and your house have been sliding downhill?"

"That is what has happened," said I. "But I cannot understand it. It seems to me the most amazing thing that ever took place on the face of the earth."

"It is very queer," said she, "but hurricanes do blow away houses, and that must have been a hurricane we had last night, for the wind was strong enough to loosen any house. I have often wondered if that house would ever slide downhill."

"My house?"

"Yes," she said. "Soon after it was built I began to think what a nice clean sweep it could make from the place where it seemed to be stuck to the side of the mountain, right down here into the valley."

I could not talk with a girl like this; at least, I could not meet her on her own conversational grounds. I was so agitated myself that it seemed unnatural that any one to whom I should speak should not also be agitated.

"Who are you?" I asked rather brusquely. "At least, to whom does this house belong?"

"This is my mother's house," said she. "My mother is Mrs. Carson. We happen just now to be living here by ourselves, so I cannot call on any man to help you do anything. My brother has always lived with us, but last week he went away."

"You don't seem to be a bit astonished at what has happened," said I.

She was rather a pretty girl, of a cheerful disposition, I should say, for several times she had smiled as she spoke.

"Oh, I am astonished," she answered; "or, at least, I was. But I have had time enough to get over some of it. It was at least an hour ago when I was awakened by hearing something crack in the yard. I went to a window and looked out, and could just barely see that something like a big building had grown up during the night. Then I watched it, and watched it, until I made out it was a whole house; and after that it was not long before I guessed what had happened. It seemed a simpler thing to me, you know, than it did to you, because I had often thought about it, and probably you never had."

"You are right there," said I, earnestly. "It would have been impossible for me to imagine such a thing."

"At first I thought there was nobody in the house," said she, "but when I heard some one moving about, I came down to tell whoever had arrived not to make a noise. I see," she added, with another of her smiles, "that you think I am a very strange person not to be more flurried by what has happened. But really I cannot think of anything else just now, except what mother will say and do when she comes down and finds you and your house here at the back door. I am very sure she will not like it."

"Like it!" I exclaimed. "Who on earth could like it?"

"Please speak more gently," she said. "Mother is always a little irritable when her night's rest has been broken, and I would not like to have her wakened up suddenly now. But really, Mr. Warren, I haven't the least idea in the world how she will take this thing. I must go in and be with her when she wakes, so that I can explain just what has happened."

"One moment," I said. "You know my name."

"Of course I know your name," she answered. "Could that house be up there on the hillside for more than a year without my knowing who lived in it?" With this she went indoors.

I could not help smiling when I thought of the young lady regretting that there was no man in the house who might help me do something. What could anybody do in a case like this? I turned and went into my house. I entered the various rooms on the lower floor, and saw no signs of any particular damage, except that everything movable in each room was jumbled together against the front wall. But when I looked out of the back door I found that the porch there was a good deal wrecked, which I had not noticed before.

I went up-stairs, and found everything very much as it was below. Nothing seemed to have been injured except the chimney and the porches. I thanked my stars that I had used hard wood instead of mortar for the ceilings of my rooms.

I was about to go into my bedroom, when I heard a woman scream, and of course I hurried to the front. There on the back porch of her house stood Mrs. Carson. She was a woman of middle age, and, as I glanced at her, I saw where her daughter got her good looks. But the placidity and cheerfulness of the younger face were entirely wanting in the mother. Her eyes sparkled, her cheeks were red, her mouth was partly opened, and it seemed to me that I could almost see that her breath was hot.

"Is this your house?" she cried, the moment her eyes fell upon me. "And what is it doing here?" I did not immediately answer, I looked at the angry woman, and behind her I saw, through the open door, the daughter crossing the hallway. It was plain that she had decided to let me have it out with her mother without interference. As briefly and as clearly as I could, I explained what had happened.

"What is all that to me?" she screamed. "It doesn't matter to me how your house got here. There have been storms ever since the beginning of the world, and I never heard of any of them taking a house into a person's back yard. You ought not to have built your house where any such thing could happen. But all this is nothing to me. I don't understand now how your house did get here, and I don't want to understand it. All I want is for you to take it away."

"I will do that, madam, just as soon as I can. You may be very sure I will do that. But—"

"Can you do it now?" she asked. "Can you do it to-day? I don't want a minute lost. I have not been outside to see what damage has been done, but the first thing to do is to take your house away."

"I am going to the town now, madam, to summon assistance."

Mrs. Carson made no answer, but she turned and walked to the end of her porch. There she suddenly gave a scream which quickly brought her daughter from the house. "Kitty! Kitty!" cried her mother. "Do you know what he has done? He has gone right over my round flower-garden. His house is sitting on it this minute!"

"But he could not help it, mother," said Kitty.

"Help it!" exclaimed Mrs. Carson. "I didn't expect him to

help it. What I want—" Suddenly she stopped. Her eyes flashed brighter, her mouth opened wider, and she became more and more excited as she noticed the absence of the sheds, fences, or vegetable-beds which had found themselves in the course of my all-destroying dwelling.

It was now well on in the morning, and some of the neighbors had become aware of the strange disaster which had happened to me, although if they had heard the news from Mrs. Carson they might have supposed that it was a disaster which had happened only to her. As they gazed at the two houses so closely jammed together, all of them wondered, some of them even laughed, but not one offered a suggestion which afforded satisfaction to Mrs. Carson or myself. The general opinion was that, now my house was there, it would have to stay there, for there were not enough horses in the State to pull it back up that mountainside. To be sure, it might possibly be drawn off sidewise. But whether it was moved one way or the other, a lot of Mrs. Carson's trees would have to be cut down to let it pass.

"Which shall never happen!" cried that good lady. "If nothing else can be done, it must be taken apart and hauled off in carts. But no matter how it is managed, it must be moved, and that immediately." Miss Carson now prevailed upon her mother to go into the house, and I stayed and talked to the men and a few women who had gathered outside.

When they had said all they had to say, and seen all there was to see, these people went home to their breakfasts. I entered my house, but not by the front door, for to do that I would have been obliged to trespass upon Mrs. Carson's back porch. I got my hat, and was about to start for the town, when I heard my name called. Turning into the hall, I saw Miss Carson, who was standing at my front door.

"Mr. Warren," said she, "you haven't any way of getting breakfast, have you?"

"Oh, no," said I. "My servants are up there in their cabin, and I suppose they are too much scared to come down. But I am going to town to see what can be done about my house, and will get my breakfast there."

"It's a long way to go without anything to eat," she said, "and we can give you some breakfast. But I want to ask you something. I am in a good deal of perplexity. Our two servants are out at the front of the house, but they positively refuse to come in; they are afraid that your house may begin sliding again and crush them all, so, I shall have to get breakfast. But what bothers me is trying to find our well. I have been outside, and can see no signs of it."

"Where was your well?" I gasped.

"It ought to be somewhere near the back of your house," she said. "May I go through your hall and look out?"

"Of course you may," I cried, and I preceded her to my back door.

"Now, it seems to me," she said, after surveying the scene of desolation immediately before, and looking from side to side toward objects which had remained untouched, "that your house has passed directly over our well, and must have carried away the little shed and the pump and everything above ground. I should not wonder a bit," she continued slowly, "if it is under your porch."

I jumped to the ground, for the steps were shattered, and began to search for the well, and it was not long before I discovered its round dark opening, which was, as Miss Carson had imagined, under one end of my porch.

"What can we do?" she asked. "We can't have breakfast or get along at all without water." It was a terribly depressing thing to me to think that I, or rather my house, had given these people so much trouble. But I speedily, assured Miss Carson that if she could find a bucket and a rope which I could lower into the well, I would provide her with water.

She went into her house to see what she could find, and I tore away the broken planks of the porch, so that I could get to the well. And then, when she came with a tin pail and a clothes-line, I went to work to haul up water and carry it to her back door. "I don't want mother to find out what has happened to the well," she said, "for she has enough on her mind already."

Mrs. Carson was a woman with some good points in her character. After a time she called to me herself, and told me to come in to breakfast. But during the meal she talked very earnestly to me about the amazing trespass I had committed, and about the means which should be taken to repair the damages my house had done to her property. I was as optimistic as I could be, and the young lady spoke very cheerfully and hopefully about the affair, so that we were beginning to get along somewhat pleasantly, when, suddenly, Mrs. Carson sprang to her feet. "Heavens and earth!" she cried, "this house is moving!"

She was not mistaken. I had felt beneath my feet a sudden sharp shock—not severe, but unmistakable. I remembered that both houses stood upon slightly sloping ground. My blood turned cold, my heart stood still; even Miss Carson was pale.

When we had rushed out of doors to see what had happened, or what was going to happen, I soon found that we had been needlessly frightened. Some of the broken timbers on which my house had been partially resting had given way, and the front part of the building had slightly descended, jarring as it did so the other house against which it rested. I endeavored to prove to Mrs. Carson that the result was encouraging rather than otherwise, for my house was now more firmly settled than it had been. But she did not value the opinion of a man who did not know enough to put his house in a place where it would be likely to stay, and she could eat no more breakfast, and was even afraid to stay under her own roof until experienced mechanics had been summoned to look into the state of affairs.

I hurried away to the town, and it was not long before several carpenters and masons were on the spot. After a thorough examination, they assured Mrs. Carson that there was no danger, that my house would do no farther damage to her premises, but, to make things certain, they would bring some heavy beams and brace the front of my house against her cellar wall. When that should be done it would be impossible for it to move any farther.

"But I don't want it braced!" cried Mrs. Carson. "I want it taken away. I want it out of my back yard!"

The master carpenter was a man of imagination and expedients. "That is quite another thing, ma'am," said he. "We'll fix this gentleman's house so that you needn't be afraid of it, and then, when the time comes to move it, there's several ways of doing that. We might rig up a powerful windlass at the top of the hill, and perhaps get a steam-engine to turn it, and we could fasten cables to the house and haul her back to where she belongs."

"And can you take your oaths," cried Mrs. Carson, "that those ropes won't break, and when that house gets half-way up the hill it won't come sliding down ten times faster than it did, and crash into me and mine and everything I own on earth? No, sir! I'll have no house hauled up a hill back of me!"

"Of course," said the carpenter, "it would be a great deal easier to move it on this ground, which is almost level—"

"And cut down my trees to do it! No, sir!"

"Well, then," said he, "there is no way to do but to take it apart and haul it off."

"Which would make an awful time at the back of my house while you were doing it!" exclaimed Mrs. Carson.

I now put in a word. "There's only one thing to do that I can see!" I exclaimed. "I will sell it to a match factory. It is almost all wood, and it can be cut up in sections about two inches thick, and then split into matches."

Kitty smiled. "I should like to see them," she said, "taking away the little sticks in wheelbarrows!"

"There is no need of trifling on the subject," said Mrs. Carson. "I have had a great deal to bear, and I must bear it no longer than is necessary. I have just found out that in order to get water out of my own well, I must go to the back porch of a stranger. Such things cannot be endured. If my son George were here, he would tell me what I ought to do. I shall write to him, and see what he advises. I do not mind waiting a little bit, now that I know that you can fix Mr. Warren's house so that it won't move any farther."

Thus the matter was left. My house was braced that afternoon, and toward evening I started to go to a hotel in the town to spend the night.

"No, sir!" said Mrs. Carson. "Do you suppose that I am going to stay here all night with a great empty house jammed up against me, and everybody knowing that it is empty? It will be the same as having thieves in my own house to have them in yours. You have come down here in your property, and you can stay in it and take care of it!"

"I don't object to that in the least," I said. "My two women are here, and I can tell them to attend to my meals. I haven't any chimney, but I suppose they can make a fire some way or other."

"No, sir!" said Mrs. Carson. "I am not going to have any strange servants on my place. I have just been able to prevail upon my own women to go into the house, and I don't want any more trouble. I have had enough already!"

"But, my dear madam," said I, "you don't want me to go to the town, and you won't allow me to have any cooking done here. What am I to do?"

"Well," she said, "you can eat with us. It may be two or three days before I can hear from my son George, and in the meantime you can lodge in your own house and I will take you to board. That is the best way I can see of managing the thing. But I am very sure I am not going to be left here alone in the dreadful predicament in which you have put me."

We had scarcely finished supper when Jack Brandiger came to see me. He laughed a good deal a about my sudden change of base, but thought, on the whole, my house had made a very successful move. It must be more pleasant in the valley than up on that windy hill. Jack was very much interested in everything, and when Mrs. Carson and her daughter appeared, as we were walking about viewing the scene, I felt myself obliged to introduce him.

"I like those ladies," said he to me, afterwards. "I think you have chosen very agreeable neighbors."

"How do you know you like them?" said I. "You had scarcely anything to say to Mrs. Carson."

"No, to be sure," said he. "But I expect I should like her. By the way, do you know how you used to talk to me about coming and living somewhere near you? How would you like me to take one of your rooms now? I might cheer you up."

"No," said I, firmly. "That cannot be done. As things are now, I have as much as I can do to get along here by myself."

Mrs. Carson did not hear from her son for nearly a week, and then he wrote that he found it almost impossible to give her any advice. He thought it was a very queer state of affairs. He had never heard of anything like it. But he would try and arrange his business so that he could come home in a week or two and look into matters.

As I was thus compelled to force myself upon the close neighborhood of Mrs. Carson and her daughter, I endeavored to make things as pleasant as possible. I brought some of my men down out of the vineyard, and set them to repairing fences, putting the garden in order, and doing all that I could to remedy the doleful condition of things which I had unwillingly brought into the back yard of this quiet family. I rigged up a pump on my back porch by which the water of the well could be conveniently obtained, and in every way endeavored to repair damages.

But Mrs. Carson never ceased to talk about the unparalleled disaster which had come upon her, and she must have had a great deal of correspondence with her son George, because she gave me frequent messages from him. He could not come on to look into the state of affairs, but he seemed to be giving it a great deal of thought and attention.

Spring weather had come again, and it was very pleasant to help the Carson ladies get their flower-garden in order—at least, as much as was left of it, for my house was resting upon some of the most important beds. As I was obliged to give up all present idea of doing anything in the way of getting my residence out of a place where it had no business to be, because Mrs. Carson would not consent to any plan which had been suggested, I felt that I was offering some little compensation in beautifying what seemed to be, at that time, my own grounds.

My labors in regard to vines, bushes, and all that sort of thing were generally carried on under direction of Mrs. Carson or her daughter, and as the elderly lady was a very busy housewife, the horticultural work was generally left to Miss Kitty and me.

I liked Miss Kitty. She was a cheerful, whole-souled person, and I sometimes thought that she was not so unwilling to have me for a neighbor as the rest of the family seemed to be; for if I were to judge the disposition of her brother George from what her mother told me about his letters, both he and Mrs. Carson must be making a great many plans to get me off the premises.

Nearly a month had now passed since my house and I made that remarkable morning call upon Mrs. Carson. I was becoming accustomed to my present mode of living, and, so far as I was concerned, it satisfied me very well. I certainly lived a great deal better than when I was depending upon my old negro cook. Miss Kitty seemed to be satisfied with things as they were, and so, in some respects, did her mother. But the latter never ceased to give me extracts from some of her son George's letters, and this was always annoying and worrying to me. Evidently he was not pleased with me as such a close neighbor to his mother, and it was astonishing how many expedients he proposed in order to rid her of my undesirable proximity.

"My son George," said Mrs. Carson, one morning, "has been writing to me about jack-screws. He says that the greatest improvements have been made in jack-screws."

"What do you do with them, mother?" asked Miss Kitty.

"You lift houses with them," said she. "He says that in large cities they lift whole blocks of houses with them and build stories underneath. He thinks that we can get rid of our trouble here if we use jack-screws."

"But how does he propose to use them?" I asked.

"Oh, he has a good many plans," answered Mrs. Carson. "He said that he should not wonder if jack-screws could be made large enough to lift your house entirely over mine and set it out in the road, where it could be carried away without interfering with anything, except, of course, vehicles which might be coming along. But he has another plan—that is, to lift my house up and carry it out into the field on the other side of the road, and then your house might be carried along right over the cellar until it got to the road. In that way, he says, the bushes and trees would not have to be interfered with."

"I think brother George is cracked!" said Kitty.

All this sort of thing worried me very much. My mind was eminently disposed toward peace and tranquillity, but who could be peaceful and tranquil with a prospective jack-screw under the very base of his comfort and happiness? In fact, my house had never been such a happy home as it was at that time. The fact of its unwarranted position upon other people's grounds had ceased to trouble me.

But the coming son George, with his jack-screws, did trouble me very much, and that afternoon I deliberately went into Mrs. Carson's house to look for Kitty. I knew her mother was not at home, for I had seen her go out. When Kitty appeared I asked her to come out on her back porch. "Have you thought of any new plan of moving it?" she said, with a smile, as we sat down.

"No," said I, earnestly. "I have not, and I don't want to think of any plan of moving it. I am tired of seeing it here, I am tired of thinking about moving it away, and I am tired of hearing people talk about moving it. I have not any right to be here, and I am never allowed to forget it. What I want to do is to go entirely away, and leave everything behind me—except one thing."

"And what is that?" asked Kitty.

"You," I answered.

She turned a little pale and did not reply.

"You understand me, Kitty," I said. "There is nothing in the world that I care for but you. What have you to say to me?"

Then came back to her her little smile. "I think it would be very foolish for us to go away," she said.

It was about a quarter of an hour after this when Kitty proposed that we should go out to the front of the house; it would look queer if any of the servants should come by and see us sitting together like that. I had forgotten that there were other people in the world, but I went with her.

Frank R. Stockton

We were standing on the front porch, close to each other, and I think we were holding each other's hands, when Mrs. Carson came back. As she approached she looked at us inquiringly, plainly wishing to know why we were standing side by side before her door as if we had some special object in so doing.

"Well?" said she, as she came up the steps. Of course it was right that I should speak, and, in as few words as possible, I told her what Kitty and I had been saying to each other. I never saw Kitty's mother look so cheerful and so handsome as when she came forward and kissed her daughter and shook hands with me. She seemed so perfectly satisfied that it amazed me. After a little Kitty left us, and then Mrs. Carson asked me to sit by her on a rustic bench.

"Now," said she, "this will straighten out things in the very best way. When you are married, you and Kitty can live in the back building,—for, of course, your house will now be the same thing as a back building,—and you can have the second floor. We won't have any separate tables, because it will be a great deal nicer for you and Kitty to live with me, and it will simply be your paying board for two persons instead of one. And you know you can manage your vineyard just as well from the bottom of the hill as from the top. The lower rooms of what used to be your house can be made very pleasant and comfortable for all of us. I have been thinking about the room on the right that you had planned for a parlor, and it will make a lovely sitting-room for us, which is a thing we have never had, and the room on the other side is just what will suit beautifully for a guest-chamber. The two houses together, with the roof of my back porch properly joined to the front of your house, will make a beautiful and spacious dwelling. It was fortunate, too, that you painted your house a light yellow. I have often looked at the two together, and thought what a good thing it was that one was not one color and the other another. As to the pump, it will be very easy now to put a pipe from what used to be your back porch to our kitchen, so that we can get water without being obliged to carry it. Between us we can make all sorts of improvements, and some time I will tell you of a good many that I have thought of.

"What used to be your house, " she continued, "can be jack-screwed up a little bit and a good foundation put under it. I have inquired about that. Of course it would not have been proper to let you know that I was satisfied with the state of things, but I was satisfied, and there is no use of denying it. As soon as I got over my first scare after that house came down the hill, and had seen how everything might be arranged to suit all parties, I said to myself, 'What the Lord has joined together, let not man put asunder,' and so, according to my belief, the strongest kind of jack-screws could not put these two houses asunder, any more than they could put you and Kitty asunder, now that you have agreed to take each other for each other's own."

Jack Brandiger came to call that evening, and when he had heard what had happened he whistled a good deal. "You are a funny kind of a fellow," said he. "You go courting like a snail, with your house on your back!"

I think my friend was a little discomfited. "Don't be discouraged, Jack," said I. "You will get a good wife some of these days—that is, if you don't try to slide uphill to find her!"

Frank R. Stockton

OUR ARCHERY CLUB

When an archery club was formed in our village, I was among the first to join it. But I should not, on this account, claim any extraordinary enthusiasm on the subject of archery, for nearly all the ladies and gentlemen of the place were also among the first to join.

Few of us, I think, had a correct idea of the popularity of archery in our midst until the subject of a club was broached. Then we all perceived what a strong interest we felt in the study and use of the bow and arrow. The club was formed immediately, and our thirty members began to discuss the relative merits of lancewood, yew, and green-heart bows, and to survey yards and lawns for suitable spots for setting up targets for home practice.

Our weekly meetings, at which we came together to show in friendly contest how much our home practice had taught us, were held upon the village green, or rather upon what had been intended to be the village green. This pretty piece of ground, partly in smooth lawn and partly shaded by fine trees, was the property of a gentleman of the place, who had presented it, under certain conditions, to the township. But as the township had never fulfilled any of the conditions, and had done nothing toward the improvement of the spot, further than to make it a grazing-place for local cows and goats, the owner had withdrawn his gift, shut out the cows and goats by a picket fence, and, having locked the gate, had hung up the key in his barn. When our club was formed, the green, as it was still called, was offered to us for our meetings, and, with proper gratitude, we elected its owner to be our president.

This gentleman was eminently qualified for the presidency of an archery club. In the first place, he did not shoot: this gave him time and opportunity to attend to the shooting of others. He was a tall and pleasant man, a little elderly. This "elderliness," if I may so put it, seemed, in his case, to resemble some mild disorder, like a gentle rheumatism, which, while it prevented him from indulging in all the wild hilarities of youth, gave him, in compensation, a position, as one entitled to a certain consideration, which was very agreeable to him. His little disease was chronic, it is true, and it was growing upon him; but it was, so far, a pleasant ailment.

And so, with as much interest in bows and arrows and targets and successful shots as any of us, he never fitted an arrow to a string, nor drew a bow. But he attended every meeting, settling disputed points (for he studied all the books on archery), encouraging the disheartened, holding back the eager ones who would run to the targets as soon as they had shot, regardless of the fact that others were still shooting and that the human body is not arrow-proof, and shedding about him that general aid and comfort which emanates from a good fellow, no matter what he may say or do.

There were persons—outsiders—who said that archery clubs always selected ladies for their presiding officers, but we did not care to be too much bound down and trammelled by customs and traditions. Another club might not have among its members such a genial elderly gentleman who owned a village green.

Frank R. Stockton

I soon found myself greatly interested in archery, especially when I succeeded in planting an arrow somewhere within the periphery of the target, but I never became such an enthusiast in bow-shooting as my friend Pepton.

If Pepton could have arranged matters to suit himself, he would have been born an archer. But as this did not happen to have been the case, he employed every means in his power to rectify what he considered this serious error in his construction. He gave his whole soul, and the greater part of his spare time, to archery, and as he was a young man of energy, this helped him along wonderfully.

His equipments were perfect. No one could excel him in, this respect. His bow was snakewood, backed with hickory. He carefully rubbed it down every evening with oil and beeswax, and it took its repose in a green baize bag. His arrows were Philip Highfield's best, his strings the finest Flanders hemp. He had shooting-gloves, and little leather tips that could be screwed fast on the ends of what he called his string-fingers. He had a quiver and a belt, and when equipped for the weekly meetings, he carried a fancy-colored wiping-tassel, and a little ebony grease-pot hanging from his belt. He wore, when shooting, a polished arm-guard or bracer, and if he had heard of anything else that an archer should have, he straightway would have procured it.

Pepton was a single man, and he lived with two good old maiden ladies, who took as much care of him as if they had been his mothers. And he was such a good, kind fellow that he deserved all the attention they gave him. They felt a great interest in his archery pursuits, and shared his anxious solicitude in the selection of a suitable place to hang his bow.

"You see," said he, "a fine bow like this, when not in use, should always be in a perfectly dry place."

"And when in use, too," said Miss Martha, "for I am sure that you oughtn't to be standing and shooting in any damp spot. There's no surer way of gettin' chilled."

To which sentiment Miss Maria agreed, and suggested wearing rubber shoes, or having a board to stand on, when the club met after a rain.

Pepton first hung his bow in the hall, but after he had arranged it symmetrically upon two long nails (bound with green worsted, lest they should scratch the bow through its woollen cover), he reflected that the front door would frequently be open, and that damp drafts must often go through the hall. He was sorry to give up this place for his bow, for it was convenient and appropriate, and for an instant he thought that it might remain, if the front door could be kept shut, and visitors admitted through a little side door which the family generally used, and which was almost as convenient as the other—except, indeed, on wash-days, when a wet sheet or some article of wearing apparel was apt to be hung in front of it. But although wash-day occurred but once a week, and although it was comparatively easy, after a little practice, to bob under a high-propped sheet, Pepton's heart was too kind to allow his mind to dwell upon this plan. So he drew the nails from the wall of the hall, and put them up in various places about the house. His own room had to be aired a great deal in all weathers, and so that would not do at all. The wall above the kitchen fireplace would be a good location, for the chimney was nearly always warm. But Pepton could not bring himself to keep his bow in the kitchen. There would be nothing esthetic about such a disposition of it, and, besides, the girl might be tempted to string and bend it. The old ladies really did not want it in the parlor, for its length and its green baize cover would make it an encroaching and unbecoming neighbor to the little engravings and the big samplers, the picture-frames of acorns and pine-cones, the fancifully patterned ornaments of clean wheat straw, and all the quaint adornments which had hung upon those walls for so many years. But they did not say so. If it had been necessary, to make room for the bow, they would have taken down the pencilled profiles of their grandfather, their grandmother, and their father when a little boy, which hung in a row over the mantelpiece.

However, Pepton did not ask this sacrifice. In the summer evenings the parlor windows must be open. The dining-room was really very little used in the evening, except when Miss Maria had stockings to darn, and then she always sat in that apartment, and of course she had the windows open. But Miss Maria was very willing to bring her work into the parlor,—it was foolish, anyway, to have a feeling about darning stockings before chance company,—and then the dining-room could be kept shut up after tea. So into the wall of that neat little room Pepton drove his worsted-covered nails, and on them carefully laid his bow. All the next day Miss Martha and Miss Maria went about the house, covering the nail-holes he had made with bits of wall-paper, carefully snipped out to fit the patterns, and pasted on so neatly that no one would have suspected they were there.

One afternoon, as I was passing the old ladies' house, saw, or thought I saw, two men carrying in a coffin. I was struck with alarm.

"What!" I thought. "Can either of those good women—Or can Pepton—"

Without a moment's hesitation, I rushed in behind the men. There, at the foot of the stairs, directing them, stood Pepton. Then it was not he! I seized him sympathetically by the hand.

"Which?" I faltered. "Which? Who is that coffin for?"

"Coffin!" cried Pepton. "Why, my dear fellow, that is not a coffin. That is my ascham."

"Ascham?" I exclaimed. "What is that?"

"Come and look at it," he said, when the men had set it on end against the wall. "It is an upright closet or receptacle for an archer's armament. Here is a place to stand the bow, here are supports for the arrows and quivers, here are shelves and hooks, on which to lay or hang everything the merry man can need. You see, moreover, that it is lined with green plush, that the door fits tightly, so that it can stand anywhere, and there need be no fear of drafts or dampness affecting my bow. Isn't it a perfect thing? You ought to get one."

I admitted the perfection, but agreed no further. I had not the income of my good Pepton.

Pepton was, indeed, most wonderfully well equipped; and yet, little did those dear old ladies think, when they carefully dusted and reverentially gazed at the bunches of arrows, the arm-bracers, the gloves, the grease-pots, and all the rest of the paraphernalia of archery, as it hung around Pepton's room, or when they afterwards allowed a particular friend to peep at it, all arranged so orderly within the ascham, or when they looked with sympathetic, loving admiration on the beautiful polished bow, when it was taken out of its bag—little did they think, I say, that Pepton was the very poorest shot in the club. In all the surface of the much-perforated targets of the club, there was scarcely a hole that he could put his hand upon his heart and say he made.

Indeed, I think it was the truth that Pepton was born not to be an archer. There were young fellows in the club who shot with bows that cost no more than Pepton's tassels, but who could stand up and whang arrows into the targets all the afternoon, if they could get a chance; and there were ladies who made hits five times out of six; and there were also all the grades of archers common to any club. But there was no one but himself in Pepton's grade. He stood alone, and it was never any trouble to add up his score.

Yet he was not discouraged. He practised every day except Sundays, and indeed he was the only person in the club who practised at night. When he told me about this, I was a little surprised.

"Why, it's easy enough," said he. "You see, I hung a lantern, with a reflector, before the target, just a little to one side. It lighted up the target beautifully, and I believe there was a better chance of hitting it than by daylight, for the only thing you could see was the target, and so your attention was not distracted. To be sure," he said, in answer to a question, "it was a good deal of trouble to find the arrows, but that I always have. When I get so expert that I can put all the arrows into the target, there will be no trouble of the kind, night or day. However," he continued, "I don't practise any more by night. The other evening I sent an arrow slam-bang into the lantern, and broke it all to flinders. Borrowed lantern, too. Besides, I found it made Miss Martha very nervous to have me shooting about the house after dark. She had a friend who had a little boy who was hit in the leg by an arrow from a bow, which, she says, accidentally went off in the night, of its own accord. She is certainly a little mixed in her mind in regard to this matter, but I wish to respect her feelings, and so shall not use another lantern."

As I have said, there were many good archers among the ladies of our club. Some of them, after we had been organized for a month or two, made scores that few of the gentlemen could excel. But the lady who attracted the greatest attention when she shot was Miss Rosa.

When this very pretty young lady stood up before the ladies' target—her left side well advanced, her bow firmly held out in her strong left arm, which never quivered, her head a little bent to the right, her arrow drawn back by three well-gloved fingers to the tip of her little ear, her dark eyes steadily fixed upon the gold, and her dress, well fitted over her fine and vigorous figure, falling in graceful folds about her feet, we all stopped shooting to look at her.

"There is something statuesque about her," said Pepton, who ardently admired her, "and yet there isn't. A statue could never equal her unless we knew there was a probability of movement in it. And the only statues which have that are the Jarley wax-works, which she does not resemble in the least. There is only one thing that that girl needs to make her a perfect archer, and that is to be able to aim better."

This was true. Miss Rosa did need to aim better. Her arrows had a curious habit of going on all sides of the target, and it was very seldom that one chanced to stick into it. For if she did make a hit, we all knew it was chance and that there was no probability of her doing it again. Once she put an arrow right into the centre of the gold,—one of the finest shots ever made on the ground,—but she didn't hit the target again for two weeks. She was almost as bad a shot as Pepton, and that is saying a good deal.

One evening I was sitting with Pepton on the little front porch of the old ladies' house, where we were taking our after-dinner smoke while Miss Martha and Miss Maria were washing, with their own white hands, the china and glass in which they took so much pride. I often used to go over and spend an hour with Pepton. He liked to have some one to whom he could talk on the subjects which filled his soul, and I liked to hear him talk.

"I tell you," said he, as he leaned back in his chair, with his feet carefully disposed on the railing so that they would not injure Miss Maria's Madeira-vine, "I tell you, sir, that there are two things I crave with all my power of craving—two goals I fain would reach, two diadems I would wear upon my brow. One of these is to kill an eagle—or some large bird—with a shaft from my good bow. I would then have it stuffed and mounted, with the very arrow that killed it still sticking in its breast. This trophy of my skill I would have fastened against the wall of my room or my hall, and I would feel proud to think that my grandchildren could point to that bird—which I would carefully bequeath to my descendants—and say, 'My grand'ther shot that bird, and with that very arrow.' Would it not stir your pulses if you could do a thing like that?"

"I should have to stir them up a good deal before I could do it," I replied. "It would be a hard thing to shoot an eagle with an arrow. If you want a stuffed bird to bequeath, you'd better use a rifle."

"A rifle!" exclaimed Pepton. "There would be no glory in that. There are lots of birds shot with rifles—eagles, hawks, wild geese, tomtits—"

"Oh, no!" I interrupted, "not tomtits."

"Well, perhaps they are too little for a rifle," said he. "But what I mean to say is that I wouldn't care at all for an eagle I had shot with a rifle. You couldn't show the ball that killed him. If it were put in properly, it would be inside, where it couldn't be seen. No, sir. It is ever so much more honorable, and far more difficult, too, to hit an eagle than to hit a target."

"That is very true," I answered, "especially in these days, when there are so few eagles and so many targets. But what is your other diadem?"

"That," said Pepton, "is to see Miss Rosa wear the badge."

"Indeed!" said I. And from that moment I began to understand Pepton's hopes in regard to the grandmother of those children who should point to the eagle.

"Yes, sir," he continued, "I should be truly happy to see her win the badge. And she ought to win it. No one shoots more correctly, and with a better understanding of all the rules, than she does. There must truly be something the matter with her aiming. I've half a mind to coach her a little."

I turned aside to see who was coming down the road. I would not have had him know I smiled.

The most objectionable person in our club was O. J. Hollingsworth. He was a good enough fellow in himself, but it was as an archer that we objected to him.

There was, so far as I know, scarcely a rule of archery that he did not habitually violate. Our president and nearly all of us remonstrated with him, and Pepton even went to see him on the subject, but it was all to no purpose. With a quiet disregard of other people's ideas about bow-shooting and other people's opinions about himself, he persevered in a style of shooting which appeared absolutely absurd to any one who knew anything of the rules and methods of archery.

I used to like to look at him when his turn came around to shoot. He was not such a pleasing object of vision as Miss Rosa, but his style was so entirely novel to me that it was interesting. He held the bow horizontally, instead of perpendicularly, like other archers, and he held it well down—about opposite his waistband. He did not draw his arrow back to his ear, but he drew it back to the lower button of his vest. Instead of standing upright, with his left side to the target, he faced it full, and leaned forward over his arrow, in an attitude which reminded me of a Roman soldier about to fall upon his sword. When he had seized the nock of his arrow between his finger and thumb, he languidly glanced at the target, raised his bow a little, and let fly. The provoking thing about it was that he nearly always hit. If he had only known how to stand, and hold his bow, and draw back his arrow, he would have been a very good archer. But, as it was, we could not help laughing at him, although our president always discountenanced anything of the kind.

Our champion was a tall man, very cool and steady, who went to work at archery exactly as if he were paid a salary, and intended to earn his money honestly. He did the best he could in every way. He generally shot with one of the bows owned by the club, but if any one on the ground had a better one, he would borrow it. He used to shoot sometimes with Pepton's bow, which he declared to be a most capital one. But as Pepton was always very nervous when he saw his bow in the hands of another than himself, the champion soon ceased to borrow it.

There were two badges, one of green silk and gold for the ladies, and one of green and red for the gentlemen, and these were shot for at each weekly meeting. With the exception of a few times when the club was first formed, the champion had always worn the gentlemen's badge. Many of us tried hard to win it from him, but we never could succeed; he shot too well.

On the morning of one of our meeting days, the champion

told me, as I was going to the city with him, that he would not be able to return at his usual hour that afternoon. He would be very busy, and would have to wait for the six-fifteen train, which would bring him home too late for the archery meeting. So he gave me the badge, asking me to hand it to the president, that he might bestow it on the successful competitor that afternoon.

We were all rather glad that the champion was obliged to be absent. Here was a chance for some one of us to win the badge. It was not, indeed, an opportunity for us to win a great deal of honor, for if the champion were to be there we should have no chance at all. But we were satisfied with this much, having no reason—in the present, at least—to expect anything more.

So we went to the targets with a new zeal, and most of us shot better than we had ever shot before. In this number was O. J. Hollingsworth. He excelled himself, and, what was worse, he excelled all the rest of us. He actually made a score of eighty-five in twenty-four shots, which at that time was remarkably good shooting, for our club. This was dreadful! To have a fellow who didn't know how to shoot beat us all was too bad. If any visitor who knew anything at all of archery should see that the member who wore the champion's badge was a man who held his bow as if he had the stomach-ache, it would ruin our character as a club. It was not to be borne.

Pepton in particular felt greatly outraged. We had met very promptly that afternoon, and had finished our regular shooting much earlier than usual; and now a knot of us were gathered together, talking over this unfortunate occurrence.

"I don't intend to stand it," Pepton suddenly exclaimed. "I feel it as a personal disgrace. I'm going to have the champion here before dark. By the rules, he has a right to shoot until the president declares it is too late. Some of you fellows stay here, and I'll bring him."

And away he ran, first giving me charge of his precious bow. There was no need of his asking us to stay. We were bound to see the fun out, and to fill up the time our president offered a special prize of a handsome bouquet from his gardens, to be shot for by the ladies.

Pepton ran to the railroad station, and telegraphed to the champion. This was his message:

"You are absolutely needed here. If possible, take the five-thirty train for Ackford. I will drive over for you. Answer."

There was no train before the six-fifteen by which the champion could come directly to our village; but Ackford, a small town about three miles distant, was on another railroad, on which there were frequent afternoon trains.

The champion answered:

"All right. Meet me."

Then Pepton rushed to our livery stable, hired a horse and buggy, and drove to Ackford.

A little after half-past six, when several of us were beginning to think that Pepton had failed in his plans, he drove rapidly into the grounds, making a very short turn at the gate, and pulled up his panting horse just in time to avoid running over three ladies, who were seated on the grass. The champion was by his side!

The latter lost no time in talking or salutations. He knew what he had been brought there to do, and he immediately set about trying to do it. He took Pepton's bow, which the latter urged upon him. He stood up, straight and firm on the line, at thirty-five yards from the gentlemen's target; he carefully selected his arrows, examining the feathers and wiping away any bit of soil that might be adhering to the points after some one had shot them into the turf; with vigorous arm he drew each arrow to its head; he fixed his eyes and his whole mind on the centre of the target; he shot his twenty-four arrows, handed to him, one by one, by Pepton, and he made a score of ninety-one.

The whole club had been scoring the shots, as they were made, and when the last arrow plumped into the red ring, a cheer arose from every member excepting three: the champion, the president, and O. J. Hollingsworth. But Pepton cheered loudly enough to make up these deficiencies.

"What in the mischief did they cheer him for?" asked Hollingsworth of me. "They didn't cheer me when I beat everybody on the grounds an hour ago. And it's no new thing for him to win the badge; he does it every time."

"Well," said I, frankly, "I think the club, AS a club, objects to your wearing the badge, because you don't know how to shoot."

"Don't know how to shoot!" he cried. "Why, I can hit the target better than any of you. Isn't that what you try to do when you shoot?"

"Yes," said I, "of course that is what we try to do. But we try to do it in the proper way."

"Proper grandmother!" he exclaimed. "It doesn't seem to help you much. The best thing you fellows can do is to learn to shoot my way, and then perhaps you may be able to hit oftener."

When the champion had finished shooting he went home to his dinner, but many of us stood about, talking over our great escape.

"I feel as if I had done that myself," said Pepton. "I am almost as proud as if I had shot—well, not an eagle, but a soaring lark."

"Why, that ought to make you prouder than the other," said I, "for a lark, especially when it's soaring, must be a good deal harder to hit than an eagle."

"That's so," said Pepton, reflectively. "But I'll stick to the lark. I'm proud."

During the next month our style of archery improved very much, so much, indeed, that we increased our distance, for gentlemen, to forty yards, and that for ladies to thirty, and also had serious thoughts of challenging the Ackford club to a match. But as this was generally understood to be a crack club, we finally determined to defer our challenge until the next season.

When I say we improved, I do not mean all of us. I do not mean Miss Rosa. Although her attitudes were as fine as ever, and every motion as true to rule as ever, she seldom made a hit. Pepton actually did try to teach her how to aim, but the various methods of pointing the arrow which he suggested resulted in such wild shooting that the boys who picked up the arrows never dared to stick the points of their noses beyond their boarded barricade during Miss Rosa's turns at the target. But she was not discouraged, and Pepton often assured her that if she would keep up a good heart, and practise regularly, she would get the badge yet. As a rule, Pepton was so honest and truthful that a little statement of this kind, especially under the circumstances, might be forgiven him.

One day Pepton came to me and announced that he had made a discovery.

"It's about archery," he said, "and I don't mind telling you, because I know you will not go about telling everybody else, and also because I want to see you succeed as an archer."

"I am very much obliged," I said, "and what is the discovery?"

"It's this," he answered. "When you draw your bow, bring the nock of your arrow"—he was always very particular about technical terms—"well up to your ear. Having done that, don't bother any more about your right hand. It has nothing to do with the correct pointing of your arrow, for it must be kept close to your right ear, just as if it were screwed there. Then with your left hand bring around the bow so that your fist—with the arrow-head, which is resting on top of it—shall point, as nearly as you can make it, directly at the centre of the target. Then let fly, and ten to one you'll make a hit. Now, what do you think of that for a discovery? I've thoroughly tested the plan, and it works splendidly."

"I think," said I, "that you have discovered the way in which good archers shoot. You have stated the correct method of managing a bow and arrow."

"Then you don't think it's an original method with me?"

"Certainly not," I answered.

"But it's the correct way?"

"There's no doubt of that," said I.

"Well," said Pepton, "then I shall make it my way."

He did so, and the consequence was that one day, when the champion happened to be away, Pepton won the badge. When the result was announced, we were all surprised, but none so much so as Pepton himself. He had been steadily improving since he had adopted a good style of shooting, but he had had no idea that he would that day be able to win the badge.

When our president pinned the emblem of success upon the lapel of his coat, Pepton turned pale, and then he flushed. He thanked the president, and was about to thank the ladies and gentlemen; but probably recollecting that we had had nothing to do with it,—unless, indeed, we had shot badly on his behalf,—he refrained. He said little, but I could see that he was very proud and very happy. There was but one drawback to his triumph:

Miss Rosa was not there. She was a very regular attendant, but for some reason she was absent on this momentous afternoon. I did not say anything to him on the subject, but I knew he felt this absence deeply.

But this cloud could not wholly overshadow his happiness. He walked home alone, his face beaming, his eyes sparkling, and his good bow under his arm.

That evening I called on him, for I thought that when he had cooled down a little he would like to talk over the affair. But he was not in. Miss Maria said that he had gone out as soon as he had finished his dinner, which he had hurried through in a way which would certainly injure his digestion if he kept up the practice; and dinner was late, too, for they waited for him, and the archery meeting lasted a long time today; and it really was not right for him to stay out after the dew began to fall with only ordinary shoes on, for what's the good of knowing how to shoot a bow and arrow, if you're laid up in your bed with rheumatism or disease of the lungs? Good old lady! She would have kept Pepton in a green baize bag, had such a thing been possible.

The next morning, full two hours before church-time, Pepton called on me. His face was still beaming. I could not help smiling.

"Your happiness lasts well," I said.

"Lasts!" he exclaimed. "Why shouldn't it last!"

"There's no reason why it should not—at least, for a week," I said, "and even longer, if you repeat your success."

I did not feel so much like congratulating Pepton as I had on the previous evening. I thought he was making too much of his badge-winning.

"Look here!" said Pepton, seating himself, and drawing his chair close to me, "you are shooting wild—very wild indeed. You don't even see the target. Let me tell you something. Last evening I went to see Miss Rosa. She was delighted at my success. I had not expected this. I thought she would be pleased, but not to such a degree. Her congratulations were so warm that they set me on fire."

"They must have been very warm indeed," I remarked.

"'Miss Rosa,' said I," continued Pepton, without regarding my interruption, "'it has been my fondest hope to see you wear the badge.' 'But I never could get it, you know,' she said. 'You have got it,' I exclaimed. 'Take this. I won it for you. Make me happy by wearing it.' 'I can't do that,' she said. 'That is a gentleman's badge.' 'Take it,' I cried, 'gentleman and all!'

"I can't tell you all that happened after that," continued

Frank R. Stockton

Pepton. "You know, it wouldn't do. It is enough to say that she wears the badge. And we are both her own—the badge and I!"

Now I congratulated him in good earnest. There was a reason for it.

"I don't owe a snap now for shooting an eagle," said Pepton, springing to his feet and striding up and down the floor. "Let 'em all fly free for me. I have made the most glorious shot that man could make. I have hit the gold—hit it fair in the very centre! And what's more, I've knocked it clean out of the target! Nobody else can ever make such a shot. The rest of you fellows will have to be content to hit the red, the blue, the black, or the white. The gold is mine!"

I called on the old ladies, some time after this, and found them alone. They were generally alone in the evenings now. We talked about Pepton's engagement, and I found them resigned. They were sorry to lose him, but they wanted him to be happy.

"We have always known," said Miss Martha, with a little sigh, "that we must die, and that he must get married. But we don't intend to repine. These things will come to people." And her little sigh was followed by a smile, still smaller.

ABOUT THE AUTHOR

 **Frank R. Stockton** (April 5, 1834 - April 20, 1902), was an American writer and humorist, best known today for a series of innovative children's fairy tales that were widely popular during the last decades of the 19th century. Stockton avoided the didactic moralizing common to children's stories of the time, instead using clever humor to poke at greed, violence, abuse of power and other human foibles, describing his fantastic characters' adventures in a charming, matter-of-fact way in stories like "The Griffin and the Minor Canon" (1885) and "The Bee-Man of Orn" (1887), which was republished in 1964 in an edition illustrated by Maurice Sendak.

Born in Philadelphia, Stockton was the son of a prominent Methodist minister who discouraged him from a writing career. He supported himself as a wood engraver until his father's death in 1860; in 1867, he moved back to Philadelphia to write for a newspaper founded by his brother. His first fairy tale, "Ting-a-ling," was published that year in The Riverside Magazine; his first book collection appeared in 1870.

He died of a cerebral hemorrhage in 1902. His collected works, 23 volumes of stories for adults and children, were published between 1899 and 1904.

Choose from Thousands of 1stWorldLibrary Classics By

A. M. Barnard
Ada Leverson
Adolphus William Ward
Aesop
Agatha Christie
Alexander Aaronsohn
Alexander Kielland
Alexandre Dumas
Alfred Gatty
Alfred Ollivant
Alice Duer Miller
Alice Turner Curtis
Alice Dunbar
Allen Chapman
Alleyne Ireland
Ambrose Bierce
Amelia E. Barr
Amory H. Bradford
Andrew Lang
Andrew McFarland Davis
Andy Adams
Angela Brazil
Anna Alice Chapin
Anna Sewell
Annie Besant
Annie Hamilton Donnell
Annie Payson Call
Annie Roe Carr
Annonaymous
Anton Chekhov
Archibald Lee Fletcher
Arnold Bennett
Arthur C. Benson
Arthur Conan Doyle
Arthur M. Winfield
Arthur Ransome
Arthur Schnitzler
Arthur Train
Atticus
B.H. Baden-Powell
B. M. Bower
B. C. Chatterjee
Baroness Emmuska Orczy
Baroness Orczy
Basil King
Bayard Taylor
Ben Macomber
Bertha Muzzy Bower
Bjornstjerne Bjornson

Booth Tarkington
Boyd Cable
Bram Stoker
C. Collodi
C. E. Orr
C. M. Ingleby
Carolyn Wells
Catherine Parr Traill
Charles A. Eastman
Charles Amory Beach
Charles Dickens
Charles Dudley Warner
Charles Farrar Browne
Charles Ives
Charles Kingsley
Charles Klein
Charles Hanson Towne
Charles Lathrop Pack
Charles Romyn Dake
Charles Whibley
Charles Willing Beale
Charlotte M. Braeme
Charlotte M. Yonge
Charlotte Perkins Stetson
Clair W. Hayes
Clarence Day Jr.
Clarence E. Mulford
Clemence Housman
Confucius
Coningsby Dawson
Cornelis DeWitt Wilcox
Cyril Burleigh
D. H. Lawrence
Daniel Defoe
David Garnett
Dinah Craik
Don Carlos Janes
Donald Keyhoe
Dorothy Kilner
Dougan Clark
Douglas Fairbanks
E. Nesbit
E. P. Roe
E. Phillips Oppenheim
E. S. Brooks
Earl Barnes
Edgar Rice Burroughs
Edith Van Dyne
Edith Wharton

Edward Everett Hale
Edward J. O'Biren
Edward S. Ellis
Edwin L. Arnold
Eleanor Atkins
Eleanor Hallowell Abbott
Eliot Gregory
Elizabeth Gaskell
Elizabeth McCracken
Elizabeth Von Arnim
Ellem Key
Emerson Hough
Emilie F. Carlen
Emily Bronte
Emily Dickinson
Enid Bagnold
Enilor Macartney Lane
Erasmus W. Jones
Ernie Howard Pie
Ethel May Dell
Ethel Turner
Ethel Watts Mumford
Eugene Sue
Eugenie Foa
Eugene Wood
Eustace Hale Ball
Evelyn Everett-green
Everard Cotes
F. H. Cheley
F. J. Cross
F. Marion Crawford
Fannie E. Newberry
Federick Austin Ogg
Ferdinand Ossendowski
Fergus Hume
Florence A. Kilpatrick
Fremont B. Deering
Francis Bacon
Francis Darwin
Frances Hodgson Burnett
Frances Parkinson Keyes
Frank Gee Patchin
Frank Harris
Frank Jewett Mather
Frank L. Packard
Frank V. Webster
Frederic Stewart Isham
Frederick Trevor Hill
Frederick Winslow Taylor

Friedrich Kerst	Hayden Carruth	James Branch Cabell
Friedrich Nietzsche	Helent Hunt Jackson	James DeMille
Fyodor Dostoyevsky	Helen Nicolay	James Joyce
G.A. Henty	Hendrik Conscience	James Lane Allen
G.K. Chesterton	Hendy David Thoreau	James Lane Allen
Gabrielle E. Jackson	Henri Barbusse	James Oliver Curwood
Garrett P. Serviss	Henrik Ibsen	James Oppenheim
Gaston Leroux	Henry Adams	James Otis
George A. Warren	Henry Ford	James R. Driscoll
George Ade	Henry Frost	Jane Abbott
Geroge Bernard Shaw	Henry James	Jane Austen
George Cary Eggleston	Henry Jones Ford	Jane L. Stewart
George Durston	Henry Seton Merriman	Janet Aldridge
George Ebers	Henry W Longfellow	Jens Peter Jacobsen
George Eliot	Herbert A. Giles	Jerome K. Jerome
George Gissing	Herbert Carter	Jessie Graham Flower
George MacDonald	Herbert N. Casson	John Buchan
George Meredith	Herman Hesse	John Burroughs
George Orwell	Hildegard G. Frey	John Cournos
George Sylvester Viereck	Homer	John F. Kennedy
George Tucker	Honore De Balzac	John Gay
George W. Cable	Horace B. Day	John Glasworthy
George Wharton James	Horace Walpole	John Habberton
Gertrude Atherton	Horatio Alger Jr.	John Joy Bell
Gordon Casserly	Howard Pyle	John Kendrick Bangs
Grace E. King	Howard R. Garis	John Milton
Grace Gallatin	Hugh Lofting	John Philip Sousa
Grace Greenwood	Hugh Walpole	John Taintor Foote
Grant Allen	Humphry Ward	Jonas Lauritz Idemil Lie
Guillermo A. Sherwell	Ian Maclaren	Jonathan Swift
Gulielma Zollinger	Inez Haynes Gillmore	Joseph A. Altsheler
Gustav Flaubert	Irving Bacheller	Joseph Carey
H. A. Cody	Isabel Cecilia Williams	Joseph Conrad
H. B. Irving	Isabel Hornibrook	Joseph E. Badger Jr
H.C. Bailey	Israel Abrahams	Joseph Hergesheimer
H. G. Wells	Ivan Turgenev	Joseph Jacobs
H. H. Munro	J.G.Austin	Jules Vernes
H. Irving Hancock	J. Henri Fabre	Julian Hawthrone
H. R. Naylor	J. M. Barrie	Julie A Lippmann
H. Rider Haggard	J. M. Walsh	Justin Huntly McCarthy
H. W. C. Davis	J. Macdonald Oxley	Kakuzo Okakura
Haldeman Julius	J. R. Miller	Karle Wilson Baker
Hall Caine	J. S. Fletcher	Kate Chopin
Hamilton Wright Mabie	J. S. Knowles	Kenneth Grahame
Hans Christian Andersen	J. Storer Clouston	Kenneth McGaffey
Harold Avery	J. W. Duffield	Kate Langley Bosher
Harold McGrath	Jack London	Kate Langley Bosher
Harriet Beecher Stowe	Jacob Abbott	Katherine Cecil Thurston
Harry Castlemon	James Allen	Katherine Stokes
Harry Coghill	James Andrews	L. A. Abbot
Harry Houidini	James Baldwin	L. T. Meade

L. Frank Baum
Latta Griswold
Laura Dent Crane
Laura Lee Hope
Laurence Housman
Lawrence Beasley
Leo Tolstoy
Leonid Andreyev
Lewis Carroll
Lewis Sperry Chafer
Lilian Bell
Lloyd Osbourne
Louis Hughes
Louis Joseph Vance
Louis Tracy
Louisa May Alcott
Lucy Fitch Perkins
Lucy Maud Montgomery
Luther Benson
Lydia Miller Middleton
Lyndon Orr
M. Corvus
M. H. Adams
Margaret E. Sangster
Margret Howth
Margaret Vandercook
Margaret W. Hungerford
Margret Penrose
Maria Edgeworth
Maria Thompson Daviess
Mariano Azuela
Marion Polk Angellotti
Mark Overton
Mark Twain
Mary Austin
Mary Catherine Crowley
Mary Cole
Mary Hastings Bradley
Mary Roberts Rinehart
Mary Rowlandson
M. Wollstonecraft Shelley
Maud Lindsay
Max Beerbohm
Myra Kelly
Nathaniel Hawthrone
Nicolo Machiavelli
O. F. Walton
Oscar Wilde

Owen Johnson
P.G. Wodehouse
Paul and Mabel Thorne
Paul G. Tomlinson
Paul Severing
Percy Brebner
Percy Keese Fitzhugh
Peter B. Kyne
Plato
Quincy Allen
R. Derby Holmes
R. L. Stevenson
R. S. Ball
Rabindranath Tagore
Rahul Alvares
Ralph Bonehill
Ralph Henry Barbour
Ralph Victor
Ralph Waldo Emmerson
Rene Descartes
Ray Cummings
Rex Beach
Rex E. Beach
Richard Harding Davis
Richard Jefferies
Richard Le Gallienne
Robert Barr
Robert Frost
Robert Gordon Anderson
Robert L. Drake
Robert Lansing
Robert Lynd
Robert Michael Ballantyne
Robert W. Chambers
Rosa Nouchette Carey
Rudyard Kipling
Saint Augustine
Samuel B. Allison
Samuel Hopkins Adams
Sarah Bernhardt
Sarah C. Hallowell
Selma Lagerlof
Sherwood Anderson
Sigmund Freud
Standish O'Grady
Stanley Weyman
Stella Benson
Stella M. Francis

Stephen Crane
Stewart Edward White
Stijn Streuvels
Swami Abhedananda
Swami Parmananda
T. S. Ackland
T. S. Arthur
The Princess Der Ling
Thomas A. Janvier
Thomas A Kempis
Thomas Anderton
Thomas Bailey Aldrich
Thomas Bulfinch
Thomas De Quincey
Thomas Dixon
Thomas H. Huxley
Thomas Hardy
Thomas More
Thornton W. Burgess
U. S. Grant
Upton Sinclair
Valentine Williams
Various Authors
Vaughan Kester
Victor Appleton
Victor G. Durham
Victoria Cross
Virginia Woolf
Wadsworth Camp
Walter Camp
Walter Scott
Washington Irving
Wilbur Lawton
Wilkie Collins
Willa Cather
Willard F. Baker
William Dean Howells
William le Queux
W. Makepeace Thackeray
William W. Walter
William Shakespeare
Winston Churchill
Yei Theodora Ozaki
Yogi Ramacharaka
Young E. Allison
Zane Grey

www.ingramcontent.com/pod-product-compliance
Lightning Source LLC
Chambersburg PA
CBHW030122180626
46812CB00002B/520